Chambers of Death

Books by Priscilla Royal

Wine of Violence
Tyrant of the Mind
Sorrow Without End
Justice for the Damned
Forsaken Soul
Chambers of Death

Chambers
of Death

Priscilla Royal

Poisoned Pen Press

Poisoned
Pen
Press

Copyright © 2009 by Priscilla Royal

First Edition 2009

10 9 8 7 6 5 4 3 2 1

Library of Congress Catalog Card Number: 2008937748

ISBN: 978-1-59058-640-2

Poisoned Pen Press
6962 E. First Ave., Ste. 103
Scottsdale, AZ 85251
www.poisonedpenpress.com
info@poisonedpenpress.com

Printed in the United States of America

*Monty Montee, dear friend and gatekeeper to the dream,
with gratitude.*

Acknowledgments

Christine and Peter Goodhugh, Ed Kaufman of M is for Mystery Bookstore (San Mateo CA), Henie Lentz, Dianne Levy, Sharon Kay Penman, Barbara Peters of Poisoned Pen Bookstore (Scottsdale AZ), Phoebe Phillips, Robert Rosenwald and all the staff of Poisoned Pen Press, Marianne and Sharon Silva, Lyn and Michael Speakman.

Let not thine heart decline to her ways, go not astray in her paths. For she hath cast down many wounded: yea, many strong men have been slain by her. Her house is the way to hell, going down to the chambers of death.
—Proverbs 7:25-27 (King James version)

Chapter One

The tree limbs arched with the weight of ice-kissed rain, then dropped their burden with a loud crack like a bursting dam.

Prioress Eleanor flinched when the torrent hit and clutched the feverish young woman in her arms even closer. "We shall find warm lodging soon," she whispered into Mariota's ear and prayed her words sounded more confident than she felt.

Shivering, the girl groaned and muttered incoherently.

If a fire and dry shelter were not found quickly, the chill autumn's fierce storm would surely kill this young woman who had known only fifteen summers. As the numbing damp soaked through her own cloak, Eleanor began to shake. Is there any comfort for us, she wondered, and began to fall victim to gray despair.

Even her donkey now issued a low complaint. Hope must be a very feeble thing indeed, she thought bleakly, if this patient of all creatures has grown anxious.

"My lady, take this." Brother Thomas eased his horse closer to the trembling women. With a swift, efficient gesture, he lifted off his own cloak and draped it gently around them. "I erred when I suggested you seek the dry spot under the tree. I thought you would be better protected from the storm. I beg pardon for my poor judgment."

Eleanor pulled the rough, dry wool closer. Her monk was a tall, broad-shouldered man, and the cloak easily covered two small women from the lashing rain. "All err is mine, Brother, and it is I who should beg pardon for taking this ill-advised journey. You are kind, but I should not deprive you of this warmth. Two must not fall gravely ill for my own foolishness."

"Fear not," Thomas grinned. "I have this blanket for cover." He buried his nose in the thick cloth he now tossed over his head and shoulders. "It reeks of horse sweat, but that is an honest enough thing. I have never found any sin in the company of horses."

His words chased gloom some small distance from her. Eleanor laughed, covering her own nose with the monk's cloak. It held a somewhat peppery odor as if his deep red hair were made of some spice from Outremer. "Truly, this has no scent of horse," she answered, then winced with horror at the flirtatious tone in her words. Had he noted it as well? Her cheeks burned, but the heat was born of shame, not fever.

Either the storm had muted her wicked meaning or he had mercifully disregarded it. Instead of replying, the monk turned away and stared into the growing darkness of the early night as if his thoughts had slipped away from the world and back into his own soul.

"What is he thinking?" she caught herself whispering aloud, then quickly glanced at the girl in her arms. Although she feared Mariota had overheard, the girl was so ill that she was unaware of much around her. Nonetheless, Eleanor continued her thoughts in silence.

During this ill-conceived journey, Brother Thomas had proven that his soul was made of greater mettle than her own. At Tyndal Priory, when she had demanded his attendance, she knew her order was selfish and that he had obeyed with profound reluctance. Whatever his disinclination, he had repaid her unconscionable stubbornness with courtesy, humor, and kindness throughout this entire venture, a journey cursed with one problem snapping at the heels of another.

"How does the girl?" he suddenly asked, looking back over his shoulder.

"Not well. I fear for her life."

"My healing skills are so poor. I grieve for that."

"You have done what you could, Brother, and bear no fault. Had I waited on this minor matter of property, Sister Anne might have accompanied us."

"The season has been bad for fevers, and the hospital was full of the suffering. The lay brothers and sisters needed the wisdom and guidance of their sub-infirmarian."

She could not see his expression well in the failing light but no criticism of her resonated in that remark. "And the dying needed a priest's comfort as their souls prepared to face God. I took you away from those duties. For that I shall do penance."

"Any priest can hear confessions and bring forgiveness," he replied, bowing his head. "The one you assigned will serve as God demands."

But Brother Thomas soothed the weary with special comfort, and the villagers had quickly discovered this skill. His touch on the brows of the frail was soft as lamb's wool. His words often spread honey on the most bitter of souls. These had been the stories brought to her ears. So why had she allowed Satan to blind her that day with such selfishness? She knew the answer and grieved over her shame.

"My lady, you had little choice. Prior Andrew himself was recovering from the vile fever and could not travel. You needed a monk skilled in boundary disputes and the language of contracts, one who could investigate matters when modesty and rank prohibited you from doing so—or to give rarely needed counsel."

The monk's quick smile suggested that he had found pleasure in the process, whatever her misgivings and his initial lack of enthusiasm for this task. She might have reason to doubt his absolute fealty to her, but she could not dispute how often he had loyally served her with unquestioned competence.

Eleanor's lips twisted into a sour smile. His courtesy in now repeating what she had argued, that day back at Tyndal, also pleased her more than it should. Although her body might sometimes wish it otherwise, her soul had always demanded that she vow her whole being to God's service, frailties as well as strengths. That oath required she see both with sometimes painful clarity. Thus she dare not pretend that bringing Brother Thomas with her on this journey had much to do with proving his ultimate fealty to her as his prioress or with her need of his knowledge in matters of property.

"I have lost all sense of time, Brother," she said, chasing troubling thoughts as far away as possible. "How long ago was it that you sent one of our company to find us shelter?"

"An hour, perhaps more, I would judge. There was light enough to see the road when he left."

A powerful gust of wind sent a sharp-toothed sheet of rain into the small party. Brother Thomas urged his horse in front of the two women to protect them from the full force of the gale.

"Thank you, Brother," Eleanor murmured. "I shall not forget your kindness this day."

"If the man does not return soon, we must seek shelter in the forest, my lady. Even if lawless men hide nearby, surely they will leave us in peace. Either they will be seeking safe haven from this weather as well or will honor our vocation for the good of their souls."

Eleanor rested her cheek on top of Mariota's burning head. "She'll not survive the night if we cannot find better protection from the cold and wind."

"Had I recognized the signs of illness earlier, we might have stopped at an inn this morning or sent word ahead for a cart from a monastery to meet us on the road."

"And I share in that blame, but Mariota hid her illness well. I fear she did not want to slow us down and hoped she could ride well enough until we reached our own priory. Although the fever was stronger than her will, I cannot find fault with her. Her mistake in judgment was founded in concern for others." Eleanor bent forward to listen more closely to the girl's breathing. It was ragged and labored. The prioress began to pray.

The donkey, on which she and the girl rode, suddenly brayed and twitched its ears.

Thomas' horse snorted. "My lady," the monk shouted. "I hear horsemen!"

A dripping rider, followed by a small company, now rounded the bend. "Lodging has been found, my lady," the man shouted through the wind gusts. "Henry de Lacy, Earl of Lincoln, has land here. His steward begs you honor him by taking shelter at the manor."

Chapter Two

Eleanor tenderly released Mariota into the outstretched arms of waiting servants. "Carry her gently. She is so very weak," she whispered as she watched them lift their light burden up the rain-slick steps toward the brightness of the open door.

"They will take her to a fire's comfort, my lady," another servant assured her, raising a hand to help the prioress from her donkey. "The mistress was told of the illness and ordered preparations for her care."

Murmuring her gratitude, Eleanor stood for a moment in the cascading rain until her legs regained enough feeling to walk. Had she ever felt so numb? The dark, rough exterior of this manor house might look forbidding to unwelcome strangers in the night, but stone walls meant there would be fireplaces enough inside to add warmth to the sweetness of charity. When she herself stepped across the threshold, Eleanor closed her weary eyes and thanked God for granting her party this dry sanctuary from the storm.

"My lady!"

Eleanor blinked at the intensity of the greeting.

A woman rushed forward, hands open as if to seize her.

The prioress jumped back from the assault.

The dark-clad woman fell to her knees in front of the dripping prioress.

"Bless me!"

All Eleanor could do was nod. Fatigue, added to the shock of this peculiar welcome, had chased all speech away.

The woman's narrow-set eyes glittered like small beads of jet in the flickering firelight. "Are you not the Prioress of Tyndal?"

Eleanor took a deep breath and found voice enough to confirm her identity.

"God, in His mercy, has blessed us by sending you when we need you most!"

Although she was owed reverent courtesy based on her rank as a baron's daughter and as head of Tyndal Priory, Eleanor had never been greeted as if she were one of God's own angels. As she looked down at this sharp-angled face and unblinking eyes, she wondered if the woman were suffering from some great distress—or might she be quite simply mad?

Quelling her apprehension, the prioress replied: "He has granted us mercy. We were in dire need of shelter from this dreadful storm." To herself, she expressed hope that this woman's strange greeting was born of that awkward nervousness found in many pious folk when faced with another mortal who has dedicated her life to God's service. "Are you the mistress of this manor, the one who has obeyed Our Lord's commandment to offer a safe haven to those in need?"

"The famous Prioress of Tyndal!" was the woman's sole and muttered reply.

Eleanor tried another approach. "May I ask your name?"

"She is Mistress Constance."

Startled by this new voice, the prioress spun around.

A square-bodied woman, perhaps no taller than the prioress herself, stood in an open doorway some feet to the right of the fireplace. When the prioress saw her, the woman offered the obeisance due Eleanor's rank before continuing. "She is daughter-in-law to Master Stevyn, the steward in residence here. Am I correct in believing that at least one member of your company is grievously ill?"

Eleanor glanced down at the now-identified woman still kneeling at her feet. Unmoving, Mistress Constance stared up at her, mouth open and eyes wide as if she had fallen into a trance.

"The poor shivering child near the fire suffers from a high fever and has lost all reason," the prioress replied, gesturing. Although she feared she must address the cause behind Mistress Constance's extreme reaction to her arrival, Mariota's grave condition demanded immediate attention.

The older woman hurried toward the fireplace where Mariota lay on a thick straw pallet. Eleanor was close behind. Servants might have loosely wrapped Mariota in a heavy blanket but she was still lying in wet clothing. A fine mist of steam rose from her shivering body. "Wine!" the woman ordered, and a servant instantly disappeared behind a screen at the back of the hall.

"I now believe she has been ill since morning at the start of our journey but said nothing of it. When we stopped to let the horses rest and take refreshment ourselves, she refused all but a bite of food. I noticed her pallor, but she claimed to be well when I asked. At midday, Brother Thomas caught her as she began to slide from her mount. It was then we discovered that she suffered a very high fever. Now she has been severely chilled by this storm. I fear for her life."

"We must pray for God's mercy on this young soul, my lady." The woman shook her head.

If Mariota dies, I am much to blame, Eleanor thought. Is there penance enough…? She knelt at the side of her charge and rested the back of her hand against the young woman's burning cheek. Suddenly there was an abrupt tug at the back of her robe, and Eleanor turned her head, annoyance coloring her cheeks.

"This house is full of sin, my lady! As Prioress of Tyndal, you have the power to keep it from me. I must have your blessing!" Mistress Constance was still on her knees but now knelt behind the prioress and was clutching her soaked garment.

Eleanor's patience cracked. Filled with worry over Mariota and shivering herself from the storm's drenching rain, Eleanor grew angry at the rude handling and opened her mouth to admonish the woman. But the servant arrived with the wine, and the prioress' attention was drawn back to her sick charge.

"I shall make sure the poor child is settled in a warm bed and receives all the care we have available here, my lady," the older woman said, her voice soft as she took the wine from the servant's hands and raised Mariota's head so she might sip it.

The calm authority in the woman's voice cooled Eleanor's temper. At least Mariota would be cared for even if she herself must remain here, drenched and chilled to the bone, because Mistress Constance was either awe-struck or obsessed. She turned back to the impertinent woman.

"You are in error if you think I have any special power against evil, Mistress. I am not a saint..." she began.

Constance shook her head so violently, her very teeth seemed to rattle—until Eleanor realized that the sound came from the ring of keys the woman clutched in one hand. Reaching out with the other to seize Eleanor's hands, she hissed: "I'll pay for the blessing. As for the evil here, you must find a way to purge..."

"Mistress, I beg you to let me attend my sick charge this night. In the morning, we shall speak more on this. As for a blessing, I give that freely enough, but you must talk to your priest if you believe the Devil is in residence."

"Bless me now!"

Knowing that blessings were never amiss, Eleanor granted the request, although she doubted the plea was born of any need for peace in a longing soul. Sadly, she suspected a more worldly purpose, such as pride in obtaining such a thing from a religious of some rank.

Once the requested act had been done, Mistress Constance stared at Eleanor's hands for some time, then pulled herself to her feet and scurried away without uttering any word, even of thanks.

Eleanor suffered another flash of anger. Did the woman hope to find signs of the stigmata so she could gain even greater admiration from any companions? When the irritation faded, however, she felt the full power of deep fatigue and longed for sleep. Forcing her eyes to remain open, she turned back to the fireplace where the sick woman lay.

Mariota had disappeared.

An instant later, the older woman reappeared from the entryway behind which the prioress could now see stone stairs leading upward.

"She has been carried to a room in the solar with a good fire," the woman said. "The servants have beaten the mattress to soften it and warmed the sheets near the hearth to give her further ease."

"You are most kind. As for my men…"

"There is enough comfortable, dry space for them in the barn where a servant has already taken them. The horses will be cared for in the stable."

"And Brother Thomas?"

The woman's eyes began to twinkle. A smile brightened her broad face.

Had she not been so weary, Eleanor might have taken offence at this obvious sign of yet another woman charmed by her monk.

"He said he would be happy to sleep near the kitchen hearth, my lady. The manor cook chases away most who enter there, but that includes the mice, so he should be comfortable enough on a thick straw pallet. I do suspect, however, that Hilda will find joy in his holy company. I do not fear he will be made to feel unwelcome."

Eleanor's thoughts darkened as she wondered just how old this cook might be.

Chapter Three

"You are pensive, wife." Master Ranulf winced and shifted. A jagged edge in the stone floor of the chapel was cutting into his knee. Perhaps that was meant to remind him of Hell's agonies?

"I am praying, husband, as should you." Even in the flickering light of the torch on the wall, the angles of Mistress Constance's face were not softened, and she seemed to be chewing her knuckles.

"Apart from begging forgiveness for my foul mortality," he replied, "I have even greater reason to praise God tonight. His kindness knows no limits. He has sent the Prioress of Tyndal to my father's door, a woman devoted to God. My heart is full of gratitude."

With an impatient sigh, Constance rose and gave obeisance to the tortured figure on the cross before turning to leave the chapel.

Ranulf quickly followed his wife, taking time only to light a candle so they might see their way to the floor above.

As they climbed the twisting stairway to the solar, she remained quiet. Since they rarely spoke after the nightly prayer, this alone did not trouble him. Tonight, however, Ranulf sensed an unusual chill. Something was amiss, and fear kept him from daring to envision what the cause might be. Only when he had shut the door to their small chamber did she deign to enlighten him.

"This house belongs to the Devil, husband. I knew evil was in residence here, but the strength of those dark powers is stronger than I had imagined."

Something churned inside him, and Ranulf pressed his hand against his stomach. "What do you mean?"

"The prioress was most loath to grant me her blessing tonight." Her tiny eyes blinked in the smoky candlelight.

The husband stiffened. "Did she deny you?"

"Nay, but she granted my request only after I begged. Indeed, I had to offer coin."

"How much did you give her?" Ranulf's mouth had gone dry, and his words caught in his throat.

"Have you added avarice to your usual transgressions, husband? Do you value a silver penny more than your immortal soul?"

He stared at his wife. "Do I not tithe? In fact, our local priest praises my generosity. My question had harmless enough intent."

Constance stared back, her thin lips pursed in flinty anger.

"I mean only to suggest that, if this holy prioress required much, then the evil she saw would be greater than if she accepted but little." He could explain no further and fell silent.

"Oh, she did bless me freely enough in fact. It was her reluctance that troubled me."

"Why then did she hesitate?"

"Sin!" Constance spun around and pointed to the bed. "There lies one reason. You demanded satisfaction of your foul lust last month. The Prioress of Tyndal must have smelt the reek of sin that you left on my body."

"A wife owes her husband payment of the marriage debt! There is no sin in that. Even Saint Paul said it was better to marry than to burn…"

"Coupling should never be done at prohibited times!" She turned her back on him but glared over her shoulder, disgust evident in her gaze. "I was still suffering my courses, yet you would not listen."

"You bleed often, wife. As for other prohibited times, I wonder that a woman would know so many more of them than our priest does. You have never quickened, except once after we were first wed. Then the child died in the womb. Might not God finally bless us with offspring if we abstained only on those days our priest recognizes as forbidden?" He shrugged, suspecting she would still find this argument feeble.

She shook her finger at him. "Our seed refuses to unite. When will you understand that my failure to bear a child must be a sign? I have long argued that we should take a vow of celibacy and live as brother and sister. Such a marriage is holier than one where two people couple like the beasts in the field." She raised her narrow nose and sniffed.

Ranulf looked away. "I have done penance for lying with you that night."

"As have I."

For a moment, neither spoke. As often happens between any couple long married, peace can be made in silence, and the tension in the room did seem to lessen.

"Then the sin has been acknowledged, and our souls have been cleansed," Ranulf said. His lips twitched. "There must have been another reason for the prioress to be so unwilling to give her blessing."

Constance blinked and hesitated as if listening to that last sentence again. "As I have said often of late, not that anyone has heeded, the reek of evil in this house is painfully sharp. If my nostrils burn with it, and I am but a weak and sinful woman, how foul must the stench be to someone like Prioress Eleanor?"

"By our very nature, all mortals are wicked. What greater pollution do you believe exists here?" Staring at his wife, Ranulf now clutched his hands together just below his belly.

Her thin lips curled into a snarling smile. "Your father is lecherous."

"My mother led a most saintly life! Surely you cannot accuse her of conspiring in sinful ways during that marriage. As for my father's subsequent marriage to Mistress Luce, he had the right to gain greater wealth by that alliance and to lie with her for his health."

Constance snorted, her contempt for that argument obvious. "Dare you claim that your brother is not impious?"

Ranulf frowned. "Shall we condemn him so quickly? I have not yet spoken to him since his return but have prayed most diligently. You and I must beg God's mercy in that matter and not give up hope that Huet will find the strength to fling Satan's hands from his eyes."

"Your stepmother…"

"Wife! Your accusations are no more than just but, other than my brother's arrival, nothing has changed in this manor for months. Unless you have other cause to claim a greater evil, of course…" He shifted as if something had pricked him.

"Mistress Maud, that wicked woman, has come and tonight dared to greet the Prioress of Tyndal. Her presence is recent."

Ranulf exhaled, then raised his eyebrows as if hoping his wife would think him surprised at the shocking act rather than how ignorant he was of the particular evil this woman possessed.

"Had the woman any decency, she would have hidden herself in the solar! Instead, she had the audacity to suggest treatment for that sick woman in the prioress' company."

"Ah!"

"Brazen, she was! How your father tolerates her, I will never understand. Instead of urging the sick to pray that God will forgive the sins that made them ill, she brews foul potions that stink of the Devil. Women like that are his very handmaidens." She sat on the edge of the bed and rubbed her hands together.

"Yet she has had some success…"

"Oh, you are too much a sinner yourself to see it all, husband. If a mortal does not die, the cause is God's mercy. Her concoctions have no merit."

"I would never argue that the Devil's art is stronger than God's grace."

"Just how much she worships Satan you do not know," Constance muttered and fell silent, her brow creasing with dark furrows.

Ranulf licked his lips as he watched her lost in thought, then sat down on the bed and edged closer to his wife, tentatively reaching out with an encircling arm.

She drew back and crossed herself. "How dare you! Have you learned nothing?"

He bowed his head and rose. "My bowels are troubled, wife, and I must seek relief in the garderobe. Afterwards I shall go to the chapel to pray again. There will be time for your servant to prepare you for a chaste rest. When I return, I will be careful not to waken you."

After closing the door to their chamber, Ranulf walked a short distance before becoming aware he had forgotten a candle. He reached out for the wall, then leaned against the stone and began rubbing his back against the roughness. Crossing his arms across his chest, he moaned with the sharp, yet sweet, pain.

Dare he seek the garderobe tonight? Satan often sent a succubus to meet him there, and his weak flesh now swelled with aching anticipation. At least that was one sin his wife had not yet rooted out. For that he was most grateful. Her righteous wrath could be terrible, making him tremble in the winds of her fury.

If he prayed hard enough, he might conquer his weakness this time. If not, surely God understood. Mortal women were whores enough, enflaming lust in otherwise godly men, but the female imps sent by the Prince of Darkness were skilled in practices beyond any man's endurance to resist.

Pushing himself away from the wall, he stumbled onward along the familiar route to the garderobe. If he failed again to triumph over this temptation, he would spend hours in the chapel, praying for mercy as his heart cursed the day God had made Eve.

Chapter Four

"Please drink some wine, my lady."

Eleanor nodded, but her shivering was so severe she could neither speak nor reach out to take any cup. Bending over, she edged her stool closer to the fireplace where the flames snapped and danced, waving orange and golden arms as if greeting her with especial joy.

The older woman, who had led her to the solar, put the yellow earthenware jug down and opened the lid of a large oak chest. Pulling out a thick woolen blanket, she draped it carefully around the prioress.

Eleanor felt the weight, but little heat, and continued to tremble beyond any ability to disguise it.

"Forgive my presumption, for I mean no discourtesy by plain speech, but you must get out of those wet clothes, my lady."

Although warmth was beginning to seep deeper into her body, Eleanor knew her chattering teeth would belie any significant improvement. Instead of speaking, she smiled and nodded again.

"I can offer a clean shift and a simple robe. The garments are humble things, and far too large, but will bring you warmth enough until your own clothes are dry. If you will allow me to serve you in this, I would be honored."

"You are kind," Eleanor stammered, then rose with evident reluctance to leave the crackling fire.

"There is no need to move, my lady. I will bring what is needed."

In what seemed like an instant, Eleanor was divested of her storm-drenched habit and now sat in dry robes. As the woman had described, they were rough and large enough to wrap around her twice, but that only added to their comfort. She smiled with relief as the icy damp slowly surrendered its hold on her body.

"A sip of wine would chase away the last of that bone chill. Shall I fill your mazer?" When Eleanor agreed, the woman bent to pick up the jug. "My name is Maud, my lady. Do you wish something to eat?"

Tasting the wine, Eleanor noted it was smooth to the tongue and mildly spiced, although she would not have cared had it been vinegar if it warmed her. "I am grateful for your charity and good service, but I have no appetite."

Maud smiled and a dimple deepened on either side of her upturned mouth, giving her round face a pleasing affability.

Less benumbed in both mind and body, the prioress began polite conversation and studied this woman who had mercifully taken charge in the hall. In Maud's replies of ritual courtesy, Eleanor found enough wit to suggest a clever person who had learned to speak her mind without giving offense. Was she maid to the mistress, or in service so long that her authority was unquestioned by the younger servants? Her age and modest dress would suggest the latter. Eleanor tried to guess whether Maud was in her fourth decade or fifth.

"This room belongs to the Earl of Lincoln when he is here, which is rare enough," Maud was saying. "It is the warmest so I did presume to have your young charge brought here."

The prioress noted that the woman's body had settled into that square shape of those beyond the birthing years, and her plump breasts sagged, yet her cheeks were still pink and unlined, except at the corners of her mouth and eyes. With that peaked hairline and heavy brows, she might never have been called a beauty by any rank or fashion, but Eleanor suspected she had found suitors enough in her youth. The woman exuded the soft promise of ease in her arms for a man at the end of an arduous day.

"We are preparing another chamber nearby for your stay. Although this is the larger space…"

Yet there is something troubling about her eyes, the prioress thought. Although they were deep-set, that alone would not have suggested such a conclusion. Their color was probably hazel, but the ashen hue encircling them darkened the eyes to a muddy brown in the uneven light. Eleanor felt a prick of concern. Perhaps the woman was only fatigued. Or was she recovering from some illness herself?

Eleanor decided her unease was born more of her own weariness than any real cause, and quickly replied to Maud's question, now unanswered for just a moment too long. "Do not trouble yourself over another room for me. I agree with whole heart that Mariota needs the bed and the warmth of this fire. I will stay with her and be quite content with a mattress on the floor. In this season the fleas should bite less, and I note the floor is well-strewed with lavender."

The woman bowed her head but not before the prioress read her relief at Eleanor's concurrence in the decision.

"I recognize her illness as a grave one," Eleanor continued. "I do not know this area well, but is the nearby town large enough to have a physician? The weather may be cruel, but I beg that someone with those healing skills be called to attend her as soon as possible."

"I fear there is no doctor here, my lady."

Feeling the acid sting of tears, Eleanor closed her eyes and, once again, cursed her folly in not waiting until Sister Anne could accompany her as she usually did. If Mariota did not live, her death would surely rot in Eleanor's soul like a canker.

A rustling noise pulled the prioress away from these recriminations, and she looked up.

Maud had pulled open the curtains encircling a large bed. Gentle concern now softened those unsettling eyes as she looked back over her shoulder at the prioress. "With your permission, I shall gladly do what I can. My skills are feeble, but, if you pray

God for mercy, He might bless me with a talent greater than I now possess."

"Please do all you can," Eleanor replied, shaking her head in despair. Any bungling by this woman would be no worse than what she had done by putting the poor child in such jeopardy in the first place. Sighing, she tried to find hope in the knowledge that, despite his modesty, Brother Thomas did possess some healing skills and might be able give this charitable soul guidance. She rose and walked to the woman's side.

Maud bent over and touched the young woman's forehead with the back of her hand. "The fever is high," she said, "and she has fallen into a dangerous sleep. I fear her soul looks more to Heaven than this world."

"Then you can do nothing." Eleanor instantly regretted the biting tone. Her anger was born of frustration and guilt, not the woman's bluntly spoken truth.

Maud either did not hear the harsh words or graciously chose to ignore them. As she tucked the furred blanket closer around the quiet form, her reply suggested only sadness. "My lady, I cannot promise what I might accomplish. Your prayers may be the best medicine for her. Yet my physician husband, whose soul God took two months ago, trained me to be his apothecary when we first married. If I claim any small skill, I do so only because he kindly trusted me for many years."

Eleanor felt her face turn hot with embarrassment. This woman was not a servant here, as she had assumed from the simple dress and modest manner. Maud's unadorned robe befitted a new widow, and her dark look was born of grief over a dead husband. In addition, Eleanor had mistaken humility for ignorance, and she felt shame over her rude presumptions.

"I shall not only pray for God's mercy on the poor child, Mistress Maud, but that He may also bring balm to your wounded heart. As for your healing skills, I would be grateful if you would apply them to the care of this sick woman." One more realization now burst upon her. "Yet I fear I ask too much of you. Is there some other illness in the household requiring your care? Has our arrival added to burdens already here?"

"Nay, my lady. I was not summoned to cure fevers but rather as a friend to Master Stevyn's family." She then waved her hand as if chasing those words aside. "Or I should say I was often companion to his wife and mother of his children, may God bless her soul."

"Recently gone to God?" the prioress asked in a whisper, now horrified that her bedraggled party may have been given charitable hospitality by a house darkened by deep mourning. Was Mistress Maud in this remote manor on such a horrible night because of the poor woman's death throes? At least Brother Thomas could offer consolation, and she might join in the family prayers for comfort.

"My words were ill-chosen, my lady. She died two years ago."

Silence fell between them as the widow returned to her examination of the feverish girl.

As long as the unexpected arrival of extra company did not add problems to a household suffering enough from illness or death, Eleanor decided she had no need to learn exactly why Mistress Maud was here. Turning her concern back to the immediate crisis, she asked: "Will you be able to find all that Mariota needs here? The weather is too foul to travel abroad for anything."

"Master Stevyn's wife always had a fine herbal garden and cared for many of the servants herself with successful concoctions. I will seek out anyone to whom she may have taught her secrets, for no manor is without its healer. Perhaps there is some new and potent remedy for me to learn." Maud's expression brightened.

"It was kind of Master Stevyn to grant us a haven," Eleanor commented as they turned away from Mariota's bed.

"The steward is away, his return delayed by this storm, but his wife will be pleased to learn that it was done as he would have wished."

Now completely confused, Eleanor shook her head. "Did you not just say his wife had died?" She eased herself back down on the stool near the fire and braced her back against the stone wall.

"Ah, forgive me! Of course you could not know all this, and I am a poor one for explaining anything. Master Stevyn has since taken another wife, one of many fewer years than he possesses. She is the reason you find me here, for young women often need advice on marital issues from their elders, and her mother is long dead."

The prioress frowned in bewilderment. What did this woman mean? Pregnancy? The marriage debt? Surely all this would make more sense after she had slept a few hours.

"When your man arrived at the gate," Maud continued, apparently interpreting Eleanor's expression to mean displeasure at the failure of the steward's wife to greet her, "Mistress Luce had taken to her bed. Had she not done so, she would have met you at the door but will most certainly make proper amends when she rises in the morning. I shall explain that it is her husband's custom to give shelter as Our Lord demanded. She will not quarrel with the decision to do as her husband would have wished."

Eleanor nodded. None of this was her concern as guest in this house, and normally she would have cast undue inquisitiveness from her mind. But fatigue had dulled her watchfulness over idle curiosity, and Maud's words raised an odd question. How young and untutored was this wife that she would need direction in common courtesy? Then her eyes began to burn, and she rubbed them until they watered just enough to ease the rawness.

"My lady, shall I have your pack horses unloaded in the morning?"

Eleanor's head grew so heavy, she knew she was quickly losing her battle with fatigue.

"My lady?" The widow's voice was gentle.

The prioress snapped awake. "In the morning, if you would be so kind," she replied. "I fear we may have to beg the steward's hospitality until Mariota's illness takes some turn. She cannot travel. The distance to our priory is too great even with a wagon and fair weather, an unlikely enough occurrence in this dark season."

"Master Stevyn will not expect you to leave until you wish to do so. The only recompense he might beg would be your prayers. He is a good man. Overall."

That brief hesitation was not lost on Eleanor, but weariness blunted her interest in further reflection.

"I must seek out cures, my lady, but the search will not take me long." Maud folded her hands in humble supplication. "After I return, I would be honored if you'd allow me to take first watch over this young woman tonight."

The widow read her weakness well enough, Eleanor thought, and had handled the problem with courtesy. "Thank you," she managed to say, just before her eyelids shut.

Chapter Five

Mistress Luce knew the way well enough without a torch. Dread of taking a misstep on the uneven, muddy ground was not the reason her heart pounded so, but fear she most certainly felt and it excited her.

Although she wore a heavy cloak, the wind stung her face and hands. In just a few moments, she'd be warmed enough, she thought, then bit back a laugh.

And what would her husband do if he came home tonight? Pull off his reeking boots, stumble into bed stinking of horse, and fall asleep, mouth open and drool soon running from his lips. "A loving greeting indeed for his young wife," she muttered. "And if I were elsewhere than his bed, he wouldn't even notice."

But her husband would not be back. His loins weren't hungry enough for her to brave the dangerous roads. He'd rather find some inn, drink enough to fall asleep in the flea-infested straw, and probably dream of how much cattle he'd have to slaughter to get through the winter.

She snorted. He had ridden her often enough at the beginning of their marriage. Following the first nights, when she still hurt after her maidenhead was torn, she discovered a taste for coupling. Even though he had rough hands, body hair as bristly as a boar's, and his belly sagged over his manhood, she tolerated this old man. He was her husband after all. When he pulled her legs apart, she shut her eyes and imagined a smooth-skinned, taut-muscled youth mounting her. Thus she found pleasure.

Then his ardor faded. And she had not conceived.

Luce shuddered, but the wind was not the cause. How often had she played the harlot to force her husband's mind from the dull business of estate management to bedding a wife? And how rarely had it worked?

When her humors turned sluggish and black, a young midwife told her that she suffered from congestion in her womb, a common affliction of women without husbands. The woman's treatment gave her relief enough, but Luce still lacked a babe.

As she approached the low building, she saw the light flickering in the cracks between the wooden slats. The narrow door opened.

"You're late," he complained.

"And you are the better man for it," she teased, running her hand lightly down his tight belly to his swollen sex.

As he pulled her inside and shut the door, she caught herself thinking that her prudent husband should be grateful. He no longer had to pay the midwife for her treatments, and she might well give him a boy—one disinclined to monkish ways, like his other two sons, because this lad would be bred in good, hot lust.

Chapter Six

"No tasting 'til it's done!" The red-faced cook raised her wooden spoon with exaggerated ferocity as if threatening to strike, but her broad grin belied any such intent.

Folding his hands most prayerfully, Brother Thomas bowed. "But the aroma already tempts. Even a saint would weaken, and I am only a sinful mortal."

"'Tis but a simple pottage of winter roots, Brother. Nothing that a monk of your high rank would find pleasing."

"Rank, Mistress? In God's kingdom, there is no greater title than *servant*, and I am honored to bear nothing else on earth."

"Fa! I have been in my lord's service for enough years and cooked for men who have spoken to the king himself. Your speech does not belong to any man of common birth." Turning her broad back to him, she resumed stirring the soup in the iron cauldron, which was attached to a sturdy but adjustable pot hook over the fire. The contents bubbled with hearty vigor.

Thomas' nose twitched at the piquant scent. "You are wrong! The smell from that pot is so ennobling that it would free a villein and raise a king to sainthood!" He might have broken his fast an hour before, but his mouth was truly watering. "What spices do you use? The nuns in our priory kitchen would add your name to their daily prayer if you would share the secret."

The cook laughed with joy like a young girl and was about to reply when a woman's voice, brittle with disapproval, rang out.

"You spend too much time in idle chatter, Hilda. Last night, supper was cold and late. Get back to work!" The source of the complaint stood at the kitchen entrance, rigid as a stick, arms tightly folded across her breasts.

The cook turned away and gripped the wooden spoon with both hands. Her sole response was to flush a far darker red than the heat of the kitchen might justify.

Thomas studied the angular, sallow-faced woman in the doorway. His instant impression of her was not favorable. "I beg pardon, Mistress, and ask that you blame me alone if there has been any failure worthy of rebuke."

Her tiny eyes narrowed as they swept over the monk from tonsure to foot and back again, but somewhere in between her expression softened. "I am Mistress Constance. My husband is the eldest son of Master Stevyn, steward to Henry de Lacy of high rank and renown." She began to lick her lips. "And who are you?"

Thomas wondered if he had somehow been transformed into a sizzling chunk of roasted venison.

A young man slipped quietly out of the shadows behind her and bent to her ear. "The monk is no wandering mendicant, Mistress."

Startled, the heir's wife yelped, her thin arms flailing wildly as she lost her balance.

The man laughed but quickly caught her before she fell. "He is Brother Thomas, and his prioress occupies the earl's chambers."

Shaking herself free of his grasp, she hissed at the young man. Although her exact words were incomprehensible, they were uttered with the vehemence of a curse.

"As I heard the tale, the late meal was your fault. Had you not been fluttering around Prioress Eleanor like some oversized moth, instead of getting her to a warm fire, she might have been less chilled and you might have had the supper when it was still hot."

Her look hard as granite and her yellowish complexion reddening to a dark orange, Mistress Constance grimaced as if she had just smelled sulfur from Hell. Then she directed a more honeyed gaze at Thomas. "Oh," she murmured, "it is your prioress who has sought shelter with us?"

"That is true."

"God has answered my prayers twice over! This house of sin has long needed a cleansing presence." She shot a malevolent glance at the young man behind her. "And now the evil has increased enough to require the intercession of more than one virtuous soul to save us."

With exaggerated caution, the young man eased his way around Ranulf's wife.

She drew back, flattening her back against the door frame as if the mere touch of his robe would defile her virtue.

"There is some bread and a piece of cheese over there, Master Huet." The cook pointed to the table at the far end of the kitchen. Confirming that Mistress Constance could not see her do so, she winked broadly at him.

"Beware, Brother, for my elder brother's beloved spouse weighs every mortal on her own scale of holiness. Prioress Eleanor's reputation has proven her to be most worthy, but you may have to spend many hours enduring her scrutiny before she deems you equal in respect.

"I honor my betters, something you might learn to do yourself," Constance barked.

Huet glanced heavenward and tore off some fresh bread, which he began to munch with unmistakable contentment.

"And my husband shall hear of your impertinence to me," Constance spat. "As for you, Hilda, attend your duties or you may find we no longer need your poor service." With that, she spun around and marched back to the manor house.

Huet dropped the bread and stretched his hand out to the cook. "I did not mean to cause trouble," he said, his voice soft with concern.

With a smile akin to that of an adoring mother, Hilda shook her head. "She's threatened to push me out the gate almost daily since she married your brother. Hasn't yet done so, as you can see." She turned to Thomas with a sheepish look. "I suffer from sinful pride, Brother, and believe there are few who do as well at my task with as much of an eye to cost. Master Stevyn and his first wife were kind enough to say so, and their guests often expressed satisfaction with the meals."

"Pride is sinful only when it exceeds merit," Thomas replied. "I would say that soup proves you are innocent of any excess."

The young man laughed. "If you be a priest, Brother, you must take my confession. Methinks any penance you'd require would be as gentle as your speech."

"And I would guess that you have some experience of priests?" Thomas replied, gazing with pointed interest at the man's head.

Huet instinctively stretched a hand over a slight indentation in his hair and flushed in silence.

The cook sat down on the bench and clutched the young man's arm with protective affection. "Whatever has happened, I cannot think he is at fault. A mischief, he might be, but he's a good lad at heart," she protested.

"I did not mean to suggest otherwise."

"The good monk knows no one in this place, Hilda." The man patted her hand. "There is no need to defend before any accusation has been made."

Jerking her head toward the kitchen door, the cook frowned. "Your sister-in-law suggested enough, lad, and others might also speak harshly of you with just as little cause. Softer words in a stranger's ear first are never amiss."

"Nor are honest ones." Huet turned back to the monk, all merriment dismissed from his expression. "In truth, I took no final vows, Brother. The tonsure has nearly grown out, and a falcon would be jealous of your keen eyes in noticing it."

"As guest in this manor, I have no cause to pry. That would be poor thanks for charitable hospitality." Thomas reached his hand out in peace.

Huet took it.

Thomas concluded he could do worse than to respect the cook's good opinion of the steward's younger son.

Content that the monk had no wish to condemn her favored lad, Hilda pushed herself from the table. "Then I must find enough chickens for the evening meal, lest Mistress Constance complain next that I am starving the master's guests." With that, she departed to seek some aged hens.

"Will you share this with me, Brother?" Huet gestured at what was left of the round loaf. "There is ale as well, and that cheese is dry enough to cry out for some."

Thomas nodded and cheerfully sat down with the man.

"You honor courtesy by asking no questions, Brother, but I must confide my whole story to my father in due course. Until then, I confess a wicked but delightful pleasure in telling my sister-in-law nothing." Huet poured the amber liquid into two pottery cups and passed one to the monk. "Despite her oft-repeated abhorrence of any hint of sin, Mistress Constance would take a knife to my soul if she thought she could learn the reasons for my return. In fact, my sins are dull enough, but she is convinced they are so loathsome that I have seen her salivate while imagining the horror."

Thomas grinned.

"I should not accuse my elder brother's wife of hypocrisy, for I do believe she honestly fears Hell, but I have oft wondered if she protests the evil in others just a bit too eagerly." He cut into the cheese wheel and dug out a crumbly orange chunk to offer the monk.

"Does your brother share this eagerness?"

"Ranulf reminds me of our dead mother in his ardent faith, although she chose to follow Our Lord's more charitable commands. As his example, my brother took the desert fathers. Like them, he roars against sin."

"I am surprised he did not wish to enter a monastery."

Huet chuckled. "Ranulf suffers from lust, Brother. He was wise enough to know he must marry for he is incapable of celibacy."

Remembering the look Mistress Constance gave him, Thomas hoped the wife pleased Ranulf more in the marital bed than the husband obviously satisfied his wife. "I grieve that they have found so little peace in God's love," he replied gently.

"And you show more charity than I ever have, Brother. Yet, for all his faults, my brother is kin to whom I owe a dutiful love. Ever since their marriage, however, he has grown more rigid in his ways, a change that I blame on her influence." He shrugged. "Did you look closely at her beady eyes? I have seen rats with a sweeter gaze. Whenever I meet her, I am transformed into a hunting cat and feel compelled to bat at her like prey." He bent his fingers into claws and swatted at a piece of bread.

"I heard that!" Hilda marched in from the courtyard and tossed her chosen fowl to a young girl for plucking and gutting. "Be careful, lad, or your father will take you to task for tormenting her," she said, glancing over her shoulder as she picked up a heavy knife.

"I doubt he'll pay me much mind, except to demand I prove myself no wastrel despite the abandonment of my studies. My father has enough to worry him with his new wife." Huet bit his lip as if he had not meant to say the last aloud, especially in a stranger's hearing.

Although his curiosity was pricked, Thomas pretended to have heard nothing of interest.

"I'll not make ill comment about Mistress Luce," the cook snorted, then looked down at one naked bird just placed on the table. She picked it up and tossed it back to the girl. "There are still pin feathers on this! Did I not teach you to singe them? Are you asleep?"

Comparing the woman's words to her tone, Thomas decided Hilda had been quite artful in expressing an unfavorable opinion of her mistress without the danger of condemnation.

"But your sire has a right to an explanation," the cook continued, and to add emphasis, she cracked through the joint of a chicken thighbone with a mighty thwack.

"Aye, but I confess I have yet to find the words."

"Talk to Mistress Maud, then. She's come to help the mistress and always did have a weakness for you despite your wicked tricks. She'll find a way for you to soften up the master."

"Our good cook thinks me awfully bad," Huet whispered loudly to Thomas.

"Only when he was a boy and would slip into the kitchen to steal bites of my pastry."

For just a moment, Thomas saw a little boy reflected in the man's eyes.

"I thought she'd blame the mice," Huet said.

The cook put her hands on her hips and glared at Huet with mock anger. "Mice have tiny teeth. I know a boy's mark from that of any rodent!"

Thomas roared with laughter. "I tried that myself as a boy and failed as well!"

"But she never told my mother." Huet went over to the cook and gave her a kiss on the cheek.

She blushed and quickly grabbed another fowl, whacking it neatly in half with one blow.

"Did your mother die very long ago?"

"What does it matter?" Huet then waved those words aside. "Forgive those callous words, Brother. I should have said that a son may learn to live with the grief, but he never ceases to miss a mother even when he believes her soul must surely be in Heaven."

For just an instant, Thomas wondered where his own mother's soul might be and quickly nodded with sympathy.

"Although I encouraged my father to marry again for his comfort and prosperity, I did not like his choice. Mistress Luce is near to my age and nothing like her honored predecessor." His brow darkened, and he stared at the fireplace where the soup pot continued to bubble with dogged enthusiasm.

Thomas watched him with increasing interest. Although courtesy did forbid questions, he wondered much about this younger son.

Huet looked back at the monk, his melancholy lightening from black to gray. "I have been told that a member of your company is gravely ill, Brother. Although I shall sincerely pray for her recovery, her sickness will require you to stay with us until she has regained health. I confess to some pleasure at the thought of your company." He tilted his head and now grinned mischievously. "Though I fear you may learn more about this family than you might perhaps wish."

"No dark secrets, I hope?" Thomas replied in like manner, but he was jesting only in part.

Huet's smile was equally inexact.

Chapter Seven

Eleanor awoke with a jolt, but her eyes focused with painful slowness. The light in the room was gray as an old man's hair, but the steady brightening proved the hour was after dawn rather than that fading grimness of coming night.

All was silent.

Terrified, the prioress jumped up from the bench against the wall and hurried to the bed. Bending over, she put her ear close to Mariota's almost colorless lips. The girl's breath was audible and ragged but steady, her skin dry and hot to the touch.

"But alive still," Eleanor said, anger with herself for falling asleep replacing the fear she had just suffered. At least God had been merciful, and her charge's soul had not left her frail body during the badly kept watch.

The wooden door creaked open.

"Is all well?" Maud whispered, slipping into the room.

"She sleeps."

The widow put the back of her hand against the girl's forehead. "Her fever is still too high. Would you hold her head just so for a moment?" She reached over to a ewer on a stand next to the bed and poured water into the basin. Dampening a cloth, she wrung it out and washed the girl's face. "We have tried an infusion of masterwort root and hope she will take some barley broth soon when she is alert enough to sip it. I hope that meets with your approval."

"You must follow the path you have found most successful," Eleanor said.

The corners of Maud's lips twitched upward at the confidence shown. "If this fails, we shall try other remedies to chase the excess heat from her and restore the balance of her humors. Cooked onions are often successful in these conditions." Smoothing the cloth out to dry on the stand, she gazed at the girl with evident concern. "At least she is young and looks strong enough to fight against this ill."

Eleanor closed her eyes. "I fear I slept toward morning."

"You need not fall ill yourself, my lady, and I think your prayers will have done this child more good than staying awake. As you see, she has survived the night. Had there been a crisis, the harsh rattling would have awakened you. There is no mistaking the sound of Death's chains when he comes to drag souls off for judgment."

"All my prayers were for her last night," Eleanor replied, "and I thank you for forgiving one who showed even greater carelessness than the five foolish virgins waiting for the bridegroom."

"My manner may be too blunt on occasion, my lady, but I meant no ill. A servant should have been assigned to stay with her while you slept. I saw how you stumbled with fatigue…"

"…and thus you took a far longer vigil than you allowed me, demonstrating both wisdom and kindness. It may have been my responsibility to watch all night, but I now see the imprudence in even considering it." She smiled to dispel any fears that she had been insulted by the widow's decision.

Maud chose not to reply and instead indicated that the prioress should lay the girl's head back down on the pillow. "Might you wish to break your fast now that I am here to watch your charge?"

The words may have been posed as a question, but Eleanor recognized it as a transparently disguised command. But a prudent one, she decided, without taking offence. Stubborn adherence to what she perceived as her duty would only add to the burdens on this household if a fever struck her down too.

"Might you direct me to the main hall? I fear I paid little heed to how we came to these chambers when we arrived last night."

◇◇◇

Once in the lower hall, Eleanor found all appetite had fled, and she found no pleasure in the one bite of cheese, its sharp flavor enhanced by warm bread fresh from the oven. At least the weak ale chased away some of the chill she had caught, sleeping against the damp stone of the chamber wall. Pouring more into her cup, she sipped. The bitter taste matched her mood. Perhaps she should delay her return to Mariota's side until she could lighten her own troubled spirit. At least she would try.

Dawn may have completed its announcement of the reluctant day, but the light remained dull and unenthusiastic. Most servants had left the hall to perform whatever duties they had been assigned and most probably with regret at the loss of this warmer haven. Eleanor prayed that they be given some respite on such a foul day. And stormy it most certainly was, she had noted on her way here, with intermittent rain slashing at any living thing within reach of the high wind.

At least the stone walls of the manor offered good protection against both draft and wet. Eleanor noted, however, that this main floor, where the manor court must be held, was aisled with wooden pillars that resembled trees where the bracing split to support the flooring of the solar above. Although the design was pleasing in its suggestion of a wooded grove, the presence of the aisles proved the house was older than the more modern use of stone walls would suggest.

Had the owner's sole desire been to make this a warmer manor or had he some other purpose for rebuilding the walls? Stone was most certainly a stronger defense against attack than wood. She must ask the steward about the history of this place, Eleanor decided. Although it was doubtful that the Earl of Lincoln had any traitorous intent or would even consider using such a minor residence as defense, she would pass the information on to her father in case he found the strong, new walls of interest to those loyal to the king.

She had delayed long enough, she decided. After all, she must relieve the physician's widow and let her attend the steward's wife. Willing herself to rise, the prioress left the hall.

The stairwell to the solar was steep and the steps narrow, even for the prioress' small feet. A clever device, she realized. Armed men would find the ascent more difficult here than in her father's castle of Wynethorpe. Thus the steward's family would be well protected. She nodded in appreciation of the design.

Near the top, where a window offered a view of the fields and outer buildings, she stopped. The opening had been fitted with a shutter, but that now banged against the wall with each gust of wind.

Perhaps it had been carelessly shut and the storm had finally blown it open, Eleanor thought, and tried closing it to keep the chill from the rooms in the solar. The alignment was askew, or else the boards were warped with the rain; thus she struggled awkwardly with the heavy wood. Finally, she gave up and sat in the window, putting her back to the recalcitrant shutter as if testing her ability to make the object obey her. "Indeed," she muttered to herself, "if I cannot force my own being to obey, how dare I hope that anything else will surrender to my command?"

What a foolish creature she was! Again she condemned her folly for taking this journey. The property issue on priory land so far from Tyndal could have waited for resolution until wild storms were rare and some warmth had returned to the earth. If she had been wiser and delayed the matter, Sister Anne and Prior Andrew could have accompanied her. Instead, she cared only that Brother Thomas be forced to come and stay close to her side.

She still loved this man—in all the wrong ways. When her prayers for relief from lust were answered, she was often grateful that Brother Thomas was at her priory, for their different natures allowed them to work most efficiently together in God's service. The rest of the time, she was obsessed with hunger to couple with the monk.

In the beginning there had been a certain sweetness to the longing. More recently, her lust had made her feel like a decaying corpse, and the rotten stink of her sin assaulted her nostrils with such foulness that she was surprised the stench had not spread throughout the entire priory.

As a counterweight, however, her vow of chastity remained stubbornly sincere. A child when she first promised to remain a lifelong virgin, she had not understood the full meaning of what she had sworn. Now she did. Yet she never took vows lightly. If Satan, with God's permission, set her body alight with these searing flames to test her steadfastness, she would battle the Prince of Darkness with the passion of a true knight and win the joust whatever the cost in physical suffering. After all, her body was only a shell that housed her immortal soul.

Nor would she ever tempt a man into sharing her wickedness. Even though she often questioned the sincerity of Brother Thomas' own calling, Eleanor had no reason to doubt that he had laudably kept his own vows. Thus she might choose to test her fortitude—or please herself, if she were ruthlessly honest—by keeping him close while she fought against her sinfulness, but she would never try to make him break his oath. At least she prayed she never would.

These thoughts began to stab too painfully at her heart, so she chased them off with the image of Mariota. Had she sinned by bringing the girl with her? Of course she could have asked another nun to provide proper attendance, but in this matter at least, she had meant well.

Mariota's family had begged entry for her at Tyndal, hoping she would become a nun. Eleanor had had doubts from the beginning about the strength of the young woman's calling. Even the girl's mother had whispered some fear that her daughter might not be willing to completely forsake the world to serve God. Nonetheless, there was a generous dowry for the priory if Mariota stayed, and Eleanor was well aware that no religious community survived long without such beneficence.

With all her other pressing responsibilities, however, there had been little time to gain the young woman's confidence in order to talk with her as needed. Eleanor suspected the girl might simply not know what she wanted. There was no doubt that a life of prayerful service profited family souls, and God rejoiced when mortals rejected the violence and sins of a secular world. Yet choosing the religious life with no calling often brought its own problems, and Eleanor had no wish to force young women to take on a life they would grow to hate, a loathing that often infected a community like some plague.

In any case, the decision regarding Mariota's future must be made soon. Eleanor had hoped the enforced companionship on this trip would allow the young woman to confide in her, and thus the prioress might suggest a clearer path for the girl. With this journey so cursed, however, even that plan had been thwarted, and now the poor child lay sick and in danger of dying.

Eleanor leaned her head back against the wooden shutter and groaned. How much she needed advice and direction herself!

On one hand, she had Brother Thomas longing to leave the priory and become a hermit for at least a year. On the other, she had a girl with a fine dowry who might have come to Tyndal with no calling at all.

She cursed her frailties!

Instead of granting her monk's request, she had ordered him to come on this trip where she could see him every day. Rather than sending Mariota home to think about her vocation, she had let her sit with the novices for far too long, hoping she would simply discover a calling.

"I am a fool," she muttered. "Greedy, selfish, and imprudent. Have I considered what is best for their souls? Nay, I have only thought of my own desires and the wealth of my priory." Sighing in frustration, she looked down on the manor land.

The fields were barren, all crops long harvested and either sold or stored in one of the outer buildings. To the left she could see a road crossing through a pasture, then where it veered abruptly toward the gate to the courtyard. Ruts, dug deep by wagon wheels, had filled with rainwater, making the way treacherous with slippery mud. Her party had been fortunate, Eleanor thought, that none of their horses had fallen or broken a leg last night.

A movement below and to her right caught her attention, and she cautiously slipped closer to the other side of the window to see more clearly.

Two people stood together near the thatched and steepled barn. In spite of the vile weather, neither appeared inclined to seek shelter.

How curious, Eleanor thought.

One of the pair was a woman, judging by her size and dress. Her robe was brightly colored and stood out against the rain-blackened wood of the barn. The other, a man, was clothed in a duller hue.

While the prioress watched, the man slid his hands down the woman's back, tucked them firmly under her buttocks, and pulled her hips against him. She clutched him yet closer, then threw her head back as he began to kiss her neck.

"And ardently enough to warm any body on such a day," Eleanor said aloud, surprised at the wanton display.

Suddenly the couple jumped apart.

Eleanor followed the direction of their gaze and saw several riders turning down the road toward the manor gate.

The woman picked up her robe and fled toward a low-roofed building, which the prioress guessed might be the stable. Her companion walked slowly to open the gate, then stood in the road where he waited to greet the lead horseman.

Gripping the rough stone for balance, Eleanor bent further out of the window. She could just see into the courtyard.

The rider was dismounting with observable stiffness and the steadying hand of the woman's companion.

The bright-robed woman now raced from the shelter of the stable, arms wide to embrace the horseman. "Dearest husband, you are safely returned!"

Had anyone noticed what she had seen just a moment before? Perhaps the couple had been sufficiently hidden from the view of all but her, Eleanor concluded.

The horseman apparently had not seen anything untoward. He embraced the woman willingly enough, before slipping his arm around her shoulders and limping out of sight.

"I wish I had not witnessed that," Eleanor murmured, sliding out of the window and back into the shadows of the stairway. Giving the shutter a pat as if granting some form of absolution, she left it hanging open and climbed the last couple of steps.

Surely the woman must be Mistress Luce. Although many religious might rightly consider the apparent lapse of virtue a proper matter to address, Eleanor decided that both courtesy and wisdom demanded she say nothing about what she had beheld. As a guest, she had no wish to bring dissention to a house that had granted refuge and aid to her desperate little company.

"The woman has a confessor," she murmured, while fervently hoping that the errant wife would seek both counsel and penance before her actions festered into even greater evil.

Chapter Eight

Despite wind so freezing that his nose ran, Thomas bent his head and walked through the courtyard mud with determination, while humming something Brother John had been teaching the novice choir at Tyndal.

A calico cat from the kitchen raced past him, in pursuit of some real or imagined prey, then skidded and tumbled into a puddle. As the creature shook herself, Thomas grinned. "Prioress Eleanor's orange cat would never display such lack of feline dignity," he teased affably.

Scrubbing with vigor, the cat pointedly ignored him.

Thomas slogged on, delighted at his remarkably bright spirits on this glum morning. Considering his long-entrenched gloom, this change should perhaps trouble him, but he decided that sort of logic came from Satan. The Fiend would rather any mortal be cursed with such hopelessness that the soul took on the burnt hue of the Evil One himself. The monk banished his doubt. After all, if he chose to analyze it with more care, the root of his happier mood was easy enough to discover.

After he had been shown to the kitchen last night, and dried himself by the hearth fire, he shared a late supper of hot soup and fresh bread with the cook and the kitchen servants. Although the arrival of the prioress' party, and the anticipated return of Master Stevyn, would mean extra work on the morrow, the servants took advantage of whatever ease they could enjoy before dawn.

And the company had most certainly been a merry one, reminding Thomas of boyhood days spent with the cook who raised him after his mother's death. Adding to the cheerfulness was the addition of Master Huet, younger son to the steward, who had just arrived himself the night before.

From a few overheard remarks by the servants, the monk concluded that the son's return had been quite unexpected, but the man was greeted with great delight nonetheless. Of course Thomas had recognized the grown-out tonsure at the time, an observation he found rather disturbing, but no one else seemed bothered and thus he dismissed his curiosity. If the others found joy in Huet's company, a man they knew far better than he, perhaps he should respect their view.

That had, in fact, been easy enough, for Thomas was soon beguiled by the man's graceful charm and quick wit. Now he shuddered in retrospect. Didn't the Devil have that kind of charm, numbing the soul to danger as he transformed his vile and sinful shape into one of more pleasing appearance?

Yet he had sensed no particular evil in Huet, either last night or this morning. Indeed, Huet had joined the servants with a humility uncommon in those of higher station. Many monks were rarely as modest, and imps most definitely never.

And Huet was a good storyteller, with many interesting tales about his travels. What pleased Thomas most, however, was the man's singing voice. He had amused them well with songs he had learned along the route, especially during his stay in Arras. The subject of the songs had been worldly love, but that did not matter to Thomas and most certainly not to Hilda, who alternately clutched her heart and wept joyfully over the lovers' trials in the romance of Aucassin and Nicolette.

Later, after the hearth fire had been banked and the company left to find sheltered corners and another body for warmth enough to sleep until sunrise, the cook had made a bed for Thomas near the hot ashes, then wrapped herself in a blanket and was soon snoring on the bench. It was just as the monk was also drifting off to sleep that Huet slipped into the kitchen and knelt by Thomas.

"May I share this space with you, Brother? The fleas in the hall are fierce," he had whispered. "I have brought a thick blanket large enough to wrap around us both. It will keep the draft away."

Another time Thomas might have rejected the offer, fearing even the innocent touch of another man, but tonight he was too weary from the hard journey to protest when Huet wrapped the two of them securely together inside the soft wool. Despite any misgivings, Thomas soon fell into the most peaceful sleep he had had since his days in London, and, for once, he suffered no dreams.

When he awoke the next morning, Thomas knew he had slept through at least two Offices. Huet was still snoring as the monk slipped out of his embrace.

I am not the only laggard, he thought with gentle amusement, looking down on the steward's younger son. Then he tenderly tucked the blanket closer around the sleeper so the young man would not suffer any chill.

Now Thomas caught himself singing, at least in muted voice, a very earthy chanson heard from the steward's son last night. He already owed penance for his failure to observe the Offices, but this quite secular expression only added to his failings. God might well understand that he meant nothing by this choice of song beyond an expression of his current happiness, but Thomas decided he had best follow the example of Saint Benedict and find some physical labor to do for swift atonement.

Thus he turned toward the stable. Being fond of the four-legged beasts, he would offer to tend the horses and especially his prioress' donkey.

As he hurried alongside the manor house, he was assailed by a rank odor and, looking down, saw the arched hole in the wall. "The night soil from the garderobe needs removal," he muttered and put a hand over his nose. In the heat of summer, flies and the stink would be unavoidably foul enough, but the recent bad weather had clearly prevented adequate cleaning. "At least the latrines at Tyndal drain into a fast-running stream," he muttered, grateful that their superior design prevented these problems.

The stench so distracted him that he did not hear the commotion until he rounded the corner.

There were several horsemen near the courtyard gate.

Thomas tensed. Was something amiss? He stopped to watch.

Near the stone steps leading to the manor house door, a manservant helped an older man dismount from his horse.

"Dearest husband, you are safely returned," a female voice cried out.

Thomas looked in her direction and saw a brightly robed young woman, arms wide, approaching the man. Was this Huet's father?

"Wife," the man replied. His flat tone and perfunctory embrace conveyed no enthusiasm.

The monk watched the steward lean on the woman and limp toward the manor door. Had they not addressed each other, he might have concluded that they were neither kin nor close friends, for all the affection either showed the other. Aye, she had embraced him, Thomas thought, but the gesture was cold, nothing more than a formal greeting. Nor had the steward shown any especial joy at her greeting, and his arm around her shoulders seemed placed there solely to give his stiff joints ease.

"Ah, but none of this is my concern," Thomas muttered, and turned away. At least his offer of help in the stables would surely be greeted with relief, considering the number of horses needing care. He smiled at the prospect of hard labor.

◇◇◇

When Thomas walked into the high-roofed, timbered structure, he saw a tall man leaning on his pitchfork and staring at a donkey as if the beast had just sprouted a horn in the middle of its gray forehead.

"That is Adam," the monk said. "The creature belongs to Prioress Eleanor."

"Eve rides Adam?" The man spun around, his mouth twisted into a lewd grin, and then realized he had addressed his jest to the wrong man. "A monk? Where did you come from?"

"Not from the Garden of Eden," Thomas replied. "Were it otherwise, I would have failed to understand your insult to my prioress."

"I intended no evil, Brother."

From the man's obvious embarrassment, Thomas decided he did mean little by his ill-mannered words and had merely spoken without thinking. He nodded acceptance of the apology. "I came to see if you needed extra hands to help with these horses."

"You accompanied the prioress who arrived in the storm last night?"

"Aye."

"Monks may have callused knees but rarely work-hardened hands."

Thomas grinned and stretched out his hand, palm up. "Mine may have softened in the last several weeks, but they will soon harden again with familiar work."

The man squinted at the monk's hand, then shook his head with some surprise. "I'm Tobye, groom to the steward and his family."

"Brother Thomas of the Order of Fontevraud."

"What can you do? Surely you didn't come here to muck out horse shit. If I can catch any of the younger boys, I make them do it." Tobye looked around. All lads had vanished.

Thomas rolled up his sleeves and looked around for another pitchfork. Now that the groom was standing straight, the monk realized how huge he was. Thomas himself was bigger than most men, and well-muscled enough, but this fellow had broader shoulders and was taller by some inches. He was grateful his vocation demanded the avoidance of violence for this was one man he would not wish to fight.

The man shrugged, found the extra tool leaning against the wall, and handed it to the monk. "Does your prioress truly ride that worthless creature?"

"She's a little woman." Thomas led the insulted beast to an empty stall nearby and returned to pitch fouled straw into a mound outside the donkey's allotted space.

"Are you are such a poor Order that she cannot afford even a sway-backed nag?"

Adam brayed loudly.

Tobye glared at the perpetrator.

"Our prioress refuses to ride a horse. If you are a good judge of the beasts, look over there." He pointed to the sleek creature in a nearby stall. "As you can see, I am but a simple monk, but that is the horse I rode on our journey."

The groom shook his head in amazement, then bent to his task as well.

The two worked in silence until the stalls were cleaned and fresh straw put down for the priory mounts, including Adam the donkey.

"I don't understand," Tobye muttered.

"What troubles you?"

"I know of no convent on this road, certainly not one that could afford to have its priest ride that fine horse."

"Have you heard of Tyndal Priory? It is close to Norwich."

He blinked. "That sounds like the monastery where Master Stevyn's first wife went when she fell ill. Although the lay brothers had no cure, the mistress praised the tonic they gave her to ease pain."

"We have a hospital at Tyndal. Prioress Eleanor is the leader there."

"A convent of nuns then?"

"Our Order is a double house…"

"With a woman in charge?"

"The mother house is in Anjou, and our founder…"

"French." Tobye spat.

"The Order is much favored by those who rule England."

The man blinked. "And you are mucking out a stable? What vile sins have you committed? I can think of no other reason than penance for this work."

"Many men, who dedicate themselves to God, do respect the vows taken."

Tobye jabbed the fork tines several times into the earth to clean them. "My tongue has a keener edge to it than is wise for a man of my low status. I beg pardon for any offense, Brother."

Thomas grinned. "Candor is a trait I may value, but I gather you have made enemies with it?"

"Not so much for that, Brother." He winked.

Opting to ignore the lewd inference, Thomas turned down his sleeves and put up the pitchfork. "As long as you do not offend your master."

Tobye fell silent, his face darkening.

"A good master?" Thomas asked, sensing the change in the man's mood.

"As good as some," was the enigmatic reply.

"I am a guest here and did not mean to pry."

The groom shrugged. "Your help was welcome, Brother, but I won't count on it tomorrow. Surely your prioress will have need of her priest."

The monk was confused by the rude dismissal but decided to let the matter be and quickly left the stable.

Watching Thomas walk away, the groom's eyes narrowed. When the monk had disappeared around the stone wall of the manor, Tobye spat into the mud.

Chapter Nine

"My lady!"

Startled by the screech, rather akin in volume and pitch to the cries of mating cats, Eleanor spun around.

Mistress Constance stood but a few feet behind, her fists knotted against her chest, and her expression suggestive of either rapture or apoplexy.

Taking a deep breath, the prioress willed herself to remain calm and nodded. Speech, she decided, might be ill-advised considering her dislike of the woman.

"Mistress Constance. Wife of Master Stevyn's eldest son, Ranulf. When you first arrived, I met you at the door…"

Eleanor took pity and interrupted the gasping recitation. "I remember you well, Mistress." An honest enough statement, she thought, and continued in the same innocuous vein. "The shelter we were offered was an act of mercy. I shall not forget the kindness."

"Ah!"

How sad, the prioress thought, as compassion now demanded entry to her heart. This woman might be wearisome, but she also lacked all joy, even in her faith. When mortals faltered with decaying age, terror over their sins often shimmered in their gaze, but surely Mistress Constance was only a few years older than Eleanor herself. Did merriment never dance in those eyes or laughter soften the angular features of her face? Faith might demand a healthy fear of doing evil to others, but, when Jesus turned water into wine at Cana wedding feast, he had shown that God allowed joy to reign equally in moral souls.

Joy? Now that she thought more on it, she realized that she had heard no child's laughter in the manor house. Perhaps this woman's sallow face and nervous manner were born of barrenness—or the death of too many babes, let alone so many other possible sorrows. A more gentle charity might be due this poor creature, Eleanor thought, and struggled to banish her annoyance. "We are well-met, Mistress. I seek the steward's wife. Perhaps you might direct me to her?"

The woman waved a hand in front of her face as if a plague of flies had just descended. "Mistress Luce could be anywhere, my lady. Like many youthful creatures, she has little patience with duty and often lacks firm purpose. Fortunately, she has me to direct the servants in the work God made them to do." She pointed her nose upward, a feature that matched her chin in sharpness. "As you must know yourself, servants are like children. They require close supervision if they are to do their duty and not steal the plate."

Eleanor shut her eyes. Her charitable resolve now began a determined retreat. "I defer to your superior knowledge."

Constance had the grace to blush.

"Taking on such arduous duty is most praiseworthy, Mistress, and I am aware that our unexpected arrival has added to your already significant burden," Eleanor continued, biting her lip to remind herself that a civil tone was required. "As you surely understand, however, I owe due courtesy to the mistress of this manor, Master Stevyn's wife."

Mistress Constance nodded, then must have realized how propitious an opportunity this was to talk further with the Prioress of Tyndal. Her face brightened. "I shall help you find her!" she said, and gestured for the prioress to follow.

As the woman took Eleanor to several places where Mistress Luce might be found, Constance chattered breathlessly about her own many duties, before explaining in yet more detail why the mistress of the manor was rarely at any of locations visited.

After seeing the linen storage, buttery, kitchen, and even where furs were kept in the garderobe to keep them safe from moths, Eleanor had had enough and found a way to extricate herself. Taking advantage of a momentary intake of breath, Eleanor quickly thanked Constance for her trouble and hurried away, climbing the steps to the solar and the room where Mariota lay. It was there she actually found Mistress Luce, in the company of Mistress Maud.

◇◇◇

When she pushed open the wooden door, however, both women cried out, alarmed by the unexpected arrival.

Maud was the first to bow her head in greeting when she saw the prioress. Luce remained rigidly still, face pale and eyes narrowed as if resentful over the intrusion.

What have I interrupted? Eleanor asked herself, noticing the pallor in each woman's face.

Maud begged leave from the prioress to depart, then disappeared without any word to Mistress Luce.

Walking to the edge of the bed, Eleanor decided the wisest course would be to ignore any tension between the two women. "How does the patient fare?" she asked mildly.

Mistress Luce raised her eyebrows as if surprised at the question, then followed the prioress to the bedside.

Mariota still lay on her back, eyes shut, covers tucked up around her chin. When Eleanor touched her forehead, however, she realized the fever had eased. "God be praised!" she whispered. "She is better."

"The widow does have some skill with the sick," Luce replied, her tone mocking. "Moreover, she has decided which of my servants should sit by this girl's side when you need respite."

The prioress stepped back and silently studied Master Stevyn's wife.

Luce's expression was both defiant and scornful. Her lips twisted into a thin smile.

Although Mistress Constance had described this woman as a young and flighty creature, Eleanor saw only anger, perhaps resentment, but no immature petulance. In addition, Mistress Luce was as possessed of as much passion as Ranulf's wife was devoid of it. "I am happy to have found you, Mistress," she said aloud. "Expression of my gratitude for your charity is long overdue. I fear our arrival has settled a great burden on your household."

"I had little to do with giving you shelter, my lady. My daughter-in-law may have been of service, although she usually succeeds only when others with greater ability grow impatient with her incompetence and do the tasks themselves. The woman who just left often forgets her place here, but she is probably more worthy of your thanks. As mistress of this manor, however, I must take the blame when things go ill, so perhaps I should take credit as well in balance." There was no warmth and little grace in her smile. "You are most welcome to our poor hospitality until your charge is strong enough to travel. My husband would have it no other way."

Eleanor replied with due courtesy, all the while amazed at how different Mistress Constance and Mistress Luce were. If she had cause to wonder at the rigidity and lack of any joy in Mistress Constance, she was equally surprised at Mistress Luce's angry soul—and the dangerous passion she had shown for a man not her husband.

Was Master Stevyn such a brutish spouse that resentment had bloomed like gangrene in her heart? Was she truly deficient in her duties, as Ranulf's wife had suggested? Was she so ruled by lust that she let others, like Mistress Maud, take over what she herself should do? And why allow an outsider, a physician's widow, perform a wife's duties and not some longtime servant? Yet this adulterous wife did not strike Eleanor as a frivolous or even a lazy woman. Her wiry, albeit short, stature almost vibrated with energy.

She realized she had remained silent for too long. "I will add you to our prayers for this profound generosity," the prioress said aloud. Although she questioned much in this manor, Eleanor knew she would have to quiet her curiosity since neither the health nor the safety of her charges was at stake.

"Such repayment will be sufficient. We have no need for more. My husband manages this land quite profitably, and the Earl of Lincoln shows his pleasure in useful ways," Luce replied. "Now I must attend my husband who is resting after his arduous journey home." With that, she turned abruptly and left the room.

Perhaps she had no cause to pry into Mistress Luce's soul, but Eleanor could not resist following her quietly and peeking around the door to see which direction the steward's wife had taken.

After the woman disappeared down the steps, Eleanor went to the window and waited until she saw Luce in the courtyard below, walking toward the stable. Unless Master Stevyn had chosen to nap amongst his horses, his wife was probably going to meet her lover.

Chapter Ten

Although night is the time when imps lewdly dance in the guise of shadows and the Prince of Darkness fills wicked souls with the desire to do evil unto other mortals, it is also the hour of dreams, often bitter but on occasion sweet.

Some claim that soft dreams are God's way of reminding us that good may still rule during the season of Evil's dominion. Others believe that such sweetness in the dark hours comes from Satan himself, cursed by the memory that he was once one of God's most powerful angels.

Whatever the truth might be, the dreams of those mortals, safely surrounded by the walls of Master Stevyn's manor, were gentle enough that following night.

Mariota fell into the deeper sleep of healing, her dreams perhaps reflective of hope that she might still live.

The Prioress of Tyndal remembered only one dream in which Mistress Maud, who had taken over the sick watch, slipped from the room. A dream it most certainly was, she decided, for the physician's widow was sitting by Mariota's bed when Eleanor woke for prayer.

As for Thomas, he fell asleep once again in the arms of Huet who seemed to hold him even closer than he had the night before. At some time in that night the young man left their mutual but chaste bed, and the monk awoke to regret the resultant chill. Then he too rose to chant the early Office and thank God that he had been blessed for once with no dreams at all.

And what were Tobye's dreams that night, sleeping alone in the warm straw of the stable, before a figure crouched over him and slit his throat?

Chapter Eleven

Was it a scream that woke Eleanor, or the shouting from the courtyard?

She sat up and stared through the darkness of morning toward a flickering light. Someone was standing in the doorway.

"Have you heard, my lady?" Maud's voice trembled.

"What has happened?" Eleanor slipped out of the linen cover on her mattress and quickly glanced at Mariota.

The girl turned over and mumbled but did not fully awaken.

"I'm not sure," the widow continued in a low voice. "Yet I did hear a cry of *murder* and knew you must be told." She pressed a hand to her throat and leaned back to look outside the door toward the stone stairs.

An old servant, puffing and red-faced even in the torch light, appeared at Maud's side. "Stay within, for God's sake," she hissed. "There is evil about!"

"Wait!" Eleanor said, hurrying to the entrance. "Explain what evil you mean?"

"Tobye, the groom, is dead."

The widow remained expressionless for a long moment, then gasped. "What cause? I noted no signs of illness when I saw him yesterday."

"Murdered, my ladies, murdered." With the promise of an interested audience, the servant began to elaborate, waving a dimpled hand in enthusiastic emphasis. "Blood splattered everywhere.

Gutted like a deer, I've heard." She bent forward, fingers cupped at her mouth as she whispered hoarsely: "Someone else said his privates were chopped…" Suddenly remembering that one of her listeners was a nun, the servant coughed, then finished her tale but omitted the other rumored details. "Master Stevyn had ordered horses for an early hunt. When they were not at the manor door, he went to the stable and found the body. Now, Sir Reimund is here with his men."

"Then he shall want the hall made ready, with table and benches down and ale for his throat, so he can speak with us all," Maud interrupted. "On what task were you sent?"

"To tell the mistress the news."

"Do not forget to ask her what orders she has for preparing the hall downstairs."

"She won't…" The servant's mouth puckered eloquently enough, but she fell silent as she looked sideways at Eleanor, perhaps fearing further speech would reveal a household secret to a stranger, even if the outsider was a religious.

"Then seek Mistress Constance."

The woman grimaced.

"And if you cannot find her, come see me here."

"That I shall," the woman replied before scurrying off.

Eleanor and Maud retreated into the chamber and shut the door. "Methinks she will return soon enough for direction from you," the prioress said, splashing icy water on her face, then reaching for her wimple.

From the courtyard, they could hear increasing commotion.

"I am an old friend of the family, known by the household servants even before Mistress Luce was born. Although I hold no authority here and do know my place…But you have met both Mistress Luce and Mistress Constance, thus most certainly understand the difficulty."

The dilemma I do, even if the root cause remains hidden from me, Eleanor thought as she touched her face around the wimple to make sure both head and neck were properly covered. "The servants will need your guidance and counsel today. Mariota seems well enough to be left alone in my care. If you will instruct me on the dosage of her medicine and…"

"You are most kind, my lady, but I would be wise to remain here myself. In doing so, I may escape condemnation as a meddling creature but shall be where any servant, who needs advice, can find me swiftly."

"Then I will seek those who may need God's comfort in the face of this horrible and most unnatural deed," the prioress replied, keeping her expression free of her appreciation for Maud's clever ploy.

The widow looked away as if fearing her blunter views of the two women might be read in her eyes.

What was her true opinion of Mistress Luce? The steward's wife had referred to Maud's assumption of authority with sarcasm, albeit with a hint of respect compared to the blundering of Constance, but the widow had been reasonably cautious in her own comments about the true mistress of the household. Was Maud aware of the relationship between Tobye and the steward's wife? If so, she must know how Luce would react to the news of her lover's death.

How grieved might the master's wife be? As the image of Brother Thomas came to mind, Eleanor knew that his death would shatter her heart. On the other hand, if Luce's affair with the groom was simply a means to ease a throbbing between the legs…

She decided to change the subject and walked to the window. "Who is Sir Reimund?" she asked, gazing down at those milling about in the courtyard.

"The sheriff of this county."

Hearing hesitancy in the widow's voice, Eleanor was reminded of the ever-absent sheriff in her own land. The dead King Henry displayed many virtues in her opinion, but his sheriffs had grown notoriously corrupt during his reign. Raising an eyebrow, she turned around. "Forgive me, but might I ask if he is a man not known for his energy in pursuit of justice, or even one lacking in some honesty?"

Maud took a sudden interest in one broken thread in her sleeve. "He serves the needs of this manor well enough, my lady, for he knows to whom the land belongs. As for honesty, the sheriff has never taken a bribe to my knowledge." She snapped the thread in two, then met the prioress' gaze. "We have learned that his methods of investigation in any crime vary according to the rank of the aggrieved. For this killing, we may expect a swift resolution. He will look to the servants."

The prioress glanced back into the courtyard, seeking the sheriff. None below was dressed with an eye to fashion or elegance, as might be expected of a man filled with ambition. Near the stable and standing by a fine black horse, however, there was one in close conversation with someone whose neck was respectfully bent. "Does he not have a crowner to assist him in his inquiries?"

"Aye, but I would not look to that one for any cleverness. This is no local gossip, for my late husband treated the man often enough for cuts and bruises. The crowner is best known for the amount of ale he drinks than any crime he has solved. I doubt you'll find him in the company below. He's rarely sober enough to mount a horse."

But Eleanor's attention was suddenly directed away from sheriffs and crowners. Down in the courtyard, to the left of the one she assumed was Sir Reimund, she saw Brother Thomas talking to another man. She might not be able to hear what was said, but the gestures were eloquent enough. The man had shoved her monk, and Thomas had just raised his fist.

The Prioress of Tyndal dashed from the room.

Chapter Twelve

Eleanor stood at the entrance to the manor house and tried to find some safe pathway through the turmoil.

A few paces from her, their piles of soiled linen stuffed into woven baskets, two laundry women chattered, pale faces close together.

To their right, several men argued, their gestures wild and their loud voices suggesting the disagreements were growing less than amicable.

Horses neighed. Babes cried.

And, somewhere in this madness of fear, a man's unshriven soul had been sent to Hell.

The prioress shuddered, as if Satan himself had just brushed her cheek with impious touch.

"My lady!"

Startled, Eleanor turned to face the stranger who had appeared by her side.

"I am Ranulf, eldest son of Master Stevyn. You should not be in this profane place, even with proper attendance." He scowled with evident disdain as he looked around. "Of which I see none."

She stiffened at his presumptuous tone. How dare this man tell her where she should and should not be? On the other hand, she did not want to imagine what he would think if she told him she had come to stop her monk from getting into a fistfight. "A man has been unlawfully slaughtered," she chose to say. "I wish to bring God's comfort to his family." After all, she had intended to seek them out.

"The Devil was his only kin." He gestured at the crowd. "And here before you are many more the Evil One can claim as his own, vile creatures that should be frying in Hell's fires." His jabbing finger stopped to point at a plump, middle-aged woman, whose face was red with weeping as she clutched her fists to her heart.

What cause had this woman to mourn Tobye's death, Eleanor asked herself, or were her tears born of shock and fear?

"Let me escort you from this obscene display." Ranulf placed himself in front of the prioress as if intending to herd her backwards like some recalcitrant sheep. "A woman dedicated to God's service rejects this evil world for good reason, and your presence here is most improper."

A firestorm of anger at this impudence roared through her. "You are very kind to remind me of the corruption my soul may suffer," she replied through clenched teeth, "but I…"

Like a prayer answered, the crowd parted and revealed the solution to her predicament. Over by the stable, the prioress saw that her monk was not rolling in the mud, trading blows with another man; he was still standing, albeit with fist firmly held prisoner by his other hand, and shouting. The object of his wrath had turned his back.

"Brother Thomas stands over there," she said to Ranulf. "I would consider it an act of charity if you brought him to my side."

Refusing to budge from his position in front of the prioress, he muttered, "I cannot leave you without protection here."

She glared and folded her arms into her sleeves.

"Brother Thomas!" the man bellowed. The pitch was high enough to penetrate the crowd noise.

When the monk spun around and saw Eleanor, his expression shifted from anger to a thankful obedience.

She exhaled with relief and gestured for him to join her. "I owe you gratitude, Master Ranulf," she said when Thomas was a few steps away. "I must no longer keep you from your more pressing duties. As you will agree, with a priest by my side, I now have suitable protection from the wickedness here."

Ranulf hesitated longer than was proper, but he did finally bow and march off.

Thomas frowned as he watched the man leave.

"The steward's eldest son," Eleanor explained, her eyes following Ranulf's progress across the courtyard.

"A grim face," Thomas said. "When I heard him shout, I first thought someone had stepped on a goat's teat."

The prioress swiftly covered her mouth to keep laughter back, but the monk had seen the smile and grinned with companionable amusement.

"For this lack of charity, we must both do penance, Brother," Eleanor replied, recognizing that she had failed to color her words with proper sternness. Ranulf might have been rude, but he had only meant to offer her protection and an escort away from harm. It was cruel to mock the steward's son. After all, she was a nun and had no obvious cause to be in this place. If she were to point her finger at the greatest sin in this brief encounter, she would have to choose her own puffed-up pride.

"I have met his wife," Thomas said.

"As have I."

The two glanced at each other.

"Methinks he merits our prayers, Brother," Eleanor replied.

The monk nodded, having the grace to turn away and hide this grin. "What may I do to serve you, my lady?"

"The reason I am here, thus causing Master Ranulf such distress, was something I saw from that window." She tilted her head. "Please explain why you were about to strike that man?"

"I beg forgiveness…"

"When we return to our priory, I am sure Brother John will provide his usual wise counsel and remind you that it is the meek who shall inherit the earth. However, even though no monk, especially a religious of Tyndal, should ever trade blows with another mortal, I must hear the cause for your singular behavior today."

"You have been told that a man was murdered?"

"One who worked in the stables: Tobye."

"When I heard the commotion, I rushed into the courtyard and learned that his body had been found in the stable. Then I saw the sheriff's men pulling the corpse outside." He gestured toward the stable door. "I feared evidence had been destroyed by that thoughtless act and tried to explain my concerns to one of the men involved."

"Perhaps Sir Reimund had already examined the site before he ordered the body removed."

"I do not believe so. According to the cur I questioned, the sheriff did not want Master Stevyn offended by the splattered gore when he came to identify the body. Thus he ordered the wound covered and the corpse dragged over there."

As she looked in the direction the monk was indicating, Eleanor realized that Ranulf had not left the courtyard. Instead, he was standing next to the man with the black horse and seemed to be discussing something with great passion. Nearby, the dead body lay in the mud.

"As you see, Tobye's corpse still lies like some slaughtered animal for anyone to stare at. When I asked that the body be handled with greater respect at the very least, I was mocked. I fear I lost my temper."

"We can do little about evidence which is no real concern of ours, Brother, but I shall ask that the dead man be taken away so his body may be properly prepared for burial."

He bowed his head. A muscle twitched in his cheek.

Eleanor realized her tone had been dismissive, yet she did understand just how angry her monk was. Without doubt, she shared the feeling and felt a prick of irritation over the carelessness shown. Their own Crowner Ralf would never have been so lax about searching for evidence. But the crime was not theirs to solve, and thus they had no right to intervene.

That acknowledged, she thought, no one should show such callous disregard for any man's dead body. God treated all souls equally, whatever their rank on earth, and the soul would seek to reclaim its body at the resurrection. To mistreat Tobye's corpse, as the sheriff was doing, touched on the blasphemous. She shut her eyes, trying to calm her growing outrage. Surely the man would not take his obvious disdain for the lower ranks so far as to defile…

She spun around and faced the monk. "I have some information that I should probably share with Sir Reimund," she said, keeping her voice low.

"Indeed, my lady?" Anger was still evident in the high color of his cheeks.

"I have cause to suspect that Tobye was committing adultery with Master Stevyn's wife."

His head shot up, but he was too shocked to speak.

"I saw them together just before the steward and his men returned to the manor. Their behavior was such that no reasonable man would say their relationship was solely that of servant and mistress."

"Then Master Stevyn must be a suspect in this murder," he whispered back.

"I fear so, yet this sheriff may not share that belief."

"Surely he cannot ignore what you witnessed. Stranger though you may be here, you are still the Prioress of Tyndal."

"And one who is no stranger to this manor has told me that Sir Reimund will do his best to avoid troubling the powerful. If the Earl of Lincoln holds Master Stevyn in high regard…"

"…the sheriff will seek some way to discount any suggestion of his guilt."

"Thus I question the wisdom of revealing what I saw." Eleanor gave Thomas an inquiring look. "At least until I can weigh the measure of Sir Reimund for myself and see how this matter proceeds."

"In the meantime, what do you want me to do?" The monk's eyes sparkled with anticipation.

How I do love this man, Eleanor exclaimed to herself as she watched eagerness paint his face with a boy's excitement. But when she spoke to him, her words betrayed nothing but calm purpose. "Accompany me to the sheriff, then step away and I shall play a game or two with him. The very least we should be able to accomplish is proper treatment of the corpse. Perhaps I shall also learn that Sir Reimund is more amenable to a just resolution of this crime than rumor suggests is likely."

"My lady, I am most eager to do whatever you wish!"

Eleanor was grateful that Brother Thomas had bowed for her cheeks had grown too hot with pleasure at those words.

Chapter Thirteen

Sir Reimund frowned when he saw a tiny nun walking toward him. Surely God had not suddenly dropped him into a convent's cloister. Might she be a vision?

The creature now stood in front of him, hands modestly tucked into her sleeves. He shut his eyes, hoping the apparition would be gone when he looked again.

She was no vision.

He bowed.

A phantasm would have been preferable. He had dealt with evil often enough that the Devil himself might arrive for a friendly supper and he would be little bothered. But a nun? Solving a murder on a manor run by the Earl of Lincoln's steward without setting either earl or steward against him was difficult enough. Now he had to get this Bride of Christ back to the chapel where she belonged without offending God.

Eleanor nodded her head in acknowledgement of his courtesy. "Forgive me, Sir Reimund, but I have heard that the Prince of Darkness has caused some wicked soul to commit murder in this place."

"You did understand correctly, Sister, and thus I most ardently pray that you return to the chapel and beseech God for mercy. Your immediate intercession with Him shall give us the strength needed to find the perpetrator."

"Pray, I most certainly shall. First, however, I must beg a favor."

"If you want a gift for your convent, I will consider it amongst the other worthy requests I receive almost daily." He stared down into the gray eyes looking up at him. "I will send a suitable person to the chapel later to hear you out on this." He turned away, feeling oddly discomfited by her look.

"My request has nothing to do with gold or property."

He squeezed his eyes shut against a deluge of frustration. "A most persistent member of her ilk," he muttered under his breath. "God preserve me from that kind."

"Sir Reimund..."

He spun around. "This is no place for a woman dedicated to God's gentler service. I will have you escorted away immediately." While seeking out one of his men to attend him, he gripped her arm as he might any common woman who had gotten in his way.

As if a lightning bolt had just coursed through her, Eleanor went rigid with shock.

Perhaps it was the stiffening of her arm that awoke him to the profanity of his act, but Sir Reimund suddenly froze, then painfully willed open each offending finger and stepped back.

Eyes blazing with fury, the prioress remained speechless.

Sweating despite the chill air, the sheriff looked around. A monk stood just beyond a circle of men. Sir Reimund sighed as if a sharp attack of indigestion had just eased. "Brother," he called out in a voice tight with tension, "will you please lead this lost sister to a safer haven?"

Thomas looked at the woman in question. "If my lady wills it."

"My lady?" Sir Reimund gazed around the courtyard. What woman of rank had just arrived? Then he looked down at the nun he had so offended, and, for the first time, noted the signet ring on her now exposed finger.

◇◇◇

Watching apprehension blanch his face, Eleanor willfully allowed wicked pleasure to fill her soul. "I am Prioress Eleanor of Tyndal," she said, "granted hospitality here when a member of my party fell too ill to travel farther in the storm."

"I know of your father, my lady." The sheriff's cheeks now became mottled. "I hope I have not offended for such was never meant." He stiffly bowed.

Eleanor answered his concern with an ambiguous inclination of her head and caught the mild curse he muttered under his breath. "The favor I ask is a simple thing. I did not wish to interrupt your work, but the poor dead body, lying there in the mud, cries out for pity. I beg your permission to have it borne to the chapel. If you and your men are finished examining the sad corpse for clues, will you not allow the mercy? It seems a cruelty to let the body lie there in public view as if it belonged to some common criminal."

"Gladly." He shouted for two men close by to approach. "These will carry the dead man away as you wish. In fact, there is little enough the body has to reveal. The method of killing is common enough amongst those of low rank, and I expect we shall have the murderer in custody before long."

Which poor, and most probably innocent soul will you weigh down with chains, the prioress wondered, the thought chilling her. Mistress Maud seemed to have the true measure of this man. Although she had intended to tell him what she had witnessed from that window, doubts stopped all speech. The sheriff's outrageous behavior to her, when he knew she was a religious but not her rank, suggested he had little regard for those he deemed of little merit. Would he not toss aside any information that threatened an easy solution and one that would offend no one of high station?

There was another concern that troubled her as well. With the death of King Henry, a shift in power at court was inevitable. There was no guarantee that her father's former influence would continue under King Edward. If the winds were changing even before the new king's return, and Sir Reimund was cognizant of the fresh direction, he might choose either to ignore her testimony or somehow use it for ill if he saw political advantage in doing just that.

Prudence suggested she delay giving her evidence until she was sure it would be used in a proper manner.

"You said you were staying here because a member of your party had fallen ill?"

Eleanor tensed. Sir Reimund's expression reminded her of the look in a feral creature's eyes before it killed the prey. "One of my charges, a young woman from our priory who seeks advice on entering God's service with us," she replied uneasily.

"And does she mend?"

Why would this man suddenly show such interest in the health of a potential nun? Did he know her family? "She remains ill," she said warily, "although there are hopeful signs of improvement."

"Ah! That means you must remain here for some time. I shall have a man sent to guard you."

"There is no need," she protested. "I was accompanied by several men and am sure you will require the services of all yours."

"Your safety is my responsibility while you are in this shire, my lady. If I did not assign one of mine to protect you, and you came to some grief, I would suffer well-deserved censure for my carelessness. The man I will select shall be discreet and respect your vocation, but he must remain nearby at all times until this foul killer is captured."

She had been bested! Eleanor seethed. This man, who must spend time at court, had apparently learned more about her than her father's position. Why had she not realized this? Her aunt had told her that her exploits against those in Satan's thrall had reached many ears. Sir Reimund had obviously heard the tales of how she had brought some to justice.

"After these men have removed the corpse to the chapel and out of profane sight, I am sure you will want to follow immediately and pray for the poor man's soul." With a deep bow, he turned and walked away, his bearing confident as if he had just won at chess.

Eleanor watched him, grinding her teeth with fury. This sheriff was no fool. Although she had never intended to meddle, he must have feared she might do just that. By placing her under guard, however reasonable that might seem, he effectively prevented her from doing anything that might embarrass him or keep him from making a quick arrest, one made with minimal concern for justice but maximum benefit to his ambitions.

"But you erred in your judgment of me," she muttered, "and now shall pay both for your insult and your presumption."

A lanky young man approached, most probably her guard.

She smiled sweetly at the sheriff's man. As she remembered her brother once saying, an army might lose battles but still win the war.

Chapter Fourteen

Eleanor and Thomas knelt by the corpse and begged God's mercy for Tobye's soul. Yesterday, the man might have been handsome enough to entice any woman to tumble with him in the stable straw. Today, his mutilated body proved inspiration only to hungry maggots and priests seeking an image for a sermon on mortal decay.

"Might your guard join us here?" the monk asked in Latin, with no change in intonation from that of prayer.

Without hesitation, the prioress answered in Latin as if replying to a priest's call for a congregational response. "He waits outside and gladly enough. I told him we wished to pray alone for the groom's unshriven soul. The guard must be new at this work because his face turned green at the sight of this poor man's slit throat, then paled at the thought that his spirit might still be hovering. Fortunately," she added with evident amusement, "you do not fear ghosts, as I learned at Amesbury."

After all this time, Prioress Eleanor's Latin proficiency should not surprise him, but Thomas knew that most women of religious vocation, even those holding high rank, had little knowledge of it. Now that she had reminded him of the events at Amesbury, however, he remembered Sister Beatrice, a woman possessed of a most formidable mind and education, who had taught Prioress Eleanor and just happened to be her aunt.

"How I wish Sister Anne were here," he replied, hoping his hesitation did not suggest he had changed his mind about wandering spirits.

"She has tutored you well enough, and I have long trusted your ability to note significant details. Please be quick in your examination of that body, however, lest my guard grow suspicious or someone else joins us in this small chapel. Convey in Latin what this sad corpse tells you."

Rising quickly, Thomas walked over to the body and stood where he could keep the chapel door in view. He pulled the rough sheet down just far enough to expose Tobye's naked chest, then began touching his cheeks and neck.

Eleanor continued intoning prayers.

"He has not yet fully stiffened." He checked the hands, arms, chest, and shoulders. "I cannot be sure, since I did not see the body where it lay, but I see no evidence of a struggle. No blood on the fingers nor obvious flesh under the nails, only the usual mud and dirt. No unusual cuts, bruises or scratches."

The prioress gave a short answer to suggest they were continuing the call and response of a set prayer.

The monk now bent to study the throat cut. "If the groom was asleep when he was attacked, either a man or a woman might have slit his throat. It was cleanly done, which suggests little or no hesitation about committing the deed. That points to a man, one who hunts or has experience in battle. The killer must be skilled with a knife to cut so efficiently and quickly, nor was it deeper than required to send the soul to judgement. Thus I might conclude the deed was not done in the heat of anger." Fearing he had heard a sound, he glanced up.

Eleanor looked over her shoulder as she continued her prayers, then gestured for the monk to continue.

Thomas examined the head before quickly pulling the sheet over the body. "That is all my poor skills tell me." Quietly returning to his prioress' side, he knelt and whispered, "The lord of this manor could surely have killed the man who had put horns on his head."

"Or else a woman, skilled with cutlery, who became enraged when another supplanted her in the bedding straw. We must look further into this crime," she continued to chant.

Puzzled, Thomas looked at his prioress. "I am your servant in all things, my lady, but will you give me leave to ask a question?"

"Granted, Brother."

"How far will we pursue this? I understand that the king's man has a certain reputation, but reason also argues that those who live here know the nature and relationships of their fellows better than we. Surely they will provide good evidence and force the king's man to render a proper justice. As strangers, I question our efficiency in this matter. As guests, do we have the right to interfere?"

Eleanor glanced at the door behind them. It remained shut. "Were this king's man as conscientious as our crowner, we would reveal all we know and let him find the killer. Based on my brief conversation with him, however, I think he lacks a certain integrity. Yet his high position in this county may cause many to be anxious about retaliation if they present evidence which does not suit his purpose. Fear of retaliation may shatter their honorable intentions and render them silent."

Thomas still looked troubled.

"Yet you would be right to question me further, Brother. My ardor for probing deeper into the matter is partly born of my own sinful craving for retribution. This king's man showed disrespect for my vocation before he knew my rank. If he has so little regard for the sanctity of a simple nun, he will show equal contempt for justice if it interferes with his ambition. The courtesy demanded by our position as guests may be affected by that."

Thomas' face flushed. "What did he do?"

"You had stepped away on my command," she continued, answering his unspoken concern, "and thus could not have seen him grasp my arm, an indignity no man commits against a woman dedicated to God." Her Latin now fell again into the cadence of chant. "But feel no anger on my behalf. Honor shall be assuaged if he is forced to look beyond his self-interest to find the murderer. As we had decided before, we need not solve the crime, but we must set him irrevocably on the path he should take, whatever direction he may prefer. The difference between our original intent and the current one is only the force with which we shall push him. That purpose can only succeed if we produce proof which he cannot hide and of sufficient strength that he cannot dispute it."

"What do you wish of me, my lady?"

"First, examine the stable for any evidence since no one seems to have done that. Next, learn what gossip is about, for you are sleeping in the kitchen and have access to many of the servants here. Take care not to arouse suspicion in this and remember that someone wields a knife with stealth and efficiency. You must not fall victim to the killer."

"And you, my lady? Will you also take care? I fear that you will not remain apart from these troubles."

"Do I not have yon lout outside the door in constant attendance?" Eleanor sighed. "Yet he bears no blame for the duty he was commanded to perform. Perhaps he may even prove more useful in protecting me than stopping me from doing what this king's man feared I might. You and I shall meet for prayer before breaking fast tomorrow, and we shall chant the Office as well as our findings in this matter of justice."

As one they loudly sang, "Amen!"

Thomas carefully opened the chapel door, and the pair stepped outside. There was no sign that anyone had lingered outside to overhear, but Eleanor's confidence in her assigned protection diminished when she looked at her guard.

All their caution to speak in a tongue he would not understand was unneeded.

The man was sound asleep.

Chapter Fifteen

"How does Mariota?" Eleanor shut the chamber door quietly behind her.

Maud raised a cautionary finger to her lips and signaled for the prioress to follow her out of the room. When the widow saw the sheriff's man leaning against the wall outside, however, she stepped back in dismay.

"Nothing more untoward has occurred," Eleanor said. "Sir Reimund ordered a guard to protect me until Tobye's murderer is captured." Her voice gave no hint of her opinion about this gesture.

The man yawned, then flushed with evident embarrassment when his still sleepy eyes focused on the widow. "I beg…"

Maud waved his attempted apology aside. "I know the lad," she explained to the prioress. Her composure restored, she turned her back to the man and lowered her voice. "The girl's fever has broken, but she remains perilously weak. The barley broth seemed to help, and I did persuade her to sip some made of chicken, a remedy I have found to be more effective against a fever than those made of other meat. Still, she has little appetite and strength. Just before you arrived, she fell asleep again. May God be thanked, however, her breathing is easier."

"There is reason for optimism?"

"When a fever snaps, there is always cause to hope, but Death is most stubborn, as we all well know. His rattling breath is still loud in the room."

Eleanor nodded. "I shall give you relief by taking my turn watching over her. Since morning, you have had no respite and must be very weary."

"Have you broken your fast, my lady?"

Eleanor bristled at the woman's question but quickly prayed for calmer humors to return. After the sheriff's insolence, her pride ached as if suffering an open wound against which salt had just been rubbed. She had grown too sensitive, she decided. The question had been brusquely asked, but she could truly find no ill intent.

"I beg forgiveness if I caused offense, my lady." Maud's pink cheeks deepened in color as the prioress remained silent. "My husband used to chide me about my thoughtless speech."

"No disrespect was noted. I was only lost in some trivial thought," Eleanor replied, relieved by the apology. Not only was she grateful for the widow's competent care of Mariota, as well as her intervention when they all staggered in from the storm, but Eleanor had always preferred blunt honesty to falsehood sweetened with honeyed phrase. "Kind intent is never thoughtless," she added with a smile.

The widow exhaled in obvious relief.

"As for nourishment, perhaps you would share some bread with me." Eleanor gestured toward the stairs leading below. "I would welcome your company, and I assume you trust the servant you left in the chambers to be competent in her care of my charge."

"If I did not, I never would have let her..." Maud firmly shut her mouth.

"Nor did I have any cause to doubt your decision."

The two women smiled at each other, relieved to be in perfect understanding.

Walking toward the stone stairs, Eleanor did not bother to look over her shoulder.

Indeed, her guard was close behind.

◇◇◇

When the trio arrived in the hall downstairs, the widow ordered a servant to bring some ale with fresh bread and led the prioress to a trestle table set by the fireplace. Eleanor invited the young guard to share the offerings when the jug and platter were put down in front of them.

His stomach growling thanks to match his words, he clutched a handful of bread, a pottery mug filled with new ale, and cheerfully settled at the far end of the table. Munching loudly, he left the prioress and the widow to chatter away as he perhaps assumed all women, whatever their rank or vocation, were wont to do.

Maud shivered despite the merry fire that snapped close by. "I pray this murder will not cause fear to invade the hearts of you and your party, my lady. This should be a place of refuge and no one should suffer unease." She gestured toward the hall door. "Not that there haven't been quarrels enough in my memory, but no more than is usual between men and most certainly never a slaying. We may all sin, but we are not prone to breaking that particular commandment against killing other mortals!"

"And I pray that the steward will not regret his kindness, concluding that our arrival has cursed him and somehow brought this wickedness about."

"Master Stevyn is not superstitious, my lady." Her eyes twinkled. "Some might even reproach him for not having sufficient faith in spiritual things, although his first wife most certainly made up for any lack."

"Earlier, Brother Thomas and I knelt by Tobye's corpse for some time, praying for his soul. We hoped that God would look favorably on our feeble pleas for mercy. Was the man especially wicked? I ask in case we did not pray long or ardently enough."

"He was no greater sinner than most of us, my lady." She rubbed her forefinger against her chin as she considered the prioress' question. "A good man with horses. I'll give him that. Never mistreated the beasts and had skill enough for healing their ills."

Eleanor leaned forward, desiring to give the impression that she was just enjoying a good gossip, should anyone nearby care.

The guard seemed quite unconcerned as he continued to gnaw his food with evident content. Even the complaints of his growling stomach had muted.

"Had Tobye served this manor long?" the prioress asked. "The loss of a valued servant would be a great one."

"Valued? Well, I suppose by Master Stevyn, a man that loves his hunting and will forgive much if his horses are healthy." She shifted her weight on the bench, then quickly sipped her ale. "As for me, I found the fellow rude."

"Indeed?"

"My words were ill-chosen, my lady. He did what was required and served the steward well. That was all anyone expected of him. In truth, he rarely spoke much, unless a fair woman came by. Then he was all smiles and bows and pleasing phrases."

Eleanor did not think the widow's reddened complexion was caused by the warming fire. Was it jealousy or sadness she heard in the woman's words? As the prioress looked at Mistress Maud's face, she concluded once again that she might not have been a beauty in her younger days, but surely she had had enough charm with those dimples and pink cheeks that young men smiled, bowed, and graced her with pretty enough phrases. Was it youth the widow now missed, resenting the loss more than she did Tobye's flattering attention to others? Or did the serpent of jealousy coil around her heart?

A chill now coursed through the prioress as she suddenly realized how quickly youth must pass. For those without her faith and vocation, how did they cope if the heart still longed for love songs after the hair had grayed and the breasts sagged?

"Did the women like him in return?" Eleanor shaded her words with tolerant amusement.

"Master Stevyn's first wife did not allow idle flirtations." A shadow played on the widow's face. "He supported her in this."

"Yet the groom must have had his conquests nonetheless."

"There have been rumors, but no wailing babes to prove the truth of them. Perhaps most were innocent enough. The cook took a liking to him, but she is no young girl and has never allowed any lover to come closer than the width of the kitchen table. No aging maidenhead was shattered there."

Eleanor raised the cup of ale and sipped to hide her interest in this news. A cook was skilled with knives, for cert.

"Hilda may have slipped Tobye the occasional extra tidbit from the kitchen," Maud continued, "but the master was wise enough to turn his eyes away from such insignificant acts."

And might this Hilda have lost her reason when she discovered who shared her beloved's bed?

"Tobye was clever enough to know the peril of offending a good master. He would have been discreet."

Did Maud not know about Mistress Luce? Or was she aware of the adultery and wished to protect the wife from some stranger's reproach? Eleanor remained silent about her suspicions and what she had seen near the outlying buildings. "A wise groom for a wiser master," she replied instead.

"A man who might have had cause to learn hard lessons, my lady, but who amongst us has not?"

The prioress raised an eyebrow at that and was about to ask what she meant, but Maud now pointedly changed the topic to the amount of rain the area was suffering compared to prior years.

Why had she so swiftly moved away from the subject of Tobye's murder? Not that Eleanor failed to understand why a widow, in particular, might not wish to dwell long on any more death, especially a frightening and cruel murder, but the prioress did wonder whether unease was the motive. Instead, did Maud fear she might let some secret slip?

But now was clearly not the time to pursue the issue further, thus Eleanor chatted amiably, pushing all darker thoughts aside, as if she truly cared about the rain.

Chapter Sixteen

"Who are you and what are you doing here?"

Thomas dropped a handful of bloody straw and jumped to his feet.

The man standing in front of him was angular and grizzled, his face scarred with red pits, and his green eyes so deep-set that their color had a darker cast. Master Stevyn was a horse-loving man who bore a marked resemblance to his favored beast. Even his breath came in snorts of evident displeasure.

"I am Brother Thomas, a member of the party accompanying Prioress Eleanor of Tyndal Priory who was given shelter here in your absence."

The man continued to scowl. "And if you are a monk, tell me what cause you have to be in this stable, kneeling in the dirt like some beggar hunting for scraps inside animal droppings. Have we failed to feed you properly?"

Thomas pointed to the nearby horses and donkey. "This manor has shown us praiseworthy charity. When I learned of your groom's cruel death, I offered my help and asked permission to tend our extra mounts. With that small service, I hoped to ease the burden our stay has added."

"It seems to me that Tobye's filthy soul has greater need of your prayers than the horses have for the currying. Others will benefit from a little extra work, for idleness is never far from being a resident vice here—or so my son insists." He jabbed his thumb at a man of equally angular shape who stood behind him, stiff as a stick. "Although I confess my nose scents nothing of the Devil's foul stink. I smell only honest horse shit here."

As the monk looked around, he realized that the men, who had been working a few stalls away just a few moments ago, were no longer visible. Perhaps they had shown some wisdom. He slipped his hands into his sleeves and remained silent as the younger man stepped forward.

"Ranulf, eldest son of the Earl of Lincoln's most honored steward," the narrow-faced man announced.

And, as I remember, a pretentious sort and justly married to the pinch-mouthed Mistress Constance, Thomas concluded. *In comparison to Ranulf, the monk preferred the father, despite his boorish speech and crude jests. Master Stevyn might be a rough-hewn man, but his easy bearing also spoke of competence. The son twitched too much.*

Without warning, Ranulf threw his head back and bellowed.

"'S Blood," his father muttered.

A half-dozen men reappeared from stalls. One climbed down a ladder from the loft.

"You lazy sons of bawds and cushions! How dare you let a man of God sully his hands with donkey offal while you sneak off to drink and swyve your pocky whores?"

One man scratched his chin. Another idly kicked at a few bits of broken straw.

Gesturing hither and thither, Ranulf roared his commands.

These were orders for such simple horse care that any man would have learned the tasks as a boy, Thomas realized. *These men could probably do them in their sleep, as they may well have done from time to time.* He quickly swallowed a chuckle.

At last the steward's son was satisfied that he had turned chaos to order, and he turned to Thomas. "You may go back to your prayers, Brother. Worry not about these scoundrels. I shall keep close watch on them and make sure your few beasts get proper care."

With that, he spun on his heel and marched away, robe swaying with his exaggerated swagger.

"Do as your conscience wills, Brother," the father snorted, his eyes expressing weary displeasure, and then followed his son out of the stable.

Thomas turned to one of the men standing beside him. "My apologies for any grief I have caused by coming here."

The man blew his nose through his fingers and flipped the outcome at the spot Master Ranulf had just left. "No matter, Brother. He'd have found some reason to yell whether you were here or not."

"Will he return later to see how well you have obeyed?"

"Nay. He hasn't the wit to know whether we have or not, but he does love to bawl like some lost bull calf for the cow's udder." The man scratched at his armpit. "If God hears this simple man's prayer, Mistress Constance will lie on her back and teach him a better occupation than troubling us with his nonsense."

"And Master Stevyn?"

"He knows we need no direction on things we do daily."

"Then I'll finish with that stall," Thomas said, gesturing at Adam the donkey. The beast responded with an arched tail.

The man grinned, his teeth a shocking white against his grime-darkened skin, and tossed the monk a pitchfork before bending to the task of digging out nearby soiled straw himself.

"Tobye will be missed," the stableman said after a long silence. "He always could handle that one."

"Master Stevyn said nothing when his son berated you all. Are father and son much alike?"

"Don't let his manner fool you, Brother." The stableman coughed and leaned on his pitchfork to catch his breath. "The old master can be hard in his ways and speech, yet he has always been fair, and there is little about the running of this land he doesn't know. Last harvest, a pestilence struck many here. One villein's wife died, leaving him with two swaddled babes to tend for a day until his sister came to help. Master Stevyn stripped to a loincloth like the rest of us and replaced the man in the fields. He may not have offered comfort to the man but neither did he punish or reproach him in any way for not giving his labor that once."

Thomas nodded, the description firming the impression he had gotten of the steward. "Why does he tolerate his son's foolishness then? Is he so fond of his eldest?"

"Fond? Nay, not so much," he grunted, "but what choice has he? Master Ranulf is the heir. Methinks we are wiser to get used to the fool's ways and learn how to work around them. This eldest was born with too little of his father's nature and too much of his mother's." His expression turned sheepish. "Begging your pardon, Brother, but she did spend a good deal of time on her knees in prayer and consequently birthed a monk. We all knew she was a good woman, and I believe she must have grieved not to have given her husband a better firstborn."

"What of the second son?"

"Master Huet?" He laughed. "Now he was spawned with stronger seed, and we all now say he's more the man by far. A few scoffed, suggesting he was a cokenay with that fair skin and his sweet singing, but they changed their own song quickly enough when he gave them a one-fisted love tap and they awoke with a blackened eye, staring at the clouds. The Earl of Lincoln took a liking to the lad as well, which is why he paid his way at university." He gestured westward. "Methinks both Master Stevyn and our lord would rather have the second son as steward than Master Ranulf, but the earl'll find a place somewhere for Master Huet in his service."

"Which should happen soon since Master Huet has returned and must be done with schooling." Thomas knew better but was curious to hear what rumors were already about.

The man bent closer and spoke in low tones. "I've heard that he wandered about in France for some months before he came back and finally confessed he had escaped the Latin exercises. But none of us ever thought he'd take to monkish ways. That's one with hot enough loins to seed babes all over the shire, begging your pardon."

Thomas laughed as he tossed a load of clean straw into the donkey's stall. "Any proof of that before he was sent across the Cam?"

The man's face darkened. "The lass died of birthing. So did the babe. As I heard the tale, he turned black with melancholy and thus agreed to have his head shaved with the tonsure for his sins." Then he shrugged. "No marriage would have been possible even had he wished it. She was a villein's daughter."

"He seems cheerful enough now. Perhaps his heart has healed."

Again the man shrugged and bent his back once more to the cleaning of the stalls.

"Two brothers who could not be more different," Thomas said after a long while.

"They share their father's stubbornness, but Master Ranulf looks like his mother and took on a brittle version of her faith. As for Master Huet, he has his father's build, but, if I didn't know his mother to be an honest and most Christian woman, I'd say some spirit exchanged her babe for another in the birthing room." His brow furrowed. "If a switch did happen, it gave the master a sweet-tempered lad with the voice of angels. That change would never have been made by any evil imp, would it?"

Thomas shook his head. "If the master's first wife was a good woman, perhaps God wanted to make up for the firstborn," he suggested. "You have heard him sing?"

The man brightened. "I overheard one of Master Stevyn's guests once say that our old King Richard would have been jealous of the lad's skills, but Queen Eleanor, the Lionheart's mother, would have made Master Huet a rich man for his songs."

Thomas did not reply and slowed his pace as he finished with the stall and began to curry the donkey. Soon the stableman was done and offered to complete what the monk had started. Thomas refused, claiming he would be through soon enough, and the man left.

The monk continued to work on the donkey's coat, a task he usually found both pleasurable and soothing, but this time the work did not keep troubling thoughts from pricking at him.

He had taken an almost instant dislike to Ranulf, and he now condemned himself. The elder son might be made with edges sharp enough to cut anyone who offended him, but wasn't there merit in that? Surely his unbending spirit also gave him firm direction and method, even if it also rendered him incapable of seeing his failures or listening to different ways of managing the land. Others who had experience in the work knew well enough how to do the tasks required. As the stableman said, all a man had to do was learn how Ranulf thought and discover ways of circumventing his instructions when necessary.

Disliking the intermittent grooming, the donkey flicked his ears and snorted with vexation.

In spite of himself, Thomas laughed and scratched between the donkey's ears. "As you do well to remind me, even an ass knows how foolish it is to burden competent servants with ignorant masters," he said, "and strategy without wisdom is as destructive as no objective at all."

Perhaps he had thoughtlessly found merit in Ranulf's benighted ways because Huet seemed without any direction. The younger son was a difficult man to comprehend and that unsettled Thomas. Huet was truly as nebulous as a shape-changing imp. He might be charming but he had also demonstrated irresponsibility by showing disrespect for an influential lord who had paid for his education. Why had Huet tossed aside a fine future? For a lute-player's life? The man must be mad. Or was his witty grace but a thin-coating that hid an evil heart?

Thomas shivered. Maybe the second son truly was a changeling after all and not some gift from a sympathetic God. On the other side of that argument, Huet might also be a good youth who lacked only one wise man to guide him on a more adult path.

He wished he could simply dismiss Huet as a charming and perhaps indolent fellow, but he liked him. Too much. Satan must be making sport again, and he had suffered enough. First, the Prince of Darkness had turned the sweetness of Thomas' love for Giles into a bitter and earthly Hell. Next, the Evil One destroyed his sleep by sending rampant imps to seduce him into sinful acts, and most recently, at Amesbury, the creature had filled him with lust for another man. No sooner did he recover from the wounds of one encounter then the Devil sent another affliction. Did he not have cause to fear Huet?

He quickly checked the donkey to make sure he had finished with him.

These recent nights had been innocent enough. The two men slept in each other's arms, nothing more. Thomas, however, had found too much comfort when Huet held him closer and wondered whether the man had really done so just for the greater warmth it provided.

Did Huet know his weakness? Was he using his wiles to seduce Thomas? Or did he hope that giving him such a minor pleasure would distract him from seeing some other evil that Huet had committed? Painful though the recollection might be, Thomas did remember that the man had left the hearth the night Tobye was killed. What he could not recall was exactly when he had disappeared. The absence was far too long for any trip to the privy and long enough to commit murder. But was it early enough to have left a corpse barely stiffened?

He cursed himself. Huet might well be as innocent of evil intent as a babe, while he, an accused sodomite, cloaked the poor man with his own frailties. And hadn't the man's sweet songs and skillful lute playing given Thomas as much pleasure as the music at Tyndal Priory? The stableman was right when he said the steward's younger son had the voice of an angel. How could such a creature be wicked?

But his next thought chilled. Was he confusing pleasure in sacred things with some shallow and lewd semblance? "Dare I trust myself to know the difference?" he muttered.

As he stroked the donkey's neck, Thomas concluded he must not be taken in by Huet's clever manner and engaging talents. Nightmares born in his prison days might have effectively unmanned him, but he had cause enough to fear the aching sweetness he found in Huet's arms. Since the day he had lost Giles, his heart had never ceased to weep with loneliness, although he had become more skilled at deafening the sound.

Nevertheless, he knew how liable he was to grasp at false suggestions of ease.

"I cannot think more on this," he whispered, swallowing bitter-tasting tears. Then he forced his thoughts to another purpose, looked around, and discovered that he was quite alone.

Kneeling in the straw, Thomas retrieved the blood-stained knife he had hidden in a corner of the donkey's stall, just before Master Stevyn and his son entered the stable, and wished he had been wrong in suspecting the sheriff's men had failed to look for it.

Chapter Seventeen

Although the usual merriment was well-muted that night, the manor hall was filled for supper. Even if a murder had taken place in the nearby stable, Master Stevyn was determined to honor his guests.

A blazing fire and the stifling warmth from so many bodies weighed down on Eleanor. Her eyes grew heavy. Might she close them for just a moment? But her head dropped, and she started awake. Fortunately, her companions on either side had turned to speak with others. Her discourtesy had gone unnoticed.

A servant bent to pour more wine into her cup, then noted it was still full. In truth, the prioress had drunk but little, nor did she have much appetite.

"Does the meal displease, my lady?" The man beside her turned around, his brow etched with concern as he gestured at her trencher.

"Envy is a sin, Master Stevyn, and I am jealous that you possess such an excellent cook. Her talents are remarkable." Eleanor's smile was gracious. "If my appetite seems dulled, the cause lies in my need to do penance for covetous thoughts, nothing more."

The sound of his rumbling laugh was deep and pleasing, but the frown quickly returned. "I regret that violence has tainted your stay here, my lady."

"I grieve that this house should suffer it," she replied, trying to read the expression in his deep-set eyes.

He turned his face away.

"Sir Reimund has provided both protection and his assurance that the guilty one will soon be found. Fear does not disquiet us."

"Had our sheriff not done so, I would have guaranteed your safety, but he is a very dutiful servant of the king's justice. His diligence and concern do not surprise me." The steward studied his folded hands and still did not look the prioress in the eye.

Should she be troubled by an answer that suggested he agreed with Sir Reimund's methods, ways she found questionable because of their self-serving motivation? Or were his words nothing but the conventional phrases spoken to one who did not reside in the shire? Of course she dared not forget that this steward might be Tobye's killer and thus his motive in saying anything relative to the crime must be examined.

Caution was due, but she also found Master Stevyn likeable, although she had certainly heard enough about him to suggest he could be a hard man. Yet he reminded her of her father, brusque in manner but equally capable of easy humor, sincere courtesy, and kind acts. The comparison softened her heart further, and she pitied the steward even more for the horns his wife had bestowed upon him.

"Are you sure your cook does not hold a secret desire in her heart to serve God?" Thus she pointedly shifted the subject from the problems of murder and hospitality. Her look spoke only of goodwill. "If so, I would welcome her to Tyndal Priory."

"I will convey your willingness to have her, but I fear she finds passion primarily in the kitchen where she has served us for many years." He gestured at a servant to bring the platter of roasted fowl and to replenish nearby trenchers. "She is quite proud of her chicken, swearing she can make the oldest hen pass for a much younger one."

Eleanor nodded in appreciation but her thoughts stubbornly returned to what she had witnessed between Mistress Luce and the now dead groom.

Although she would not have called Master Stevyn a handsome man, with his pitted skin and angular features, the prioress thought he carried his late middle years with ease, and there was no aged dullness in his gray-streaked, brown hair. He radiated confidence and most certainly knew how to treat high ranking guests with warm hospitality but without extravagance.

These were all good qualities. Had Master Stevyn been her father's steward, she believed the Wynethorpe family would be well-pleased with his blend of courtesy and prudence, rewarding him accordingly. Although she assumed he had been a younger son, perhaps of some landed knight, he had the competence to gain the attention and favor of good connections. Without question, he was successful and would be a good match for any woman of proper rank like his current wife.

That might be the practical and logical view, but Eleanor knew the heart was rarely either. There was still the matter of a young wife facing the marriage bed with a husband who might disgust her. Thus she asked herself how she would have felt, had her path in life led to such an arranged marriage rather than service to God.

Considering how fiercely she had fought to take religious vows rather than marry, she feared she might not have been as compliant about the choice of groom either. Once married, however, she would have served her husband with more honor than Mistress Luce had and borne the couplings if the spouse was otherwise a worthy man. Of that she felt some certitude. Although she had suffered unbearable lust as a prioress, she had still fought to keep her vows.

Fearing her musing had kept her silent too long, Eleanor hastily added a good-humored question: "Does her secret work for mortal women? If so, I know few on this earth who would not beg for her recipe!"

Mistress Luce, seated on the other side of her husband, suddenly bent forward and laughed. "My stepson's wife, for one!" Her tone suggested no merry jest.

"If you cannot control injudicious speech, wife, be silent," Stevyn snapped, his eyes narrowing until their color resembled burnt greenwood.

"After luring your son to the church door, she owes him an heir. I only question if her womb has not shriveled, since she has yet to bear a healthy child, and wonder whether she might not own more years than claimed when all agreed to the marriage contract."

"Enough said. The matter is between husband and wife, or, as my son would prefer to think, between Man and God." His tone left no doubt that he would tolerate no further discussion from her.

Failing to gain her husband's support, she flushed with the public rebuke and turned her attention to Brother Thomas who sat on her other side.

Eleanor glanced down the table at Mistress Constance. Although the woman's rigid posture and raised chin stayed firm, the sour cherry color rising in her cheeks suggested that Luce's barb had pricked her otherwise armored skin.

"Please forgive my wife," the steward muttered. "She is newly with child. Like many women in that condition, I'm told, her humors are often unbalanced and her speech can grow foolish."

"Then that is the reason Mistress Maud is here." Eleanor winced in embarrassment for speaking aloud what should have remained private thoughts. "Those words were unfortunate. I have no wish to pry into your private matters."

The man's eyebrows collided with barely suppressed anger. "The physician's widow came at my request to advise my wife, although I fear my spouse betrays her feckless youth by refusing to take proper heed of the guidance given."

The steward's outburst was disquieting, and Eleanor tried to find words to cool that fury. "Nonetheless, Mistress Maud's presence here was fortuitous, and I owe thanks for that both to you and to God. She is a skilled healer and has done much to help my sick companion. If the young woman lives, she will owe that recovery to her."

"The widow has ever been a good woman," he replied, his expression softening, "and tried to save my first wife from an untimely death. She failed, but her lack of success had nothing to do with incompetence. God was not willing to let my first wife's pure soul stay longer amongst the sinful."

"I have heard that they were friends. Your wife's death must have been a cruel loss to you both then."

Stevyn suddenly paled. In contrast, the pits in his face became as inflamed as a child's pox.

Have I offended? Eleanor wondered, pressing a hand to her heart to calm the pounding.

"Husband!"

The steward swung around in his chair, his expression black as a gale at sea.

"Chase that stormy look from your face, my dearest lord." Luce sat back and put her hand on her belly as if suggesting such rage would endanger the product of his seed. "Brother Thomas has asked if your younger son would play a song for us. Will you not grant your guest's wish?"

Eleanor glanced at her monk, and an unbidden heat swiftly burned her cheeks. Mistress Luce had just reached over and laid a hand on his arm, her head tilted as she stared at him with openly sensual appreciation. Why is he smiling? Eleanor thought with an outrage based more in jealousy than any concern for the sanctity of his vocation.

"Forbid it!" Mistress Constance shouted. "Singing like some low-born, traveling minstrel is unsuitable for a man studying to be a priest."

"Oh, let him sing his ditties, wife," growled Ranulf, who began picking a back tooth with his fingernail. "My brother is no man and must only remember the words to songs that quieted his infant squalling."

As Eleanor looked at the couple, with their long noses and tiny eyes, she was reminded of weasels.

"I like his singing, and, if Brother Thomas has requested it, such a thing cannot be unseemly." Mistress Luce put her other hand on her husband's arm and openly caressed it.

Ranulf's eyes darted back and forth between monk and stepmother, then he leaned against the table as if suffering pains in his belly.

"Entertain us, Huet," Stevyn said, brushing aside his wife's hand. "If your voice is as pleasing as it was before you left, it may soothe your brother's annoyance over your inexplicable return."

"A sweet love song?" The younger son stood and bowed with an exaggerated gesture to his brother.

Master Stevyn's stamp was most certainly upon that one with his muscular body and green eyes, Eleanor thought with chaste enough appreciation. Despite his mild mockery of his elder brother, however, Huet's rounder face bore an agreeable gentleness that suggested a softer nature than his father possessed. Perhaps his mother had passed on all tenderness to her youngest since that quality seemed utterly lacking in Ranulf.

"Remember our guests, Huet!" the elder brother called out. "None of those bawdy things beloved by wicked students. Even you must know something more suitable for those who wisely honor God over sinful flesh."

"Something I learned on my way through Arras, then." Huet grinned. "If I sang the story of the prodigal son, would you find that proper enough, Ranulf?"

As if startled by the suggestion, the elder brother blinked, and then concurred with a cautious grunt.

No one's faith should be so devoid of joy, Eleanor thought as she considered the expressions of Ranulf and Constance. Even after Adam and Eve had been expelled from Eden for their grave sins, God had not taken away honest pleasure nor forbidden the relief of benign laughter.

The steward's youngest son picked up his small lute from under the bench, then walked to a position in front of the assembled guests at the high table. Briefly pausing to tune the instrument, he smiled and began to sing.

"What a beautiful voice!" Eleanor exclaimed in a whisper to Master Stevyn. "Did his mother…?"

"Neither of us can sing," he replied. "Soon after Huet was born, I decided he must have been God's special gift. He may have my bearing, but he has his mother's…" Stevyn fell into a musing and forgot that he had been speaking.

Eleanor sat back, completely charmed by the younger son's talented performance. With gesture and intonation, he painted each scene of the story. One moment, he was the willful lad, arguing with his father. Next, he became the grieving father, weeping as the son left home and knowing his beloved boy would suffer for his misguided decision. Huet was so skillful, she forgot where she was and instead imagined she was standing in front of some inn where the singer now played the part of the wayward lad, then errant women…

"I hope that did not offend, my lady." Master Stevyn leaned to speak softly near the prioress' ear.

"A cautionary tale, well-told, can never cause offense," she replied, reluctantly emerging from the power of the performance. Then she happily plunged back into the mood of the story.

Huet had just transformed himself into the chastened son as he dragged himself homeward with a soul both weary and fearful. How would his father greet him? Would he cast him out?

Eleanor knew the story well, but Huet's telling was so fresh that she wondered if it might not have a different ending.

With high notes of delight, the man sang of the father's joy when he saw his lost son. As he flung one arm wide, Eleanor could see father and son embrace. Even the other son's sourness at the feast, given to welcome the prodigal, was portrayed convincingly. When Huet finally came to an end, the prioress deeply regretted that the song and tale were over.

"Well done!"

Eleanor looked over and saw her monk gesturing with enthusiasm.

Next to him, Mistress Luce was so charmed that she seemed unaware that the hand she had laid on Thomas' arm had been discarded.

"I suppose you meant to mock me!" Ranulf stood, his gaunt body shaking with rage. "Like the prodigal you celebrated, you have discarded all righteousness and now come home as if you expected our father to forgive all and kill the fatted calf for your sinfulness."

"You demanded an edifying song. I gave you one. What quarrel could you have with that?" Huet's expression suggested neither consternation nor remorse.

"Why didn't you choose another? There are many enough!" The man's sallow face had turned orange with hot rage.

"Why should I consider myself a prodigal son, brother, and why should you assume your dedication to duty was as self-interested as the son in the tale just told? You know nothing of my reasons for return, and I know little of what you have done to serve our father since I left."

Ranulf pounded the table. Wine slopped over the rim of his cup. "Father, I demand you admonish Huet for the insult given me!"

"Silence," the steward now roared. "Both of you! Had Huet sung of Mary and Martha, Ranulf, you would have seen yourself as the beleaguered Martha and claimed insult because Mary won greater favor. As for you," Stevyn gestured at his younger son, "if you think you are welcomed with no punishment for abandoning your studies, then reconsider." He picked up a handful of discarded chicken bones. "This is no fatted calf, lad, and I give you no forgiving embrace. We shall speak, when my work allows it, and that will be soon enough. If I were you, I would not unpack that bundle you brought back from your senseless wanderings."

Ranulf slid back down on the bench.

Constance edged ever so slightly away from him.

Huet bowed to his father and retreated to his place next to Brother Thomas.

"I swear he paid for his way home by entertaining at inns." Stevyn muttered in such a low voice that he seemed to address neither his wife nor the prioress. "Look how he slinks back to his seat. Isn't that the way of a wily minstrel, fading out of sight when the performance does not please? 'S blood, but I have been cursed with these sons!" Briefly, he buried his head in his hands.

Mistress Luce ignored her husband, bent back in her seat to stretch around the monk, and plucked at her stepson's sleeve. Her hand brushed over Thomas' shoulder.

Digging her nails into her palms, Eleanor stopped herself from exclaiming in outrage.

Thomas, however, was utterly oblivious to the woman's closeness. He was far too involved in explaining something to Huet. The younger son was just as engaged with the monk's conversation and failed to notice his stepmother's attempt to get his attention.

Chastising herself for reacting so strongly, Eleanor exhaled.

"Huet!" Luce pleaded.

Brushing her fingers away as if they were annoying insects, Huet picked up his lute, and proceeded to demonstrate a technique on the instrument for the monk.

The stepmother gave up and sat forward again with a disgusted snort.

Brooding, Master Stevyn gnawed at a chicken thigh and did not heed his wife's displeasure.

For a woman whose lover had just been murdered, Mistress Luce seemed remarkably devoid of grief. If I were to conclude anything from her behavior tonight, Eleanor thought, I would say she did not miss the groom at all and was trying rather quickly to seduce some other man as replacement in her bed.

Even her stepson? The prioress shuddered at the idea, then turned her mind away from such a horror and asked herself if Luce had simply wearied of Tobye. If so, might she have had cause to kill him?

In addition, there were Luce's comments about Constance's marriage and age. Not only were the remarks odd, but they had a definite sexual undertone. Constance was surely little older than the steward's second wife, and the statement that she had *lured* Ranulf into marriage was curious.

Such comments pointed to significant discord, perhaps jealousy, between the two women. Was it competition over a man? Surely Master Stevyn was not the object. Had they both lusted after Tobye? Constance might present herself as sternly religious, but the prioress knew that did not mean the woman was devoid of malign lust.

Eleanor looked over at Ranulf's wife.

Nibbling at a piece of bread, the woman might have the demeanor of a modest enough spouse, but her eyes were focused on Luce and that gaze was filled with white-hot hate.

Did Ranulf notice this? Eleanor turned to read his expression.

Ranulf, however, had disappeared. His mazer was overturned, and the dark wine had spread across the white tablecloth like a pool of blood.

Chapter Eighteen

The late morning light cast shadows in Mariota's hollowed cheeks. "I have gravely sinned," she whispered before falling into a fit of coughing.

"How so, my child?" Eleanor took the young woman's hand and marveled at how quickly Death impressed his skeletal seal on mortals when illness struck. Instinctively, she grasped the girl's hand more firmly as if telling the dark creature that she would not allow him to take Mariota's soul just yet.

Although many believed evil was the root cause of illness, Eleanor was inclined to agree with her sub-infirmarian that sickness had a multitude of causes. As she looked down at Mariota, she wondered how filled with wickedness this youthful creature could truly be. Not only was the girl young, but she had comported herself with devout and respectful demeanor during her stay at Tyndal. Shaking her head, the prioress refused to condemn the young woman for falling ill.

Yet Mariota turned her face away, and tears began to weave their way down her sunken cheek.

"Surely your failing is not so heinous." Taking a soft cloth, Eleanor reached over and patted the dampness away. On the other hand, Sister Christina, the infirmarian at Tyndal, had seen cures when the weight of sin was lessened with confession. Both nuns were probably right, the prioress decided. She would encourage Mariota to talk, and, if the error qualified as a sin, Bother Thomas could assign penance and grant absolution.

"Pride kept me from admitting I suffered a fever until I had endangered all in the fury of that storm. I pray my breath has not proven as malignant as a leper's and others have not fallen ill or worse."

"Fear not. No one has." Actually, she thought, I bear far more blame for exposing all to peril since it was my ill-advised decision to take this journey in the first place.

"I have always suffered from obstinate pride, my lady. My mother often said she had to remind me, far more often than was deemed reasonable, that meek obedience is pleasing to God and is a virtue all good women should possess."

"Thus we are taught and wisely reminded," Eleanor answered, "for many of us suffer from willfulness." As she herself should know, being just such a woman. "Your mother loves you," she continued aloud, "and desires only to guide her daughter in a path that will best lead to mortal happiness."

Mariota weakly clutched the prioress' hand and began to sob.

"Child, what troubles you? Surely the reason is not just this vile fever. You have brought no grief to any!"

"I am wicked!"

"No more, I am sure, than any other."

"More! More!"

The prioress stroked her hand, trying to soothe and fearing Mariota was too frail to bear such fierce despair. What could this young woman have possibly done to warrant this severe self-condemnation?

Although Eleanor was less than a decade older, each month between them felt tripled in time to her. After her appointment to Tyndal Priory, when she was barely twenty, the prioress had faced evil far more malevolent than most people of so few years on earth could even imagine. Thus she had assumed that Mariota's guilt must involve some misstep of insignificant wickedness. Yet there was one thing that could trouble the girl, something that the prioress had suffered all too painfully as well.

"You fell in love with a man, did you not?" Fearing the girl would interpret any smile as mockery, she forced her expression to remain politely reserved.

"Who told you of this?"

"No one did, but as women we are fellow creatures and understand such things. Adam was one of God's most delightful creations, and we often find his sons irresistible." This time she risked a sympathetic upturn of the corners of her lips.

"Were you ever in love, my lady?" Her eyes then widened in horror. "Forgive me! I meant no insult! Love of God is the greatest…"

"Few escape mortal passions, but we enter the religious life because heavenly joys are greater than earthly ones," the prioress replied with deliberate ambiguity.

"I lied to you and my mother."

Eleanor nodded encouragement.

"I said I had a vocation."

"And now you doubt that?"

"I don't know what I believe."

"You are not the first to ask for time to discover if the contemplative life is suitable. Sometimes we believe it is, only to discover that we are more able to do good in the world. There is no sin in changing your mind."

"When my father lay dying, I promised God I would dedicate my life to His service."

"Did your father know of this vow?"

Mariota nodded. "He heard me and, concluding this was my intent, said he had always hoped I would become a nun."

"Did you mean to take vows?"

The young woman closed her eyes. "I was begging God to heal my father and promised to become a better person if He did. I thought to give more alms to the poor."

"Were there other witnesses to your words and your father's response?"

"My mother and brother."

"Did you explain your true intention to them?"

With a sob, the young woman nodded again. "They said I must do as my father had prayed and wished."

Eleanor squeezed the hand she tenderly held and tried to find words that would both comfort and wisely direct. "Is your mother truly convinced you have a vocation?"

"She now turns to my elder brother for advice."

This young man had accompanied their mother and Mariota to Tyndal. Perhaps two years older than his sister, he was a somberly dressed lad and displayed more gravitas than anyone of his few years or experience should reasonably possess.

"And what is his opinion?"

"I must honor my promise."

This was not a happy situation. Strict obedience to a perceived deathbed promise would be hard to set aside, yet an unwilling vocation was an open wound that often festered. Of course there were many upon whom vows had been forced, religious who possessed common faith but no zeal. Sometimes the lack was benign and a more ardent faith was even born in time. In other instances, however, corruption and sin resulted.

If Eleanor could come up with a reasonable alternative, both Mariota and Tyndal might be better served. Should she do so, she hoped the girl's brother was still enough of a boy to prove malleable in the face of an elder's advice. And Prior Andrew would be the one to counsel him in this different but still virtuous path.

"Who is the man you love?" Eleanor trusted her question was asked kindly enough to encourage more confidence from the girl.

Mariota flushed.

At least the cause is not fever, Eleanor concluded with relief. "A friend of your family?"

"And one who has grown up with my brother."

"Did your brother know of your attachment?"

"Nay, my lady, and I had no right to add another burden on him so soon after our father's death."

"Burden? I fail to understand that, unless this man did not return your affections or had insufficient means to support a wife, or was even, perhaps, vowed to another?"

"My lady, there was no impediment to our marriage. We loved each other, but my father fell ill before we could ask his permission to wed. Then my father read my words as a holy vow, and my beloved wept at the news but swore he would do nothing to offend my brother's wish to honor our father."

Eleanor heard the bitterness in Mariota's voice and wondered if she had hoped the young man would confront her family on her behalf. If so, disappointment at his refusal might explain the brief flash of anger she also saw in the woman's eyes.

There was yet one more detail, even two, that might preclude entry to the priory. "When you two talked of love, did you perchance vow marriage to each other in the present tense? Or did he bed you?" If they had taken such a vow, they were wed in God's eyes as well as in the laws of the secular world. If the girl was not a virgin, she could still become a nun, yet Eleanor might be able to argue...

"Neither, my lady."

And thus you must take on a vocation you do not wish because you were an obedient daughter and a virtuous woman, Eleanor concluded. All arguments I might have made on your behalf have been crushed.

She turned her face away so Mariota could not read her surrender.

The young woman sighed and closed her eyes as if understanding the futility of her situation whether or not it was voiced.

You may still find joy in the cloister, the prioress said to herself, and decide that love of God was ardent yet soothing to the spirit like water on a fever. Yet how could she serve as mentor when she had failed to banish her own longing for Brother Thomas?

"We shall speak more of this later, my child," Eleanor said, then realized Mariota had fallen back into a deep sleep. Eleanor stroked the girl's thin hand. If God denied Death's wish to take the young woman as his own bride, there would be time enough to discuss the future.

For several moments, Eleanor remained by the girl's side, praying that God grant Mariota peace whatever the days ahead brought. Then she summoned a nearby servant to keep watch and left the room, closing the door softly behind her.

Her devoted guard stood just outside the chambers. He turned and bowed.

Wordlessly acknowledging that courtesy, the prioress modestly tucked her hands into her sleeves.

From the courtyard, a piercing shriek shattered the silence.

Chapter Nineteen

The cook groveled in the rank mud, then clambered to her knees and seized the sheriff's wrist.

"I am innocent!"

"Take the vile creature away," Sir Reimund shouted. He stared down at Hilda with loathing and tore his hand from her tremulous grasp.

Two men rushed to obey.

"She offends all honest souls."

A man gave the sheriff a cloth.

Snatching it, he rubbed at the muck soiling his hand as if he were scouring a pot.

Stunned by the scene before them, Eleanor and her guard halted just outside the manor house entrance. The prioress gazed at the muttering, pushing crowd and wondered what she should do next. Had every servant gathered to watch the spectacle?

Somewhere dogs barked, and several chickens burst from the crowd, clucking with avian displeasure. Two men stood at the edge of the group, heads together, as if conferring over some significant thing. One straightened and roared with laughter. Nearby, a woman heavy with child cried out, a stain darkening her skirt. An older companion took her by the arm and eased her away.

From the vicinity of the stable, Master Stevyn shouted something incomprehensible. Eleanor could see his head as he began to shove his way to the center. Mistress Maud followed close behind him, effectively using sharp elbows to keep the path open even after they had passed through.

Seeing the pair, Eleanor assumed Mistress Luce was also here but could not identify the wife anywhere in the throng.

"What are you doing with my cook, Sheriff?" the steward roared.

"She killed your groom. I'm taking her to the castle jail until her trial and hanging."

The cook screamed once, began beating her breast, and then raised her eyes to the sky and howled like a terrified dog.

"Hilda?" The steward stared in amazement at the mud-stained servant. "You think she killed Tobye?"

Mistress Maud put her hands on her hips as fury stiffened her square body. "She's shown violence only to chickens and pigs, my lord. What proof have you to find her guilty of a more heinous act?"

Eleanor decided to push her way through the crowd, but so enthralled were they by the spectacle, they refused to budge.

"If I may, my lady?" her guard whispered, then stepped in front of her. "Stand aside for the Prioress of Tyndal," he snarled as he thrust people out of the way. Like awkward statues, they tilted this way and that but did shift position enough to allow her space to walk.

The sheriff strode over to meet the steward. "She's guilty enough," he said, replying to Stevyn rather than the widow who had asked the specific question. "A woman past child-bearing who lusted after a young man and was mocked by him, probably rejected for one better suited to his taste in bed. She cut his throat in revenge, an act not unusual for women like that."

"Even if she did want to lie in his arms," Maud shouted, "there was nothing more between them than her dreams."

The cook was still on her knees, her body steaming from the reeking mud and animal dung that stained her clothes. "I give you my word that I did not kill him, Master Stevyn," she whimpered. "On God's mercy and my soul's hope of heaven…"

"Don't blaspheme!" a man yelled, and Ranulf shoved two people out of his way to rush to his father's side.

"God knows I bear no blame in this murder," Hilda wailed. "When I swear my innocence on His name, I commit no sin."

"Sir Reimund," Eleanor called out in a tone that carried with authority over the heads of the crowd, "you have been asked a reasonable question. Since you have yet to respond, I must conclude that you did not hear it. Thus I shall repeat the query."

The crowd hushed and turned to hear what the Prioress of Tyndal had to say.

"What evidence do you have of this woman's guilt?" Eleanor asked. "Does she not deserve to hear the accusations in order to better answer them? Gentle King Henry was known for his mercy to sinners. Surely you do not dare to believe that his son, now our noble lord, would demand a less perfect justice?"

The sheriff' brow furrowed with dark fury and the assault on his authority. "With all due respect, my lady, I do not think this matter is any of your concern."

A loud voice from behind Eleanor replied: "God demands justice, Sir Sheriff, and no earthly king's man could ever speak for Him as truly as the Prioress of Tyndal. I, on the other hand, have more worldly cares. We shall be without dinner if you arrest our cook. Has the Earl of Lincoln or his steward so offended you that you wish to get revenge by making us suffer so?"

When Eleanor turned around, she saw Huet close by. His tone may have been tinged with merriment, but his demeanor was devoid of it.

"Our honored guest has requested no more than fairness demands," the steward replied. "In that, my younger son has argued well. What is your proof of guilt?"

Realizing he was outnumbered by those he dare not offend, the sheriff shrugged but his face paled with the effort of concession. "Her lust for the man and her outrage, when she believed he was swyving another woman, were observed by an impeccable witness. This same person saw her near the stable the night the groom was murdered, a time when the virtuous are in their beds or on their knees in prayer."

"By your own words, Sir Reimund, you have also damned this witness as a vile sinner if he saw our cook wandering about at the Devil's hour," Huet replied. "Do you think any honorable man could hear the testimony of such a wicked soul and conclude it was honest?"

"How dare you!" Ranulf bellowed.

Huet grinned. "The witness must have been you, sweet brother. What were you doing, wandering around at such an hour? Looking for a horse to ride, or perhaps you sought help to raise your lance against the Prince of Darkness?"

The color of Ranulf's face burst into apoplectic purple.

The sheriff said nothing and had apparently decided he would be well-advised to make sure his fingernails were perfectly clean.

"What have you to say for yourself?" Master Stevyn turned to Hilda, his customary roughness curiously softened.

The cook looked down at her filthy dress, then raised her reddened eyes to meet the gaze of every one in that crowd, people who would never forget this day of her humiliation. "Tobye did give me a kiss or two in payment for a few small sweets I baked," she said, "things too imperfect and unworthy of your table. Aye, I felt a sinful pleasure in those kisses, but he was far younger than I." Meandering tears whitened paths down her muddy cheeks as she wept anew. "Why should I feel jealousy when I always knew he would never love a woman like me with such a belly and hanging breasts?" Her speech dropped back to a whimper.

"Did you rage at him as you have been accused?" Stevyn's face grew pale. "Did you go to him the night he was murdered?"

As if she had just been stripped naked, she wrapped her arms around her breasts and bent her head with shame. "Aye, I did roar at him once because of the woman—*women* he thoughtlessly swyved. As for being out the night Tobye was murdered, I went to the privy once, perhaps twice."

"You were resentful because you are a woman, and lust banishes the little reason you possess," Ranulf snarled. "Your defense is guided by Satan and it is his honeyed voice, spoken with your tongue that makes your wickedness sound almost innocent."

Eleanor bit her lip. Hilda had slipped when she said she had berated Tobye for coupling with one woman, then tried to correct the error by making the number greater. Hilda was a loyal servant and would not give more information out of fear that she would lose Master Stevyn's apparent sympathy. And she probably had the right of that. She might well be called a liar or traitorously ungrateful were she to name Luce. As matters now stood, however, her heated argument with Tobye sounded like the rant of a jealous woman, not a concerned condemnation of the affair between Tobye and the steward's wife.

But was Hilda jealous? Could the cook be Tobye's killer? Eleanor rather doubted the woman's guilt. Unless Hilda was possessed of greater cunning than her demeanor would suggest, the prioress believed her innocent of this particular crime. But she was not so convinced that the woman had not been near the stable that night for some reason other than a mere trip to the privy. Her mention of that sounded hesitant as if she were desperate to find an excuse. Was there a way to question the terrified woman in private?

Huet's voice interrupted her thoughts. "Come, come, elder brother," he was saying. "Surely you know that some women don't suffer from lust at all. Is not your own wife an example of such perfect virtue?"

Ranulf's glared, his face changing hue from red to white and back again.

Eleanor concluded that Mistress Constance must be notoriously in arrears on the marriage debt.

The sheriff was losing patience and finally interjected: "All that may be argued with differing opinions amongst honorable men, but the fact remains, an unarguable fact, that this woman, who has confessed to lust before you all, was seen near the stable the night the groom was foully sent to God with all his sins riding on the back of his crooked soul. On that alone, I must arrest her."

"If you will give me leave, Master Stevyn, I must speak."

Eleanor looked up in surprise to see her monk maneuvering through the crowd toward the sheriff.

Sir Reimund opened his mouth to protest.

"Let us hear what you have to say, Brother." The steward seized the sheriff's arm with such strength that the man winced.

Thomas nodded gratitude for the permission. "The night the groom was killed, Master Huet and I shared a straw mat in the kitchen near the hearth. Since we had huddled closer to retain warmth from the dying ashes as the night went on, I awoke when Master Huet rose to attend a call of nature. I saw the cook in the kitchen, fast asleep on the nearby bench. That was the same place I had seen her lie down before I, too, fell sleep."

Eleanor overheard an abrupt intake of breath behind her but instinctively pretended she had not heard Huet's reaction.

"She could have left the kitchen and returned either before you awoke or after you had fallen back to sleep, Brother," the sheriff replied, his voice tense.

"Since I am accustomed to rising for the early Office, I stayed awake and prayed until just before dawn broke. Only then did the cook leave the kitchen but for no longer than it might take anyone to visit the latrine or do a quick morning wash before returning. By then others were about. I could hear them."

Master Stevyn raised a questioning eyebrow at the sheriff.

"That does not give her an excuse for much earlier in the night, Brother." Sir Reimund's voice shook.

Was his visible dismay caused by anger or doubt? Eleanor wondered.

"Since you surely examined the corpse and noted the extent of its stiffness, you must know that he could not have been killed too close to the time the sun set."

Instead of replying, the sheriff glowered at the guard he had assigned to the prioress, as if he had expected him to prevent interference from all others as well.

Fortunately, the man failed to see his lord's displeasure since he was bent in close conversation with a young woman.

Eleanor lowered her eyes and prayed that Thomas would rein in his tongue. She may have decided to get involved in this crime for reasons she deemed proper, but she also knew they had no explicit right to do so. Giving testimony in private was one thing, but they must tread lightly and most certainly must not reveal so publicly that they knew details they should not. Justice might be cruelly thwarted if a protest was raised because of Church interference in matters rightfully under the king's authority.

"As for witnesses, Sheriff," Huet called out, "I can add my testimony that the cook was asleep when I went to the privy. Since my bowels were loose that night, I spent some time there, or pacing nearby in discomfort, and neither saw nor heard anything untoward. Hilda was snoring when I returned. Brother Thomas was on his knees in prayer."

Thomas blinked and then nodded in silence.

"Thus we have a highly regarded witness to her probable guilt and reputable witnesses to her possible innocence," the sheriff muttered. "Where there is conflict…"

"…there is reason for caution and doubt," Master Stevyn finished. "As to the testimony of the first witness?" He turned to his eldest son. "Can you swear it was our cook whom you saw? Can you give an hour?"

"A woman slipped into the stable. When I saw her, I thought she was Hilda. Tobye greeted her with a laugh and, although I could not hear their exact words, I did note her wheedling tone. I remember thinking it odd that our cook would have any honest cause to seek out the groom at such a time and place. I confess I did not see her face, nor can I tell you the hour of the night." He folded his arms. The gesture was defiant, but his face was ashen and he could not meet his father's eye. "I was on my way to pray."

Eleanor felt a chill shoot through her. Ranulf's testimony suggested far more than a woman simply being in the general vicinity of the stable.

Mistress Maud briefly touched the steward's arm, and he bent an ear to her whisperings.

Ranulf glared at Huet. "When I rise from my bed, my sins trouble me more than my bowels, but then I am more abstemious than certain sinners amongst us. I go to the chapel from my bed, not the privy because I have gotten drunk."

And, of course, you would never stop in your rush to seek God's mercy to eavesdrop on how others are progressing in their many lusts, Eleanor thought, disgusted at the man's hypocrisy. She was not sure whether Ranulf or his wife was the more tiresome, but the former was no longer a minor irritant. Anyone who tried to shove a woman, possibly innocent of any wrongful act, to her hanging was a grave threat to justice. Yet was she so innocent?

"May I suggest a compromise, Sir Reimund?" Stevyn now asked.

"I always listen to a reasoned voice," the sheriff replied, his teeth visibly clenched as if fighting a feverish chill.

"I do not believe my eldest son's statements can be dismissed, yet we have all heard equally compelling stories that cast doubt on their precise accuracy." He looked over to Eleanor. "Since we have the Prioress of Tyndal here as an honored guest, I would like to ask her permission to involve Brother Thomas in this matter."

Well practiced in restraint, Eleanor did not visibly react. After delaying a suitable amount of time to suggest reflection, she nodded her agreement.

Stevyn bowed, then continued: "May we not keep our cook here under close guard and ask Brother Thomas to speak with Hilda about the future of her soul? A guard would make sure she did not escape, and you would have time to resolve any discrepancies between the statements given. If Hilda is guilty, she may well confess for the good of her soul or you may find a satisfactory resolution of the conflicts."

The sheriff remained silent but glanced at Eleanor as if she were to blame for this.

"Your proposal holds merit," she replied to the steward. How fortunate these people were, she thought, to have Master Stevyn to preside over the manor courts. The jury might decide the matters at hand in such situations, but his considered opinions would surely tilt them to a more just conclusion.

"Very well," Sir Reimund replied. "Let me know where the cook will be housed, and I will set a proper guard."

Stevyn pointed at a low hut nearby. "One door. No windows. It was storage, but we've just finished a larger building. This one is empty."

Mistress Maud walked to the bedraggled cook, gently lifted her to her feet, and directed Hilda through the crowd.

Eleanor noted the kindness but then grew troubled. Her vague impression that the widow had left the chambers, where Mariota lay, on the night of the groom's murder would not fade. Surely she was wrong and the memory false. Yet she could not set her question aside. If Ranulf had seen a woman with Tobye that night, a woman who was not Luce but bore a resemblance to Hilda, might she have been Maud? In truth, she hoped neither the cuckolded steward nor this healer was involved, but she knew she dare not base a fair judgment of either on such short acquaintance.

As everyone dispersed and the steward walked away with the sheriff, Brother Thomas made his way to Eleanor.

"Do you believe in Hilda's innocence?" She kept her voice low enough that the guard, who was still talking to the woman next to him, would not hear.

"I do, my lady, but I am troubled."

The prioress held up her hand for silence and walked over to her guard. "Brother Thomas has asked that we go to the chapel to pray for Hilda. Will you be kind enough to accompany us there? Afterward, I will make sure you get a good supper."

A mother's smile could not have been sweeter, but Eleanor did feel properly contrite over her use of prayer as deception.

Chapter Twenty

Mistress Constance drew back from the window overlooking the courtyard, but her legs trembled so that she could not stand. Slipping down to sit on the narrow stone step, she clasped her hands together and gnawed on her reddened knuckles.

"Cursed creatures," she hissed and closed her eyes so tight that her head pounded and Hell's scarlet flames danced against her lids. "Oh how the Devil rules here!"

And lust was surely the deadliest of his evils. Did she not see enough proof of that as a young girl? Her mother had screamed with each hard birth, until she finally died when the blood would not stop after the last dead babe. Yet she had heard her parents continue to couple like rutting goats after each childbearing. Why had they failed to learn what God was trying to teach? Giving in to lust with a man was the straightest path to death and Hell for a woman. At least she had understood that lesson.

Taking a deep breath, she pulled herself up, scraping her hands against the rough stone, and stared again down into the courtyard.

Her husband was still there, a man she hated. He pretended virtue, but she knew what he did in bed after she refused his vile demands. Payment of the marriage debt indeed! All her mother had gained from that was a very narrow grave.

And still standing in the courtyard beside Master Stevyn was Mistress Maud, a true Jezebel who wore the chaste and simple robes of widowhood while her body festered with abominable sin. That one was no better than Mistress Luce, a woman who would couple with Satan himself if a mortal man was not ready to service her.

As for Hilda, she felt no pity. Hanging was no more than the woman deserved. She had seen her pant shamelessly over Tobye. No better than a bitch in heat.

Fools! Constance snorted in contempt. They probably thought she was immune to lust and that chastity was an easy choice. But wasn't she her mother's daughter, hungering for a man between her legs just like any other wretched woman? She understood how longing twisted its way into the soul, turned it black with the gangrene of iniquity, and brought incubi to shatter a woman's peaceful dreams.

How she wished her father had listened when she begged for entrance to a convent, but he suffered as much from avarice as lust. The chance to bind her to the steward's eldest son was too tempting, and he had persuaded her to agree by suggesting that Ranulf would follow his own mother's pious example and demand only an heir or two from the marriage bed.

Instead, Ranulf had thrown her on the rushes and rammed her like a bull despite her cries of pain the night after they took vows at the church door. The babe he seeded in her died in a rush of blood a few months later, but she had survived and soon learned that her husband was easily filled with guilt for the weakness of his flesh, if not completely persuaded to deny his too frequent need to satisfy it.

Thus God had revealed how compassionate He could be to those longing to remain chaste and had shown her the way to keep her body unsullied by Ranulf's loathsome touch—at least most of the time. As for her dreams, they were minor failings compared to the brazen sins of others. She did not willingly allow any mortal man to touch her, even her husband, and kept a small whip for secret penance on those occasions when the incubi mounted her and she failed to awaken until she howled with bucking lust. Indeed, God was surely pleased enough with those atonements.

Until now.

She pressed her nails into her cheeks. Despite His patient mercy, was there anything she could do to keep Him from flinging her soul into Hell after what had happened that night?

Leaning back against the wall, she began to weep.

Chapter Twenty-One

The guard had taken Eleanor's invitation to accompany them to the chapel quite literally and was now kneeling in ardent prayer only a few feet away.

"What news have you for me?" Eleanor sang softly in Latin as she kept an eye on the guard to her left.

After hesitating over how best to respond, Thomas chanted, "The dagger and some concerns."

The first part of his answer pleased the prioress. "Tell me of the former."

"I found it hidden in the straw, where others should have discovered it had they looked, but none did, which is no better than we feared."

"Alleluia!"

Thomas buried his face in his hands and hoped he could match his prioress' discretion in this covert conversation. "The crafting is well done, yet the object bears no distinctive mark."

"Has it kin amongst the cook's tools?"

"Sadly."

"Might it have been stolen?"

He hesitated, wanting very much to say it had been. "Or not," he finally forced himself to reply. "Whether dropped by accident in the rush to escape, or deliberately left as some ruse, remains unclear."

Eleanor fell silent as she studied the guard. Although he seemed uninterested in their discussion, she began a regular litany of prayers.

Thomas dutifully followed until the final *Amen*.

The guard remained on his knees, hands clasped tightly, and apparently unaware of his companions.

"Will you ask if anyone recognizes the knife?"

"If so, I shall claim I found it near the kitchen."

Eleanor gazed up at the cross. "Be careful, lest you ask the man who did this deed. He might choose to silence you."

The likeness of one immediately came to the monk's mind, the man's arms encircling him. Then he imagined a knife pricking his breast. Thomas flinched. The vision vanished, and he nodded concurrence with her plea for caution.

The guard rose to his feet.

Their chance to exchange information had ended, but Eleanor knew her monk had more to say and that something troubled him. After all the crimes they had solved together, she knew Brother Thomas would never recoil at the prospect of facing a murderer. What else was worrying him? She would chance one last question.

"Have you left a concern unspoken?" she chanted.

Thomas visibly paled.

Although the guard's head was bowed, he now leaned against the chapel wall where he could see what the two religious did.

"Tell me quickly. We must leave."

"The younger son gave false witness today. He did not return as he claimed in the early morning. I did not see him at all until later in the day."

Eleanor's eyes widened. That might well make Huet another suspect in this killing. Yet, if he had done it, his heated defense of the cook suggested he did not want an innocent to suffer for his crime. Might that mean there was a complication to this murder? Might it even have been self-defense? Yet there had been no sign of a struggle.

She frowned. There was something else that bothered her. Why had Huet lied so publicly when he knew Brother Thomas could give witness against him?

Glancing at the guard, she saw he was showing some impatience and knew she could not ask her monk more.

"I pray that God will have mercy on his soul if he is guilty of this sin," she whispered.

"Amen," Thomas responded, turning his face away.

Chapter Twenty-Two

The current storm had passed, even the weakening rainfall had ended, but the air remained heavy with moisture. Looking across the courtyard, Eleanor wondered if she should chance a walk through that chill mist.

Mariota had fallen asleep. A servant, rhythmically twirling a spindle to twist wool into thread, sat nearby and watched over the girl. There was no reason for the prioress to stay inside after chapel, and she was never inclined to remain sedentary for long. Even if the ground was sodden, she longed for the exercise. It would help her think, and she had much to ponder.

As she walked down the steeply curving staircase to the hall below, she forced herself to confront the question of why she had gotten involved in this matter of murder. It was no business of hers. This was not priory land. The king's law ruled here. Although the sheriff may have offended her, and he did prefer the easy answer to problems, he was not dull-witted. That young guard he had assigned to make sure she did not meddle in his affairs was one proof of that.

Why did she not remember her teachings and step away, forgiving Sir Reimund his offense as she should? He could easily solve this crime—if he chose justice over furthering his own ambition. She bit her lip. Of course she doubted he would choose truth over self-interest and thus ached to thwart him. But was her reason based in a desire to render justice or was the motivation born of vanity?

After her successes in similar affairs, she may have grown conceited, believing that only she would be disinterested enough to discover the truth. If so, she must cease her involvement immediately and confess her overfed arrogance.

Yet the more she learned about the circumstances surrounding the groom's death, the more she feared some innocent would be hanged, and her soul balked at the very thought. Although she had not spoken with the cook, both Huet and Brother Thomas had argued forcefully for her innocence, and the steward had shown frank disbelief when she was arrested.

If the sheriff was finally convinced to release her, would he substitute another innocent victim of low rank? The speedy choice of Hilda suggested he would follow that pattern again and ignore the possible involvement of both the steward and his younger son. Eleanor knew she could not sit back and let that happen.

As the prioress walked through the entry door to the courtyard, she glanced behind her and realized her faithful guard was not in attendance. Then she heard a girlish squeal and saw a child race toward her, skidding to a stop just before she collided with the Prioress of Tyndal.

"My lady, please forgive my daughter! She meant no harm." The young guard was red-faced as he approached the girl and put a hand gently but firmly on her shoulder.

The child dutifully bobbed but stared round-eyed at the woman before her.

"Now ask politely for what you wanted," the father bent to whisper.

The girl, surely no more than four, put one finger in her mouth.

Eleanor knelt. A small woman by any measure, her eyes were now on a level with those of the child.

The girl grinned. "Blessing?" she asked without removing the finger.

The guard shifted nervously. "She begged to come with me today and meet you, my lady. She is usually a good child and knows how to behave with her betters. I don't know what has caused this."

"Our Lord said we should all be more like children." Eleanor smiled and made her fingers walk like a playful spider on her palm.

The girl giggled.

The prioress picked the girl up and hugged her. "She is beautiful," she said, handing her over to the guard. "Am I correct in concluding she favors her mother?"

The young man nodded but moisture rimmed his eyes. "God's angels required that her mother go into their service over a year ago. We know it was her duty, but we still miss her."

Her heart ached to learn that news, and Eleanor pressed a hand against her breast. In truth, it mattered little to the wee ones that a mother was now safely with God. A father might try to sooth the absence with gentleness, but a mother's death was a wound that never quite healed. It was a feeling Eleanor knew well. With especial tenderness, she blessed the child as she had been asked.

"Now that we have your daughter's company for my honor's sake, shall we take a walk?" The sheriff had assigned this man to watch her, but the guard had shown only courtesy to her. He seemed a good, well-intended country fellow. His help moving her through the crowd and several other small gestures had demonstrated that a soft heart came with duty.

As they gingerly stepped around puddles and over piles of multi-hued muck, Eleanor smiled at her guard who now held his daughter firmly by the hand. "Have you both eaten yet?"

He nodded. "When she knew we'd be here, Hilda always saved a trencher from the evening meal, or the harder crusts from fresh bread soaked in milk for my child. The kitchen may be in turmoil now with Hilda locked away, but one of the servants was kind enough to feed us."

"You've known the cook long?"

"She and my mother grew up together, and they remained good friends."

"Then Hilda is of local birth?"

"Aye, and her parents served the manor as did theirs before them."

"If your mother calls the cook *friend*, Hilda must be a good woman."

He started to answer but then hesitated.

Perhaps he fears a reply would be against the sheriff's wishes, Eleanor realized. "I am not seeking any information about the crime of which she is accused. Master Stevyn said she was talented at her work, and such a woman could easily have earned enough to save for marriage. I wonder that she never found a husband. Or is she a widow? I was not sure."

The tension went out of his shoulders. "I think a cooper wanted to marry her years ago, but he died when a cart turned over and broke his back. My mother sometimes jested that Hilda liked running a kitchen better than being run by any husband and thus chased all young men away with words as sharp as her carcass cleaver. Yet my mother never quite understood why the cook didn't marry. She was well-known for her gentle heart and liked by all, especially when she fed us!"

Her impression of Hilda confirmed, Eleanor decided not to pursue any more questions and laughed at the guard's jest. "Your mother sounds like a most loving friend. Tell me of your family."

And thus the two chatted companionably as they walked through the manor house gate to the bumpy road and empty fields beyond. The guard let his daughter run free but never so far that he didn't call her back to a safer distance. Eleanor was touched by how much the young widower loved his child. Although she learned that his sister had taken them in to give his motherless girl a woman's care, she saw how he delighted in the time he spent with her himself. Indeed, her guard reminded her of a younger Crowner Ralf, a man fierce enough with felons who became soft as lamb's wool when holding his baby daughter.

The prioress pointed out a low stone wall near a cluster of trees and asked if the way was treacherous. The young man assured her that the grass might be wet but the ground was firm enough, and so they walked toward it.

As they approached the trees, Eleanor noticed with some surprise that a figure was sitting on that fence in the shadow of the grove. It was a woman, bent over with her head buried in her hands.

"Forgive me," the prioress said, "but I believe that is the steward's wife. May I speak with her privately? She seems distressed and might be embarrassed, or even frightened, if you were to accompany me. Yet I do beg that you not go too far away should she be ill or otherwise need your assistance."

When he bowed and stepped back, Eleanor was touched that he so quickly understood a woman's need to speak only in another woman's ear and watched him lead his daughter into the grove where he began pointing out things for her to see and learn thereby.

Now drawing closer, the prioress saw that the woman was certainly Luce and that the woman wept. "Mistress?" she said with a gentle tone. "May I bring comfort?"

Luce leapt down to the ground but, when she saw who it was, sank against the rough stone and stared in silence at the dark, sodden earth.

Eleanor reached out with concern. "Are you ill?"

The wife's lips curled into a bitter smile. "If grief be a sickness, then I am ill. If...oh, what is the use in living?"

"If you can speak to me of your sorrow, we may find an answer together with God's help."

Luce made a fist and began to pound the damp rock with increasing force until a sharp pain caused her to cry out.

Eleanor saw a dark stain of blood on the wall. "Please, Mistress, do not let anguish conquer your soul. God weeps when His creatures suffer too much." She lingered over the choice of her next words before concluding, "And demands that we who serve Him remember that all mortals are sinners, and thus no one may cast stones of condemnation."

"Does not God curse us when we sin, even out of suffering?"

"Only if we do not regret those errors."

"What would He say, do you think, if a woman lied to her husband about a quickening womb?"

That question most certainly caught Eleanor's interest. The woman's words were cutting with sarcasm, but the question required honest reply. "If the lie was given in hope and kindness, the sin is minor enough and might be overbalanced by good intentions." She hesitated, weighing the chance of an answer if she continued. "Are you not pregnant?"

"I have demanded payment of the marriage debt often enough, but my husband has not filled my womb with life."

"Why did you tell your husband otherwise?"

"I had hoped to give him a son anyway."

"By other means."

"You are perceptive, my lady."

"And that means has gone…"

"…to Hell."

"Your husband has two sons. Was he so eager for another?"

Luce's mouth twisted with anger. "He was not, even though his eldest has no issue and his youngest was sent to be a priest. It was I who needed the son to be my comfort and support."

"I know your husband is much older and may well leave you a widow. Yet surely you could remarry, if he dies before you, and thus gain the protection of another spouse?"

"And how old may I be then? Will not another man hesitate to wed me if I prove barren in this marriage? And if I fail to have a son, who must tend me when I am so aged that I can only sit in a corner and drool like some babe myself?"

Although the words rang with anger, Eleanor heard terror quivering just behind them. "Master Stevyn has two sons," she said, "either of whom must take care of you. In addition, you will inherit a widow's due."

Luce snorted. "A widow's due? Aye, that might pay for a servant to feed me pap, should I grow helpless, but only blood kin care enough to make sure toothless crones are handled with kindness." She shuddered. "As for Master Ranulf, it might be a mercy if he left such charity to his wife. Yet there would be little benevolence in that. You have met her. Do you think her hands know aught of tenderness?"

Eleanor tilted her head to suggest sympathy.

"A dry husk inhabits the place where her heart should beat. The servants even jest that her husband must crawl on his knees and beg like a dog before she'll ever lie with him." She hugged herself as if chilled.

"What of Master Huet?" Eleanor shifted the object of the discussion, yet she wondered why Luce spoke in such a venomous tone and what had caused the hatred to grow between the two women.

"What should I think of him? He went off to be a priest. Now he is back, his tonsure gone, and he drifts without purpose, plucking his lute with a plectrum of horn. Perhaps he is not as eager for chastity as he once was, but I know not the direction he will take. A handsome man, for cert, but..." Falling silent, she lowered her eyes.

Eleanor shivered with a horrible thought. Might the steward's wife and her son-by-marriage have just become lovers? Huet had seemed indifferent to his stepmother at dinner, when she boldly tried to get his attention, but that lack of interest could have been feigned.

Might Tobye have become jealous and threatened to tell tales if they continued their incestuous beddings? Or did he demand coin? Might Huet have killed to silence the groom?

Growing frustrated with the ever-changing nature of the crime, Eleanor suddenly lost patience. There were so many evasions and veiled hints, too many paths to follow. Or was her imagination simply becoming overheated to compensate for this cold weather and thus she was making matters out to be worse than they were?

"You have committed adultery, Mistress," she snapped, tucking her hands into her sleeves to ease the chill. "Confess and repent, if you have not done so already. God forgives the contrite soul, and you may yet find yourself pregnant by your lawful husband."

"And if I do not quicken with a boy?"

And why should you be so terrified of this? Eleanor wondered, hearing the tremor in Luce's voice.

"I do not think you understand, my lady. When you are aged, you will have the priory nuns to care for you. I did not have your vocation and must depend on offspring for gentleness when I can no longer tend my needs."

"Why fear such a distant thing? How could it be worth the sin you committed in trying to ease it?"

Luce sighed with annoyance. "My parents both lost their wits. Sadly, they had borne only two girls, and it fell to my younger sister to care for them. Soon after our mother died, our father wandered into a stream and drowned. My sister had fallen asleep under a nearby tree and suffered so because of her failure to prevent his death that she hanged herself."

The prioress winced. "Surely there were servants to ease the burden. Kin? Why was she obliged to take on such a labor by herself?" She gestured at the manor lands. "They could have come here and been easily watched over."

"There were servants, but my sister did not trust them enough. We had no other living kin, and I was about to be married, my lady. How many husbands want to take on the tending of some woman's parents in their dotage? Even if willing, wouldn't an older man suffer from such daily reminders of rotting age? I believed Master Stevyn might choose another to wed, one who did not bring thoughts of mortal decay to the marriage bed, if I raised the subject of my parents with him. As you must certainly understand, I had to hide the truth and thus could do nothing to help my sister."

This time Eleanor knew that her chill had nothing to do with the dampness in the air.

"I would remain alone here for awhile." Luce now looked at the prioress with narrowed eyes, her manner bordering on insolence.

Eleanor rose and took her leave with more courtesy than was owed. As she, her guard, and his daughter walked back toward the manor house gate, she grieved that she had failed to bring either peace or contrition to the twisted heart of the steward's wife and feared the evil in this place of refuge was more sinister than she had imagined.

Chapter Twenty-Three

The musty stench of mold was strong in the windowless hut.

"I am innocent of murder, Brother." Hilda sobbed as she cowered in the corner.

"I would prove that and speed your release," he said, "but you must answer my questions fully, truthfully, and without hesitation."

Although she might not see his own tears in the dim light, Thomas rubbed all traces from his cheeks. How could a woman be transformed into this thin shadow of despair within so few hours? Yet, as he recalled his own first day of imprisonment, he knew he should understand well enough just how quickly loss of hope sucked life from a man.

"I swear I left the kitchen but once or twice the night Tobye was cruelly slaughtered. You saw me asleep when you awoke for prayer. It was so cold that my trips to the privy were brief."

Did she omit mention of Huet's testimony, knowing he had lied? Thomas was about to ask, then decided she might not want to bring attention to the falsehood, fearing it would weaken her case. Or perhaps she thought the statement of a monk would have greater merit than that of a one who had abandoned the priesthood, and thus it mattered not what the latter might say? Did she wonder why the man had lied? He opted to abandon all those uncertainties and probe for answers to more immediate questions.

"Did you ever meet with Tobye in the stable and couple in sin?"

"I have never known any man, Brother, although I confess I dreamed of it."

"Did you know the women who actually shared his bed?"

She turned her face from him, and in the feeble light he saw the profile of her hand pressed against her mouth as if to stop words from tumbling out.

"You must tell me what you know or have heard. Let me decide what information might best save your life and what can be forgotten here."

"I am a servant to this family and owe them loyalty. To speak ill of any amongst them would be a betrayal."

A most revealing response to his question, Thomas thought, considering what he had already learned about Mistress Luce. If the wife's adultery was so well known, there was little reason to doubt that Master Stevyn was also aware of the cuckoldry and, like any husband, would be disinclined to ignore it. Who might she be trying to protect: master or lady? "If you distinguish what you know from what you have heard as rumor, there are few who would find fault with you. Most certainly not I."

"What is my life worth if Master Stevyn casts me out because he learns what I have said? Even if I am found innocent of his groom's murder, I shall suffer the shame of being condemned as a faithless servant while I starve."

"Let God be the judge of your words. If your heart holds no malice and your testimony brings to light some relevant family sin, your act will have been a righteous one. He will surely protect you." Yet how reasonable was that? Thomas asked himself, knowing full well she had cause enough for fear in a world ruled by mortals. He tried unsuccessfully to silence that blasphemous whisper from his soul.

Hilda closed her eyes and silently moved her lips as if praying that the burden of this moment be lifted from her shoulders. Tears glistened on her cheeks in the pale light, but she ignored them. "I lied in the courtyard, Brother. I was jealous. Tobye had other women, for cert, and I envied them even though I could never have bedded him even if he had truly wished it. I feared Hell too much. Why is it that we long for something that we fear with equal strength? Will God forgive me for that?"

"Did you ever harm his bedfellows in any way?"

"Only in my heart, Brother, but that alone must make the Devil leap high with joy."

Sin enough perhaps, but he knew far graver ones than this woman could even imagine. "If Satan did, his prancing was short-lived. God is gentler with faults that never hurt another mortal." He waited for her to continue.

"Isn't confessing my lie about the jealousy enough?" Her voice wavered.

Thomas hoped she could see understanding and forgiveness in his smile despite the gloom. "He had other women. Who were they?"

Rubbing her hands together in tortured agony, Hilda groaned, then bent closer to him and whispered, "Mistress Luce. I know that. Once I saw her coupling with him against the wall like some common woman, but methinks there was another who came from the manor house that horrible night."

Thomas tried to hide the surprise as he asked: "Who was she?" Doubt took residence in his heart. She had heard Ranulf's claim that he had seen her in the stable. Was she now claiming that she had seen a woman too? To corroborate the testimony of the steward's eldest son, and suggest that he had been wrong only in the identification of the woman, was a clever ploy. Nay, he thought, she was not possessed of such crafty wit.

"Who was this person?" he asked again, wondering how vague her answer would be.

"I was coming out of the privy and saw a woman's shadow near the stable. Then she slipped inside. I saw only her shape, never her face." She flinched and turned away. "Aye, Brother, once or twice I did spy on him, but my intent was never to betray his lovers even though my heart ached with envy. Maybe that pain was my penance for the wicked longing of my flesh?"

"Quite possibly," he said gently, "but your sin is light enough. Tell me what else you saw or heard. You might find a readier forgiveness if the eavesdropping reveals a killer."

"In truth, my sight was limited by the hour and weather. I knew it was a woman by the length of her heavy cloak, but I could not determine if she were young or old. When I slipped up to a window and pressed my ear as close as I dared, I was unable to recognize words. She spoke too low, but I thought she whined with piteous begging. Tobye must have grown angry, for I did hear him exclaim that his member withered at the very sight of her. Then I ran away out of shame for what I was doing."

"Did her voice remind you of anyone?"

"Aye, Brother, but I would never swear it in God's name."

"But you can confide it to me in confidence, Hilda, and let me consider what is best to do next. I promise I will do nothing that will bring harm to you for a mere supposition."

She bent to his ear.

The door creaked open, and a man stepped into the room.

"How does Hilda, Brother?" the steward asked.

Chapter Twenty-Four

"My lady!" the guard's daughter cried out.

Eleanor and the child's father immediately turned to discover what had caused her to shriek so. When they saw the reason, both laughed out of amusement as well as relief.

With both arms, the child was waving at an equally small girl standing inside the manor gate. The object of this enthusiasm now bounded toward them.

"Would you give my friend your blessing as well?" The child's hazel eyes, round with anticipation, looked up at the prioress.

"With much pleasure, especially since you ask it," Eleanor replied. Just beyond the gate, near the hut where the cook was confined, she also saw Brother Thomas in close conversation with Master Stevyn.

Although the two little girls must have played together often, they bounced and squealed with happiness as if they had been separated more years than they had been on earth.

The sight chased some of the darkness from the prioress' heart, a sorrow that the violence of murder always brought her. If only we could keep that innocent joy of childhood and never be touched by cruelty, she thought, and smiled at the children who looked up at her with solemn faces, their hands dutifully folded. As she gave her blessing and felt God's love flow through her to touch the girls when she kissed each on the cheek, Eleanor hoped that they would grow old together with that same delight in friendship and comfort in each other's company.

"My lady, may I ask favor for myself?" Her guard shuffled and his face reddened as they walked into the courtyard.

From the corner of her eye, Eleanor saw a young woman and recognized her as the one he had been talking to when Hilda was arrested. She nodded, knowing quite well what his wish might be.

"I would take but a minute to greet the mother of my daughter's friend. As you see, she is near, and I promise not to cease careful watch over you."

The prioress now caught her monk's eye. "With Master Stevyn just there and Brother Thomas on his way to my side," she said to her guard, "I will be safe enough from any mortal ill. He and I shall remain here, for we must discuss some prayers we have promised." She lowered her eyes with modesty. "You need not cut short your courtesy."

With an appreciate word and grateful grin, the man walked over to see the lady whose obvious joy at his arrival betrayed her own delight in his company.

"My lady, you amaze me," Thomas said, looking in the direction of the departing guard. "How did you manage to send him away?"

"Love is a most powerful emotion, whether it be for God or another mortal. In this case, I simply bowed to the great enticement of the latter." She turned her eyes heavenward. "Let us speak in Latin," she continued in the suggested language. "Have you learned anything of interest? We must be brief, lest someone convey to another that our conversation was longer than expected between monk and prioress."

Thomas knew that anyone in that busy courtyard might find profit in relaying information to the sheriff. He inclined his head slightly in the direction of the small hut. "She witnessed the adultery, of which we were aware, and thus confirmed how wide-spread the knowledge was."

Eleanor bowed her head and nodded.

"She continues to maintain her innocence."

"Do you believe her?"

"I would swear to it for many reasons, but she does corroborate what one other claimed to have seen. Although it was not the night of the murder, she also saw an unknown woman meet the man long after sunset. She never heard her words, only the tenor of the plea, and thus she concluded that the woman was quite sotted with him. He, on the other hand, rejected her cruelly, telling her that he would never bed a woman too old to bear children."

"Did she recognize the voice?"

"She hesitated to guess, but when I pressed her further, she was about to suggest a name. Then her master entered, and she drew back. With him there, she would say nothing more to me."

"I saw you speaking at length with him. Did you learn something in that?"

Thomas frowned. "I tried to determine if he was vexed about the conversation I had had with his cook, but I failed. Either he is clever at hiding his thoughts or he had no concern. My own belief is that he is not a man to betray his feelings. Although he must surely know that his wife has been unfaithful, for instance, I have seen little evidence of it."

"Amen."

"He did tell me that the cook will be removed from here in the morning. The king's man claims there is little more to learn about the murder. Although I have stood witness to her innocence, as has another, he believes there is cause enough in other testimony to hold her in the castle prison."

"How quickly he decides such things," Eleanor snapped. "Does he think this frightened woman will flee to the forest and seek protection from brutish and lawless men?"

"Perhaps he hopes she may die of a fever in a dank cell," Thomas replied, remembering all too well some who had. "If that happens before a hearing, the true wrongdoer will escape."

Eleanor frowned as she pondered whether that person was Master Stevyn, his younger son, or even the unknown woman. "I do wonder who she thought visited a man at such a dark hour and begged so piteously." She glanced at Thomas, her eyes questioning.

"Before she is taken away, she might long for a priest to comfort her, my lady. With your permission, I will go to her." He bowed.

Her lips curled into a thin smile. "The moment for confiding a mere guess may have passed, Brother. Fear of dungeons and hanging cause mortals such terror that the need to cleanse the soul predominates over such matters, but let us pray that she still clings sufficiently to hope and thus confides the name. In any case, convey my blessing. Tonight I shall beg God to let us find the true killer before this poor innocent is condemned to an undeserved and shameful death."

Chapter Twenty-Five

The night before execution, some condemned may fall asleep, hoping to awaken from the nightmare of certainty into the dawn of improbable reprieve. Others stare with unblinking eyes at the dark walls of their prisons, begging for sweet moonlight's conquest over the blood-red sun.

Hilda saw little difference between an immediate hanging and a slow death, gnawed by rats in a dripping cell beneath a castle moat. She beat her fists against the hard, indifferent earth, her eyes wept dry and her heart drumming with terror. Words for prayer had long since failed her. Instead her soul quivered, unable to think any longer on her many sins that might send her to Hell, even if she was innocent of murder.

Suddenly, she froze.

There was a scraping noise outside the door.

That was no rodent, she realized. Was someone unbarring the door?

The wood creaked, and the door did open slowly.

A shadow slipped inside. It had a clear and mortal form.

The cook began to sweat, first from fear and then irrational hope. "Why…?"

"To save you from hanging," was the warm reply.

"You believe me?" She gasped. Her hand now pressed against a heart thundering with inexpressible gratitude.

"Are you not innocent?"

"Full of sin I most certainly am but not of the crime of murder."

"But are you guilty of unseemly gossip?"

"I do not understand." Hilda shook uncontrollably.

"Come now! Women are wont to chatter like squirrels, accusing anyone, not in their current company, of sins born solely in the fens of their unreasoned minds. Have you never done that? Do not lie, for I have overheard the chittering often enough amongst the servants."

The cook opened her mouth to speak, but she was unable to form words.

"What did you say to that priest from Tyndal? Did you prate on and on as is the wont of creatures like you?"

"He took my confession, only that!"

"Only a confession of your own frailties? Nothing of your fevered imaginings about the sins of other souls? I think you are lying, Hilda."

She shook her head.

"Give me your hand."

The cook did so but felt no comfort in the warmth of the strong grip.

"Do you swear that you did not impugn anyone?"

Eagerly, she nodded. Her hand was released.

"But you wanted to do so, didn't you?"

Hilda looked away.

"Of course you did, you frightened and wretched one. Most people would be willing enough to point the finger at someone else to save themselves from choking on the noose." The laughter that followed held no mirth.

"I did not try to save myself by so doing," the cook whispered. Her words were greeted with a long silence.

"Come with me then. You shall be freed of this place."

Hilda now eagerly took the proffered hand, rose, and turned toward the door.

That was the last thing she saw.

Chapter Twenty-Six

When Thomas saw the gate to the courtyard open and the sheriff with his company ride in, he uttered a curse for which he would surely owe penance. Sunlight was still but a promise. Sir Reimund had arrived earlier than expected.

"Shouldn't you be in the chapel praying, Brother? As we approached the manor, I heard bells announce the Office."

"This woman's soul cried out to me," the monk replied, gesturing at the dark outline of the hut. "For such a cause, God may allow postponement of my prayers."

The saddle creaked as Sir Reimund twisted to look around. "And where is your prioress? Have you sent her off to pray in the chapel, a place most proper for her to remain?"

Itching to pull this man off his horse and strike him for his insolence, Thomas folded his hands firmly into his sleeves and let his heavy silence be the sole expression of his fury.

The sheriff grinned, his teeth white against the gray light of morning. "Forgive me, Brother. I did forget the ways of your Order. Unnatural as the practice may be to most of us, she rules *you*, does she not?"

"Do not all men honor their mothers and bow to the Queen of Heaven?"

Reimund nodded, his assent perfunctory.

"In like manner, I obey my prioress, a woman who represents our Lord's mother on earth."

"Then I must beg her prayers on my behalf," the sheriff replied with a brusque courtesy that did little to hide his impatience to get on with the task at hand. "I have come for the accused. Will someone announce my arrival to Master Stevyn?"

"I need no servant to roust me from my bed at this hour," the steward called out as he rounded the side of the hut. Even against the dreary light of a struggling morning, his face was pale.

"I would offer God's consolation before she is taken off to some cold cell," Thomas said.

"She'll have priests aplenty before her hanging. I promise you that. Meanwhile, we must swiftly be on our way. Other, unsolved crimes await our attention." The sheriff gestured abruptly to one of his men. "Bind and bring her out of there."

"Grant her that mercy of a priest's comfort, Sir Reimund," the steward said. "She and her kin have served this land well for many years, and Brother Thomas may bring her solace."

Thomas was startled at the sorrow evident in the man's tone.

The sheriff studied the steward as if he were assessing the value of a bale of wool.

Have you decided if there is some advantage to gain from consent? Thomas' heart filled with more than a little anger.

Sir Reimund turned to the monk. "Give her a short prayer for the journey then, Brother. We'll remain by the open door where she may see us. Perhaps the grave nature of her foul crime will at last pain her like the prick of the knife she used to slit the groom's throat."

Pray, I must, Thomas thought with bitter regret, for I shall be prevented from asking anything that might save the poor woman's life. He walked to the hut door and waited as the assigned guard fumbled with the bar that bolted it. Finally, the man managed to raise it.

"We've come for thee, wretch," the guard called out as he stepped into the hut. Almost immediately, he stumbled backward, crossing himself in terror. "The Devil's been here!"

Shoving the man aside, Thomas rushed inside.

Hilda lay on her stomach. The air reeked with the sharp metallic odor of blood. Even in the dim light, it was obvious that her back was stained dark with it.

◇◇◇

"Surely this proves her innocence, Sir Reimund," the steward said, his tone brittle with barely controlled outrage.

His arms crossed, the sheriff scowled. "I've known a man to commit self-murder by driving his forehead against a bare nail in the wall of his cell. She probably did this to herself."

"Bring me a torch," Thomas ordered and knelt by the body.

The steward pushed his way through the sheriff's men and shouted for one of his servants to fetch one. "Quickly!" he bellowed, then swiftly backed away from the entrance. "My lady!" he said, his voice softening.

Eleanor walked into the hut. "What has happened?"

The sheriff emitted a palpable groan before turning to greet her with a token bow. "Nothing to trouble you, my lady."

"All sin is of interest to me for I obey a Master far greater than any earthly king," she retorted, "and murder is amongst God's first prohibited acts. Would that not qualify as a sin, Sir Reimund, and thus one of my concerns?" Without waiting for him to reply, she walked past him to where her monk was kneeling.

A servant rushed in with the requested torch.

"I need light here." Thomas pointed, then leaned closer as the flickering light brightened the back of the woman's head. Gently, he turned her over and touched her neck before bending to place his ear to her mouth.

"You need not do that, Brother. One of my men…"

"Be silent!" the prioress snapped.

Reimund and Stevyn glanced at each other. The steward shrugged, and the sheriff kicked at some straw before stepping away.

"I think she is still alive, my lady," Thomas said. "For how much longer, however, I cannot say."

Eleanor quickly removed her outer cloak and gave it to him. "Wrap her in that." She turned to the steward. "She must be moved from here. If her soul continues to cling to this body, she may yet point out her attacker and perhaps the one who did murder Tobye."

Stevyn went to the entrance and shouted an order.

"If only we had Sister Anne with us," Thomas whispered, wrapping the woolen cloak around Hilda as tenderly as if she were a babe.

"You must do your best, Brother, and remember what you have seen her do in like situations."

He looked at her, eyes darkened by worry, and finally nodded.

The sheriff grunted. "The woman is guilty and deserves to die, my lady. It matters not if she does so because of this wound, which she may well have inflicted on herself, or by the grace of the hangman's noose. My only regret, should she die here, is that others, who might be tempted to kill, will not see her jerking body and thus be reminded that they shall suffer the same fate if they commit a similar crime. To see the hangman at work is a fine deterrent to murder."

Several servants had just entered and now circled around Hilda. "Be gentle!" Thomas begged, helping them brace and lift the cook onto a rough wooden frame.

"Step aside, if you will," Stevyn said to Sir Reimund, "so these men may carry our Hilda to the house." Then the steward followed the servants outside.

"No one can stab themselves in the back, remove the knife, and hide it before losing all awareness," Thomas growled. "Someone did this to her and for cause. Perhaps they feared she knew or might suggest the true killer."

"Maybe she just dropped the knife in the straw," the sheriff finally said. "My men will search for it."

Thomas finally lost his temper. "And if you do not find it, shall you conclude that some other servant has a knife stained with blood? Whether that blood was animal or human would be irrelevant to you, would it not?"

"If you were not a monk, I'd throw you in prison for treasonable words against a king's man." The sheriff grabbed Thomas' habit and jerked him closer.

"He belongs to God, Sir Reimund," Eleanor said quietly. "Only the Church can order discipline against him. Yet I beg your forbearance, for we were given shelter here by Master Stevyn's household out of Christian charity. Our gratitude makes us protective of our saviors and thus prone to some rashness on their behalf. Just as you would not trespass on the rights of God's Church, however, neither do we wish to interfere with the just pursuit of the king's justice."

The sheriff released his grip.

Even though his face still felt as hot as hellfire, Thomas stepped back and bowed his head with a feigned show of meekness. At least the sheriff's men were now forced to search the hut with witnesses present. He counted that as a small victory.

Master Stevyn bent low to re-enter the hut after giving further directions about Hilda's care. Without evident emotion, he glanced at the men now shuffling around in the straw but turned to the prioress. "My last wife found much comfort at your priory and from your sub-infirmarian," he said, his voice catching slightly, "even if Sister Anne was unable to save her life. Yet we have a healer with some talent here, my lady. I have asked the physician's widow to tend to Hilda."

"A wise as well as a kind decision," Eleanor replied with the briefest of hesitations. "Brother Thomas has often assisted Sister Anne in her treatments, but a woman may treat another of her sex without offending modesty. Mistress Maud has shown much skill in the care of the poor child in our company." She bowed in acceptance of his decision.

Brother Thomas watched the sheriff's men continue to search unsuccessfully for the weapon used against the cook. The space was small enough that their hunt could not last much longer. He glanced over at the prioress.

Eleanor ignored him. "Yet she is not a physician, and I have heard there has been no one to replace her husband since his death. Although she is most skilled, she is still a woman and thus plagued on occasion with illogic and inability to clearly see the proper path to take. Might she be allowed to consult with Brother Thomas? He could offer direction if she faltered."

After a brief conference, one of the searchers went to the sheriff, who now stood just outside the hut. Although their words could not be overheard, the man's gestures suggested he was convinced of the futility in their hunt for the knife.

Thomas noticed that his prioress was also watching this interaction and suddenly realized that she had planned her discussion with the steward to last as long as the weapon search.

"As you wish, my lady. I am sure that Mistress Maud will appreciate any guidance Brother Thomas can offer her." The steward bowed.

"I am most grateful to you, Master Stevyn." She lowered her eyes. "Now we must leave and let these men continue their efforts. I have stayed far too long and shall return to the care of my young companion."

As the two monastics left the hut, the sheriff turned his back and immediately walked away so he did not have to utter even the most rudimentary courtesies to them.

On their way back to the house, however, Eleanor looked over her shoulder and saw that her guard still trotted close behind. After the attack on Hilda, the sheriff would claim that the protection was proven necessary, and thus he would continue his attempt to prevent her from interfering with his preferred investigative techniques.

Glancing back, Brother Thomas also took note of the faithful shadow and waved in a friendly fashion, then chose Latin to tell his prioress: "They found no knife, my lady."

"Nor did either of us think they might," she replied with a preoccupied frown.

"I wonder where our killer dropped this one. I cannot imagine using the blade to kill another mortal in the morning and then cutting your meat at dinner with the same thing."

Eleanor raised an eyebrow. "When the Prince of Darkness drives a man to such madness that he murders another made in God's likeness, he might well do just that."

"I fear you have the right of it, my lady." He paused before continuing. "I doubt the importance of either weapon as evidence. Although I will keep it safely hidden, the first had no distinctive markings. The second, should I find it, will most probably be equally undistinguished, thus my delight at the discovery in the stable has dampened more than this ground on which we stand."

"Nonetheless, you must search the area nearby. Even though I agree with your assessment, we must not ignore the possibility that we may both be proven wrong." Her monk's sad face made her long to cheer him. "No evidence may ever be discounted until the crime is solved."

"At least you were able to keep witnesses present while the sheriff's men searched the hut. Now it is clear that Hilda did not commit self-murder. I feared Sir Reimund would *arrange* for a knife to be found."

"There were no windows through which to toss it. No rational person would conclude that she could unbar a door, bolted from the outside, and throw away a knife with which she had stabbed herself. Although our king's man may begrudge the loss of his choice for the groom's killer, I think he might concede that the cook was attacked by someone besides herself."

"You are most generous in your assessment of his wits, my lady. I am not sure they are quite that keen, having been blunted by his ambition," Thomas replied.

Eleanor chuckled. "I assume you will confess that lack of charity, Brother, when we return to Tyndal. On the other hand, your confessor may well decide that any sin is wiped clean because your words hold some truth in them."

Exchanging amused looks, the pair continued to the manor house in companionable silence.

Chapter Twenty-Seven

"Death grasps her hand with great strength, my lady. I doubt Hilda will ever again greet fellow mortals on this earth." Mistress Maud stood back from the pallet where the cook lay, her breath almost imperceptible.

Looking down at the body, which had quickly become little more than a frail mortal shell eager to release a struggling soul, Eleanor nodded understanding. She might wish the outcome to be otherwise, but she had asked Brother Thomas to give the last rites. "You have known her long?" The prioress' voice was soft with sympathy.

"I have. She is a good woman. I never believed she killed Tobye."

"You do not think she lusted after the man and grew jealous enough to strike out?"

"Oh, she itched for him but, as sins go, hers were trifling enough. Was she jealous?" Maud's smile was cheerless. "Most likely, but she would have sooner wept over it than turned to murder. Women may dream, my lady, but men either seize what they want or destroy what they can't have." She shrugged. "Yet God made Adam before Eve, thus wise men say he was His more perfect creature. Imaginings, being womanish, must be the greater folly."

Eleanor was surprised by the well-whetted edge she heard in those words. What was the source of this woman's bitterness? But no question formed quickly enough for the asking, and she knew the cause might well have nothing to do with this crime. Perhaps she would be wiser to let the widow continue on.

"I do not doubt that Hilda suffered from her longings. The Devil may find it easier to torment youth with unrelenting lust, but I sometimes think he gains special merriment by pricking those who believe they have grown past that foolishness." Maud blinked as if surprised by what she had just said. "Yet I am sure Tobye lent his shape to incubi that tormented many other women at night, both the wrinkled and the smooth-fleshed. If thwarted lust is a motive in this murder, my lady, the sheriff may find there was a long line of women, who stood outside the stable on that night, waiting their turn to kill the groom."

Since she often hoped that age would calm her own passions, Eleanor prayed the widow was wrong about Satan's ways. "Did the cook have any enemy who might have hated her enough to attack her with intent to kill?" she asked, redirecting the conversation from her own uncomfortable thoughts.

"Hilda? Never! She slipped savories to lads and sweets to the girls. Her meals pleased those of both high and low birth. The only creatures that had cause to loathe her were fowl, and even there she chose to wring the necks of ones closest to their natural death. She took pride in making a tough old cock taste like a tender young hen."

Eleanor smiled. "So I have heard."

Maud looked down at the woman lying in bed and sighed.

"Can you think of any reason why Tobye was murdered or why Hilda was attacked so cruelly?"

"Have you found reason not to trust the sheriff to find the killer, my lady?" Maude raised an eyebrow as she studied the prioress.

Eleanor lowered her eyes with suitable meekness. "Like many women, I suffer from the weakness of curiosity. My questions are nothing more than whimsical things. As the king's man, I have no doubt that Sir Reimund will prove up to the task." Her face hidden, the prioress frowned. And why ask such a question, she wondered, when it was you who first planted the seed of doubt in my mind about his peculiar methods of seeking justice? Eleanor grew uneasy.

"He would not have assigned a guard to keep an eye on you if he thought you so harmless and docile." Maud chuckled. "Our sheriff is not the only one who knows your reputation as a woman with an unsettling and masculine mind."

Was this widow part of some trap set by Sir Reimund to catch her interfering where she should not? Had Maud's earlier suggestion that the sheriff cared most about his own interests been part of a scheme? Eleanor tried to calm herself and think logically.

Although she had gained a reputation for solving criminal matters, her greatest success involved financial solvency for her priory. Power was ever linked to coin so, if there were concerns that she was growing too influential, they were based in the increasing wealth of Tyndal.

Perhaps the sheriff believed he would gain by proving she had willfully and unjustifiably interfered with the king's matters. The ways and concerns of King Edward were still unknown to her, indeed to her father as well, for this new king was known more for changes in direction than the steadiness of his purpose. Were she to make a misstep and find disfavor with the new regime, Eleanor knew that she, her family, and her priory would be in danger. And, should she suffer a fall from grace, there might well be those at court who would rejoice and smile on the man who had brought it about.

It would be wise not to trust Maud, or to give Sir Reimund cause to complain to her superiors, she decided. She must tread more carefully than she had in this matter. After all, she had no wish to ruin her family or her priory, especially by foolish actions born more of sinful pride than anything else.

"At Tyndal Priory, I have an obligation to render God's justice," she replied with care. "In the world, I have no more authority than any other woman. This land belongs to the Earl of Lincoln and the king's law rules here. Sir Reimund has nothing to fear from any feminine interference."

"More's the pity," Maud sighed. "He is not an evil man but…" She shrugged.

Eleanor refused to be drawn into any criticism of the sheriff. "I am sure he will find Tobye's killer as well as Hilda's attacker." Eleanor fell silent long enough to let her firmly stated confidence in the man sink in. As she had learned, people are often lulled into complacency after hearing the accepted point of view expressed. She would now chance a question. "I never met the groom, but wonder that Master Stevyn kept such a man if he was so despised."

"Tobye was reliable and skilled with horses, whatever his other faults might be. My jest aside about the scorned women, I cannot say he was truly hated. A few husbands had cause to give him a beating, but the blows dealt were only hard enough to make his member droop when next he thought to smile upon their wives. There was a father or two who had wished his daughter could stand at the church door with maidenhead taut enough to bloody the marriage bed, but Tobye was clever and often able to point out other likely and equally randy youths as culprits there. He may have been less guilty of lewdness than he was accused."

"Aye, but someone most certainly hated him more than those," Eleanor said, letting her words fall as comment more than question.

Maud looked perplexed.

Deciding she had best turn away from all further inquiry, the prioress shook her head. "I pray that terror does not take residence in the hearts of those who live and work here. Murder is a frightening thing."

"There was less unease after Hilda's arrest and before she was attacked."

Eleanor could not read the expression on Maud's face quickly enough and turned her attention to the cook. An almost imperceptible rise and fall in the warm coverings over her proved life still had a hold on the sorely wounded woman.

"Although few believed she had done the deed, many were comforted by the swiftness of resolution in the crime," the widow said.

"Perhaps there will be an equally quick solution in this matter," Eleanor replied, deciding it was wiser to let the woman believe that she, too, was equally comforted by justice rendered with such shallowness. In truth, she had to bite her tongue to keep from crying out that she found no justice in that hasty arrest of an innocent.

Maud looked surprised by this answer.

The prioress nodded with due courtesy and took her leave.

◇◇◇

As she walked toward the room where Mariota lay, Eleanor felt thwarted but now realized she had another problem. If she continued to ask questions, no matter how innocently she presented them, she might endanger others in her company as well as herself. Had she the right to do such a thing to innocent people just because she questioned the sheriff's judgment?

Of course she had felt insulted by his manner toward her, even rightly so. His behavior had been unacceptable toward any woman of religious calling, let alone a prioress and a baron's daughter. That said, she must balance her response with an understanding that her worldly pride might well be leading her in a foolhardy direction.

She stopped by a window and looked down on the busy courtyard below. Smoke rose from the smithy. A woman was feeding a flock of chickens. Animal noises mingled companionably with human shouts and the din of work. There was something soothing about watching people, going about their labors as if nothing had ever troubled them. As she well knew, however, routine might suggest calm, but fear could yet be a hidden resident.

Should she tell Sir Reimund about seeing Mistress Luce in an unchaste embrace with Tobye? What about this other woman who slipped into the stable and begged some favor of the man? Who was she? If both Ranulf and Hilda had witnessed the same thing, the prioress had to believe the event probably occurred.

Eleanor glanced back at the room she had just left. Was it Maud? Hadn't this woman seemed troubled when she mentioned lust burning in one *past such foolishness*? Didn't that understanding sing of experience? Was she an older woman who longed for the embrace of a handsome man, a woman too old to bear a child?

"No," she whispered, "surely not Maud."

Despite her fears that there was some collusion between sheriff and physician's widow, Eleanor owed Maud gratitude for her care of Mariota. Had Maud's one good deed blinded her to darker elements in the woman's nature? Was Maud's name the one Hilda meant to whisper in Brother Thomas' ear?

"All mortals are sinners," she groaned, resting her cheek against the rough stone, "but some dance the earth, shouting of sweet virtue to disguise the stench of their own rotting hearts. Others suffer men's mockery because they gently embrace lepers and defend the suffering or weak with the compassion God intended. The rest wander through their lives, doing no greater evil and owning no finer virtue than any other man. Which is she?"

There were other suspects. She had not dismissed the strong possibility that Master Stevyn knew of his wife's adultery and had killed the man who set horns on his forehead. But could he be guilty of the attack on Hilda? The steward might have struck her down because she knew or had witnessed something that would send him to the hangman.

Or did Mistress Luce kill her lover because he threatened to tell her husband, should she grow quick with child, unless she gave him bright coin for his silence? Or had she faced being replaced in his bed?

Had Huet killed the groom because he was his step-mother's lover? Again, perhaps Hilda had been a witness or knew more than was safe for her.

And what about this older woman?

There was too much to consider.

"Nor do I know these people," Eleanor complained softly, "and this manor is even smaller than the village of Tyndal. Surely the perpetrator is suspected. I should no longer question Sir

Reimund's arrests for he must know far better than I who might have committed these crimes."

Yet she could not escape the fact that he had chosen to put Hilda in chains for no other apparent reason than she was convenient and would offend no one of rank. Surely he had heard rumor enough about Mistress Luce's adultery, even if it was from the bawdy jests of his men. That said, to accuse her or her husband of this crime might bring down on his head the wrath of an earl. Master Stevyn was esteemed for his skilled running of this estate. Henry de Lacy would not look kindly on the man who hanged his steward or caused Stevyn deep humiliation by publicly crowning him as a cuckold.

Eleanor pressed her fist against the stone. "My primary responsibility is for the safety of those who came with me, a journey that grows even more ill-advised each day that I insist on meddling in affairs that are not mine to resolve," she muttered. "And shall I repay the kindness of hospitality by pointing an accusing finger at those same good souls just because their motivations in killing this groom have not been questioned? What arrogance to think that I know better than those who have far greater understanding of the ways of this place! Since when has ignorance proven wiser than knowledge? And have I forgotten that I have authority over others in Tyndal Priory only because I stand as the symbol of a perfect woman and not because I am less frail than others of my sex? Dare I endanger my priory and my family with this wild imprudence?"

Having now presented herself with logical reasons why she should not continue this ill-advised pursuit of justice, she fell silent. But her heart had ever been rebellious, and in that stillness, she knew it had conceded nothing to logic or any of these reasonable concerns.

Feeling her face turn hot with frustration and fury, the prioress spun away and marched toward the room where her young charge lay healing from the winter fever.

As many had learned in the past, Prioress Eleanor was most dangerous when she was angry.

Chapter Twenty-Eight

"You look downcast, Brother. Shall I sing you a bawdy song to make you laugh, although you may have to do penance for it after?" Huet mimed a young man wooing an invisible maiden. "Or would you prefer a more prayerful one to please your soul?" The steward's younger son became an old man, bent with the pain of his sins, praying for God's forgiveness.

Thomas leaned back on the bench in the kitchen and watched with admiration. "Where did you learn such skills, Master Huet? Surely they were not taught as part of your priestly training?"

The young man's smile was enigmatic. "Have you been a monk since boyhood?"

"I became a clerk first," Thomas answered. This was not the first time he had been asked this question and had an easy enough half-truth prepared should he be asked for whom he had served and where. As his spymaster, a man who preferred more skilled deception, had warned, Thomas might be caught out with this crude stratagem one day. So far, few had ever cared to delve deeper than his first reply.

"And you were God's most dutiful servant, never sinning?"

"I sinned eagerly and often enough."

"And thus took these vows as penance?"

Thomas bowed his head, knowing silence suggested an adequate enough answer.

"Forgive me, Brother, for I meant no ill by that question. I oft speak before reason can advise otherwise."

"Nor was I offended. It was I who erred by inquiring into matters I had no right to know."

"And thus we each allow the other his secrets." Huet winked, then laughed to suggest his comment was only a jest.

Thomas was not fooled by the contrived lightness of the man's tone and turned his gaze away to conceal his wariness. Huet had lied about returning to see Hilda asleep on the bench and thus Thomas had cause to be distrustful, forcing himself to maintain an objective distance. In truth, had the circumstances of their meeting been different, he knew he would have enjoyed joisting wits with this man, whom he found both talented and companionable, but this situation did not permit such relaxation.

"Did you hear the latest news about Hilda?" Thomas asked, deliberately changing the subject.

"She is dead?"

The monk let Huet's response resonate in his ears to catch what meanings he could, but all he heard was sorrow. "Near enough, I fear," he said. Perhaps his suspicions of the man were ill-conceived. The steward's son seemed very fond of the cook and may well have lied only to save her life. "I felt some trembling in her neck and a little breath of life from her mouth, but she had bled much. I have too little skill to help her and must pray that God lets her stay a while longer on earth and identify the one who did this unconscionable act."

Huet frowned.

Involuntarily, the monk shivered. Surely Huet knew that Thomas was aware of the lie told and thus could expose the steward's son any time he wished. If the man had made up the tale solely to keep the cook from hanging, he would expect Thomas to remain silent. After all, Huet's words only provided support to the monk's and thus the lie was well-intended. Thomas had no reason to speak up.

Or was this man malevolently clever? If this son of Master Stevyn had lied because it somehow placed him safely away from both time and place of the murder, Thomas was in danger. Perhaps Huet thought the monk would remain silent out of fear that he might be the next victim if he revealed the lie, an unlikely conclusion since most murderers killed witnesses.

Suddenly, Thomas became aware of just how vulnerable he was. The two of them were alone, and leaning against the table as he was, he was off balance should Huet wish to attack him. He had no wish to die with a knife shoved into his belly before he could defend himself. Slowly, he straightened up.

Huet folded his arms and studied the monk. "I heard she tried to kill herself."

"Who told you that?" Thomas raised an eyebrow. Was the sheriff deliberately spreading this falsehood to suggest Hilda had done so out of guilt for the murder of Tobye? Must the cook remain condemned even if she was innocent?

Huet raised a matching eyebrow. "The man who protects your prioress, Brother. After she heard the commotion, and refused his advice to remain in safety, he followed her. When he reached the hut, he heard the sheriff loudly proclaim our cook had stabbed herself."

"So he hoped!" Thomas realized he had been foolish to openly criticize Sir Reimund and quickly amended his words with: "Or rather believed." What a poor attempt to change his meaning, he thought, and one not likely to fool the steward's observant son. He silently cursed his brief show of temper. "No weapon was found. I examined her and said plainly enough that she could not have wounded herself so grievously, then disposed of the knife from a hut with no windows and a door barred from without."

Huet pursed his lips and nodded.

"Why would anyone have wanted to hurt her? I have little acquaintance of the woman, but she seemed a gentle enough soul."

Perhaps Hilda had witnessed something that pointed to Huet as Tobye's killer, and the man had tried to kill her for that. After his strong defense of her in the courtyard, others would be less likely to suspect him as the true murderer.

But how could he know in advance that Sir Reimund would choose the cook as his suspect over, say, the pig boy or a laundry-woman? Surely Huet must be innocent.

Or had he simply taken advantage of the situation and found the imprisoned cook easier prey than she might otherwise have been?

In any case, until the killer was caught, Thomas could not risk casting aside any suspicion and knew that his peaceful nights, falling asleep in this man's arms, were over. If he wanted to avoid any chance of a slit throat, he had best find a bed where there were too many witnesses as protection.

"Yet you have the measure of her, Brother. Her greatest sin was giving out bits of manor food to those of us who knew her soft heart and danced like puppies for treats. She had no children of her own and adopted us all with an eager love."

"No enemies then?"

"Remember the story of devilish imps who infested the herd of swine, causing them to lose all reason and leap into the sea where they drowned? Satan may so drive a man to madness that he does things he might not otherwise do. Barring such a fiendish act, there was no one who had cause to injure her, any more than she had grounds to kill the groom."

"Maybe he tormented her more than anyone knew and she could take no more, thus cut his throat. A moment of madness, perhaps, as you have just described."

"Well argued, Brother, but I have rarely known a soul with so little anger in it. The sheriff must look elsewhere for the one whom Satan drove witless." Huet's smile was most engaging.

Thomas felt his face turn hot but was determined not to surrender to the man's charm. "You know everyone here. Had anyone more cause than she?"

"Why do you ask, Brother? It is not your concern."

Thomas swallowed hard, then forced a sheepish look. "Monks often find the world's ways incomprehensible, and we ask too many questions about it. In addition, the Prince of Darkness may not disport himself more often in the world than in priories, but we are inclined to pretend otherwise and look for reasons to support that belief."

Huet threw his head back and laughed. "You must whet your skills if you would become a teller of tales! Let me demonstrate a more persuasive demeanor." He mimicked a sly, inquisitive monk. "That look you gave me would not lead any man to conclude you were like the religious you describe."

Thomas willed himself to smile as if he had only intended a jest. "But I did make you laugh. Have I not learned that from you at least?"

Huet nodded, his expression much bemused.

Thomas sighed. "Nonetheless, the matter is certainly not my concern. I am but idly curious."

"With all due respect, Brother, I doubt that. Your question is founded in true caring, not the idle prying from which so many suffer. In reply, I would say that several had more reason to kill Tobye than Hilda. He breached maidens and rode wives. The women may have been willing enough, but their gates were owned by others, and he had no right to enter as he did, whatever the invitations. If I were Sir Sheriff, I'd look to cuckolds and angry fathers before I laid a hand on our cook."

"Any in particular?" Thomas asked, knowing he had just pushed his claim to trifling inquisitiveness a bit too far.

Huet shrugged. His eyes narrowed.

"None?"

"If you wish to satisfy what you name your *idle curiosity*, you had best ask others to raise questions. I have been too long away to know the most recent offenses. But, if you continue, I advise you to take care. There will be mortals aplenty who might not consider your interest but a simple failing of a cloistered monk." He bowed. "Now, if you will forgive me, I promised to meet with my father for our long-delayed discussion about my abrupt return home."

Thomas watched the man leave the kitchen. Were those parting words a threat or a kind warning? Rubbing his forehead, he concluded only two things after this talk with the steward's younger son: he himself had been dangerously unwise in his speech, and Master Huet was far less ignorant of manor affairs than he pretended.

Chapter Twenty-Nine

Mistress Maud was not in the chamber.

Although Eleanor's temper had waned during the short walk here, she knew it might wax again if fed by the sight of one whom she must call a suspect, no matter how unwillingly. Eleanor exhaled with relief when she saw that Mariota's sole attendant was the usual servant.

The woman set aside her mending and rose to acknowledge the entrance of the prioress. "May I serve you in any way, my lady?"

Eleanor refused but thanked her, grateful for the woman's gentle manner. It drove away the last of her unwomanly raging, allowing her to conclude that she had surely exaggerated the murkiness of the problems. Later, and with calmer spirit, she would carefully apply reason to each issue. As her aunt had taught her, anger only distorted facts. The situation could not possibly be as complex as she had thought under the influence of the Devil's fury.

"How fares this child?" she asked, turning to look at the bed.

Mariota opened her eyes. "I feel much stronger, my lady," she whispered hoarsely. "I walked to the door and back today."

Surprised at the response, the prioress cried out with delight and rushed to grasp the girl's hand.

"She also took some soup but an hour ago," the servant added as she returned to her work, the stitching so skillful that the tear was becoming quite invisible.

Eleanor studied the girl. "Then you are most certainly heal-ing." Although Mariota was still pale, her cheeks had regained some of the healthier pink they had previously borne.

"Shall we leave soon?"

There was a sadness in the girl's voice that caught Eleanor's attention. Was she still suffering over what she had recently confessed? "Not until there is sufficient lull in the storms, and you have enough strength to travel back to the priory without further endangering your health."

Mariota squeezed her eyes shut as if the meager light stung.

Eleanor gestured to the servant that she might leave them.

"I will remain outside should you have need of me," the woman replied.

The prioress waited until the door was firmly shut. "You seem troubled, my child."

"Are we alone?"

Eleanor nodded. "Speak freely and tell me what burdens your spirit."

A slight flush dusted the young woman's cheeks. "I would not speak ill of those who are kind."

Fear numbed the prioress, but she knew she dared not show it. Her mind now raced through the possible meanings, and her heart began to pound. To disguise her alarm, she carefully released Mariota's hand, patted it gently, and drew back a step. "Let me take that weight from you. If your spirit be honest in its speech, I shall decide whether those who seem benevolent are truly so or only don the convenient robes of compassion."

Mariota stared up at the ceiling and began to speak. "This morn-ing, Mistress Maud brought Master Huet to this chamber and sat while he played most beautifully upon the lute. His gentle songs of love, both worldly and spiritual, quite raised my spirits."

"I have heard him, and he owns much talent." Eleanor smiled encouragement.

"After a while, I slipped into a pleasant sleep, dreaming that my brother's friend greeted me with great happiness." She looked at the prioress as if searching for some sign, either of hope or censure.

"As we all know, God can tell us things in dreams, and this may suggest that matters have changed in your family of late," Eleanor said, then quickly added a caution. "I am not, however, as blessed as Joseph who read God's word in Pharaoh's dream."

The girl nodded. "When I awoke, I felt at peace and decided that God might truly be merciful in this matter. Then I opened my eyes." She began to tremble.

Eleanor took the girl's hand and held it with a gentleness she hoped would make further speech easier.

"I dare not draw any conclusions, my lady, but the sight did startle me."

"Tell me in simple words exactly what you saw?" The prioress fought not to betray her own apprehension.

"Mistress Maud and Master Huet were standing near the window. They were holding each other in close embrace."

Sweat trickled down her sides as if the room were overheated, but shock had numbed Eleanor to such petty sensitivity. She could only feel terror for Mariota's safety. Her mouth was too dry when she swallowed, and she repressed a coughing fit.

"Did they know you had witnessed this?"

"I think not, my lady. His back was to me, and she could not see over his shoulder. I quickly closed my eyes. After waiting a while, I made a noise as if just awakening, then hesitated until I heard some sound. When I opened my eyes, they were apart and staring out the window as if something of import had caught their interest."

Either they assumed they had escaped her notice by jumping away from each other or they knew full well she had witnessed their sin. It was the latter she feared and believed more likely.

Solutions raced through her mind and were just as hurriedly discarded. Mariota was too weak to move, yet she must no longer be left in the care of another from this household. Of course, she could take on most of the young woman's care but even she needed sleep.

"You were right to tell me of this, but there may be an innocent enough explanation," the prioress said. "Until I find out more, however, speak to no one at all about it. Should any person, including the sheriff or the two themselves, ask if you have witnessed anything curious while lying in this room, I give you permission to lie and claim ignorance. It is unlikely anyone shall do so, but wisdom forbids speaking further of it now."

Mariota nodded, but the renewed pallor in her cheeks and furrowed brow spoke eloquently enough of her thoughts.

Surely the girl has heard some of the details of the crimes committed here, the prioress thought. There was no way to keep the stories from her, and Mariota was not foolish. She knew well enough that her life was in danger once again.

Now another horrible realization struck Eleanor most forcefully

She had not exaggerated the complexity of the crimes recently committed after all. They were far more intricately entangled than she had imagined.

Chapter Thirty

As Thomas walked through the busy courtyard, melancholy fell on his spirit with the weight of a pall over a corpse. He tossed his head like a horse bitten by a fly, as if that would free him of the malignant gloom, but the darkness only dug its claws more firmly into his soul.

"A lover could not be more faithful in attendance upon me," he groaned, "or show greater jealousy over my joy in another."

That *other* was the rare happiness he had experienced on this journey from Tyndal.

Melancholia had been the usual disorder in his humors since his imprisonment. It was briefly banished after some months at Tyndal, only to return during his journey to Amesbury Priory. The agonies he had then suffered grew so unbearable that he begged Prioress Eleanor to grant him permission to become a hermit, at least for a time, after the poisoning of Martin the Cooper last summer. She refused, ordering him instead to accompany her on this matter of priory land boundary disputes.

The journey was ill-advised due both to the pestilent season and harsh weather, but his prioress rejected all argument. Rarely had he seen her more adamant and never as unreasonable. When the company set out on a blustery day, the chill wind was only a foretaste of trouble to come. Oddly enough, an increase in his anguish had not been part of it.

He had found pleasure in unknotting legal issues and providing his prioress with options for equitable solutions. Her approval of his work had been most evident, and he had enjoyed the times when they took opposite sides of each argument to establish which solution might be best. Once the issues were resolved, and the party had begun their ride back to the priory, Thomas was shocked to find he had discovered contentment.

Then Mariota fell ill, and the storm had forced them all to seek shelter at this manor. Bedded down in the kitchen, Thomas easily fell back into a pattern of life he had lived as a child. His mother dead before he could even remember her, a cook had taken him on and raised him until she also died, just before his voice broke. Kitchens had always meant love and security. Hilda, the cook, reminded him much of the woman who reared him.

And now she was dying.

He cursed. She did not deserve this. Why did some grow corpulent in the service of corrupt men while those like Hilda suffered under the heavy boot of injustice? Why did God allow it? As bitterness soured his heart, he curled his hand into a fist and raised it to shake at the sky.

Something nudged his leg.

He looked down, his thoughts instantly pulled back from that chasm of irrevocable misery where Satan delighted in pushing him.

A brown dog of mixed breed was sitting in front of him, its expression expectant as if the creature had just asked a question.

"Where is your master?"

Seeing that it had gained the monk's attention, the dog dropped the stick it held in his mouth at Thomas' feet.

"Here, Brother."

Thomas looked around and saw the speaker, a lad no older than nine summers, gaunt, with scabs and scars covering his face, neck, and hands. The boy was still recovering from a pox.

"How long have you had this fine creature?"

The boy grinned. "He was the gift promised if I lived, Brother."

The monk nodded and his heart grieved at the roughness still evident in the boy's voice.

"We came for your blessing, if you would be so kind." The boy knelt and steepled his hands.

The dog looked hopeful.

If God has let this child live, Thomas thought, surely the boy was already under His safeguard. As for the dog, the monk suspected he had the same protection as any sparrow in God's kingdom. He gave them both the peace of a blessing nonetheless.

"Are you training him?" the monk asked after the boy had risen from his knees.

"Only to fetch sticks," was the wary reply. "My father says our master would not approve if he learned to hunt."

A father who will nevertheless teach the beast to track down conies when the steward is abroad, the monk concluded. He picked up the proffered stick and threw it.

The dog spun around, scattering clumps of mud as he did, and raced after it, albeit with a limp and a hop. Now Thomas understood why this boy had been allowed to keep him. The beast was too lame to hunt.

"A clever creature?"

"He's a good watchdog."

"Barks, does he, when a stranger comes nigh?"

"Barks at Satan himself, Brother!"

Thomas raised his eyebrows in wide-eyed approval at such valor.

The boy misinterpreted the look. "Ask my father if you do not believe me." His jaw set with resolute certainty.

"I did not doubt your word, lad, but now I must ask when this fine hound chased the Prince of Darkness away. I do love a good tale!" Thomas crouched on his heels so his eyes were on the same level as the boy's.

"Last night!" The boy puffed his chest out on his dog's behalf.

"Verily?"

"See that hut over there?"

Thomas looked in the direction the lad was pointing. It was a crudely built hut near the storage shed where Hilda had been held. "Oh, yes," he whispered.

"My scabs were itching too much to sleep, and I tried not to wake my parents while I scratched. I could hear the rain had stopped and, through that window, I saw the clouds had broken. The crescent moon was just there." He pointed to a place in the sky that suggested a time perhaps an hour before dawn.

"Aye? Aye?" As his hopes increased that this demon might turn out to be a mortal killer, Thomas lost any need to feign interest in this story.

The boy reached down and stroked his dog, now resting his head against the lad's leg and panting with the effort of retrieving the stick. "Suddenly, Rabbit began to howl in such a way that my parents awoke. My mother began to whimper and even my father moaned. A lost soul was passing, they said."

Thomas had fallen into thought, calculating how long before the sheriff arrived that this had happened. If the boy was right about the position of the moon, there would have been time enough to attack the cook and escape before most were awake, but not so long that Hilda would have died from her wounds.

All of a sudden he realized the boy had grown silent and was looking at him as if expecting some reaction. "But it was not a soul, was it?" He rested his chin in his hand and concentrated on what might be said next.

"Nay, Brother. My father gestured for me to be quiet, which I obeyed, but I did roll toward the window and look out with due caution. The Devil was outside!"

"You were a brave lad. How did you recognize the Fiend?"

The boy cocked his head and took a man's stance with legs apart and fists on his waist. That the limbs were like twigs and the fists no bigger than apples made the gesture even more poignant. "Wasn't our master's cook slain by Satan himself? That's what I heard this morning, and I did see the Devil unbar the door to the shed where she was and disappear inside. My parents told me to say nothing lest the Evil One seek revenge on anyone who saw him." The boy glanced up at the monk with a troubling look. "But it is safe to tell a monk, isn't it?"

Thomas rose and reached over to grasp the boy by the shoulder. "Nothing sends the Devil dancing away faster than the protection of someone in God's service." He painted a cross on the lad's forehead. "You are wise to listen to your parents and should not tell anyone else of what you saw, but this mark will keep Satan's hand from harming you for what you have told me."

The boy grinned.

"Did you note any details about this Evil One? He takes on various shapes, you know, and sometimes the likeness of someone we have met." The question was worth asking, even if the boy had seen nothing more.

Shaking his head, the lad first denied seeing anything unusual, then frowned. His face suddenly brightened with one thought: "He was the darkest shadow I have ever seen, Brother! But the Devil would be, wouldn't he?"

Thomas ruffled the boy's hair and sent him back to the game with his dog. As he watched the pair walk away, Thomas almost danced for joy.

Although his discovery of the knife in the stable had proven of little value, he now had a sighting of the killer and a time when the deed was done. All he had to do was learn the names of the few who were abroad at that bleak hour, winnow out those with legitimate cause to be so, and question the chaff.

Chapter Thirty-One

Eleanor was impatient for a walk by herself but knew propriety forbade it. A prioress, being of high rank, might bend rules if she did so with probity and reason, but the border between acceptance and condemnation was always narrow for any woman, whether she was bound to God or some mortal man.

When she insisted on traveling across a courtyard, filled with men, to the hut where Hilda was found, she had already challenged that boundary. The shock of seeing her determined march through their midst had caused those rough-mannered men to lean away from her like the waves of the Red Sea when Moses led the Israelites to safety, but she dared not chance censure again just because she was restless. Sighing, she longed for the freedom she possessed behind the walls of Tyndal Priory.

Eleanor looked over her shoulder and saw that her devoted shadow was standing a courteous distance behind her. Just a few feet beyond, the door to Mariota's room remained open, and the servant woman could be seen embroidering a simple pattern on a cloth held taut within a small wooden frame.

The man leaned against the wall and bowed his head, thus indicating his thoughts were elsewhere and that she could assume greater privacy than his presence would otherwise suggest.

As the prioress sat down on the bench near the window, her heart softened toward the young man. He had been both sympathetic and respectful in his attendance, while remaining obedient to the orders of Sir Reimund.

She put a hand over her mouth to hide a smile. Indeed, the guard had taken those commands more literally than the sheriff had intended, diligently keeping her from harm while allowing her some freedom to do as she willed. Had he done otherwise, she feared she might well have made him suffer for it. It would have been wicked of her, and most unwomanly to rebel against his purported protection, but her tolerance for interference had become brittle of late.

Perhaps she should write Sister Beatrice for advice on how to thwart this growing obstinacy, for her aunt was a woman who also shared the attribute but had conquered it with penance by taking a far lesser position at Amesbury Priory than her abilities would have allowed. On the other hand, as Eleanor recalled her aunt's adamant refusal to change her mind about taking on the leadership of that ancient priory, she did wonder, albeit with much affection, if her aunt had truly subjugated her stubbornness or just reframed the definition.

The breeze surging through the window felt chill and damp with the promise of yet another storm. Looking outside, she watched clouds layer one upon another, like wispy veils in several shades of gray, as they scudded across the sky from the sea not that many miles away. A small patch of blue sky did peek out to the west, but the brief view only taunted the earth with hints of the warmer seasons. Indeed, as the days grew darker, icy gales would become relentless.

Eleanor shivered.

In contrast, crusaders, returned from Outremer, had told her tales of the merciless sun that blistered their skin, although the nights could be so chill that soldiers had died of the cold. Some of these men, now home and faced with autumns like this, longed to go back to such brightness. Others thanked God that they had escaped Hell. What would her brother, Hugh, think whenever he returned? Eleanor closed her eyes and offered a brief prayer for her eldest brother, a man who had grown strangely silent since the new king had left Acre.

Prayer for her brother had calmed her, and she leaned against the damp stone. Walking abroad when the air would soon grow misty with rain was ill-advised for many reasons. She would be wiser to remember that these troubling events had prevented her from honoring many Offices. A walk to the chapel would be in order.

As she rose, Eleanor glanced down on the courtyard. In one corner, she saw Brother Thomas tossing a stick for a crippled dog. Next to him was a small boy whose laughter was merry enough to cut through the activity around them. She rested her chin on her hand and watched the monk crouch down and talk with the boy who seemed quite pleased to be telling him some tale. Then the pair parted, and her monk walked briskly toward the manor house.

What a good man he was, she thought, and what pleasure she had had in his company during this journey. Although she had not been able to banish lust entirely, she had found some chaste joy in his wit and clever arguments when they debated together. Shared jests had been common, and the laughter they enjoyed seemed as effective in chasing away Satan's temptations as lying on a cold floor for an hour of prayer.

She most certainly had cause enough to bemoan this trip, and looked forward to seeing the entrance gate of Tyndal, but she would also regret trading his sweet companionship for that of accounting rolls, which were possessed of far less wit than her monk whatever their other estimable qualities.

Musing on this, she began to turn away from the window when something below abruptly drew her attention back.

Side by side, Mistress Luce and the physician's widow were walking past the hut where Hilda had been kept. The way they gestured and talked, one might almost conclude they were boon companions. Yet the prioress knew well enough, from a brief encounter with them together and several remarks made by each, that there was a dearth of affection between them.

But could she trust that conclusion? Hadn't she been proven wrong about much—or at least hadn't many of her opinions been placed in doubt?

She had erred in her judgment of Mistress Maud. The woman had seemed competent and possessed of balanced humors. After what Mariota had witnessed, however, that good impression was shattered.

Was Maud the woman seen pleading with Tobye that night? Might she have killed him because he knew of her lust for the master's younger son and either threatened to expose her as leman to a man who should be a priest, or else demanded payment for not doing so? Did the physician's widow stab Hilda because the cook knew of the affair or could name Maud as a possible suspect in the groom's murder?

If so, the woman dissembled well. Eleanor could not call to mind one gesture, look, or word that suggested any dismay in Maud's heart over the prospect that Hilda could live to give witness against her. She had given the cook her own pallet on which to lie, had tended to her with the utmost tenderness, and had wept at the idea of the woman's probable death. Was there anything in this behavior to suggest a killer?

On the reverse of that argument, Maud was well-positioned to ease Hilda into God's hands without anyone thinking twice about it. She was often alone with her and had already expressed her expert opinion that the cook would most likely die. Knowing the cook would never live to point an accusing finger at her might allow Maud to feign the innocence of grief she did not feel.

Eleanor tapped her fingers against the wall in frustration at the extent to which she had been misguided. Surely this proved how vile her arrogance was, interfering in the sheriff's business when she had no cause? Why did she think she was ordained by God to render judgments on guilt or innocence? Wasn't she but a mere woman, a flawed vessel?

Taking a deep breath, Eleanor again tried to regain calm and objectivity. Whatever her imperfections, her greatest failing in this situation had actually been the inability to distinguish between facts and conjectures.

I may have been most foolish, she thought, but I doubt God is offended because I care about justice in this matter. Surely

He disapproves when mortals conclude that their worldly ambitions are best served by letting the innocent suffer or offering them up as a sacrifice. Nay, God has never shown offence when I interfered in other crimes, and, if I have grown bloated with conceit over past accomplishments, I shall do penance.

She resettled on the bench and considered what to do next. The wisest approach would be to reassess what she had learned and not allow herself to be blinded by womanish impulse when logic must rule.

"Below are two women, walking toward the manor house." She whispered to herself with that determined simplicity a novice mistress might use to explain a new concept to an obtuse student. "Mistress Luce was Tobye's lover and is Huet's stepmother. Those are facts. Mistress Maud may be Huet's lover. That is most likely a fact but must still be counted conjecture. Although they were discovered in each other's arms, there might be some other explanation for it."

She watched Luce and Maud stop and turn toward each other. The physician's widow abruptly folded her arms and tucked in her chin as if angry or offended. The steward's wife spun around and walked off alone.

And what of Mistress Luce's conduct toward her stepson, she asked herself, that evening Huet entertained them all? Was it a fair observation to think the behavior was seductive? It most certainly was not maternal! To conclude that a stepmother would flirt with her stepson, albeit one of similar enough age, was an uncomfortable one, but Eleanor could not dismiss the possibility. If Maud learned of it, might she not be jealous? That might also mean that Mistress Luce was in danger, assuming the widow was the one who killed Tobye, if the wife let the widow know she had discovered the affair.

Eleanor now saw Maud pick up the front of her robe and run to catch up with the steward's wife. The pair met again just below the window where the prioress sat.

Eleanor leaned over to better see what was happening, praying as she did that they would not look up and see her. Their gestures suggested a heated discussion.

The surrounding commotion, normal in any courtyard, made it difficult to hear what the women were saying. In any case, no one else seemed to pay much attention to the pair. The prioress began to suspect this was such common behavior between the two that it was no longer entertaining to watch.

Suddenly, Luce raised her hand as if to strike.

Maud grimaced in anticipation of the blow.

Luce lowered her fist and drew back.

The widow hurried away. Although she did glance once over her shoulder, her expression was unreadable.

"You have dared to rise above your station," the steward's wife shouted after her. "Leave this manor and never show your face here again!"

This time, several women did turn their heads to stare at their master's wife. A man lowered his axe and then shook his head in disgust before returning to his labor of wood chopping.

Eleanor quickly looked at her guard to see if he had overheard, but he was still leaning against the wall, his eyes shut as if lost in some pleasant dream.

In Mariota's room, the servant continued to stitch.

The prioress turned back to see Maud's reaction. Surely the woman had heard Mistress Luce's words, but the widow neither replied nor stopped before disappearing around the side of the stable.

Glancing down, Eleanor saw Mistress Luce cover her eyes with one hand as if struck with a headache. The gesture lasted but a moment before she quickly lifted the hem of her robe out of the mud and climbed the stairs leading to the manor house entrance.

Eleanor decided to meet her at the door.

Chapter Thirty-Two

"My lady!" Brother Thomas called out, then saw her guard close on her heels as she emerged from the entrance to the stairwell. "I must speak with you, for my spirit is most troubled and needs guidance," he quickly added.

This was the one time Eleanor might have preferred not to meet her handsome monk, despite the joyful look on his face when his eyes met hers, but he was a man disinclined to idle talk and must have discovered something noteworthy.

With regret, she bowed her head as Mistress Luce approached.

The steward's wife hurried on without acknowledging the courtesy.

Eleanor watched the woman hasten up the stairs leading to the chambers above the hall. The lack of response was surprising. What had happened between widow and wife to cause such extreme distraction?

And what emotion could she read in the woman's face? Mistress Luce passed by so quickly there had been little time to observe her. Were those damp cheeks indicative of sorrow, or had a bitter wind caused the eyes to tear? Were the pinched lips suggestive of anger?

Perhaps she should follow, or would that gesture be interpreted as rude interference in a private matter? God's comfort might be turned aside, she decided, but no honest soul would call it impolite. She would hear Brother Thomas' news and seek to learn more about what she had witnessed between the two women in the courtyard.

"Follow me, Brother, and tell me what you have discovered," she said in Latin, and then nodded to the guard before beginning the climb back up the stairs in search of Mistress Luce.

"I have learned the hour of the attack," Thomas muttered.

"Thanks be to God," Eleanor replied with a brief look heavenward.

"I met a boy who lives with his parents near the place where our poor woman suffered her grievous wound."

"Continue," she said, grateful that he understood the need to omit names that might be recognized by her guard.

"They own a…" Thomas hesitated on his phrasing. "…a hound of Hell, one who cries out if some strange mortal draws nigh."

"May God protect us from such wickedness." Eleanor glanced back as she reached the top of the stairs. Her guard was walking a few steps behind Brother Thomas. Was his head bowed in prayer, or was the young widower thinking of a certain young woman who had clearly caught his interest? With gentle amusement, she assumed the latter.

"This creature howled at a certain hour last night as if possessed. The boy's parents were awakened, but only the boy saw the shadow of wickedness enter the place where our poor sinner lay. His parents said it must be Satan and that their son should say nothing about it, lest the Devil seek vengeance."

"Let us praise God for granting them such wisdom." The prioress nodded, continuing along the corridor.

"But I told him he could safely tell his tale to a priest but only to me."

"God will surely reveal who was abroad with the Devil at that hour, for there must be some other sinner as witness."

"Amen," Thomas replied.

Eleanor gestured for him to stay back while she approached the chambers of the steward's wife. She raised her hand to rap at a closed door.

"You needn't disturb my mistress. She has no wish to see anyone."

Eleanor spun around.

A heavy-set woman stood behind them, her narrow brow furrowed. In her hands was a tray with a pitcher and two cups.

The prioress swallowed her indignation at the servant's curt manner. Perhaps this woman had been trained in service to the sheriff's household where she learned to treat God's servants with such disrespect?

The woman pushed past Thomas and the guard. Now face to face with the angry prioress, however, she paled. "I'll ask if she will receive you, my lady," she muttered, her voice dropping nervously, and then she knocked at the door.

It opened just far enough to let the servant edge her way through before shutting with a firm thud.

Eleanor raised an eyebrow. From behind the door, she heard raised voices, although nothing of the words spoken. Close by, her guard shuffled uneasily. Her monk was silent.

Then the door opened wide enough to let Mistress Luce emerge. She stood before them without speaking, hands folded across her stomach as if protecting a quickened womb.

Eleanor gestured at the two men with her. They stepped away to give the women privacy. "I did not wish to disturb you," she said gently, "but if I might offer some words of peace…"

"You are kind, Prioress Eleanor, and I fear my servant has been less so. For her offense, I do beg pardon and have admonished her. She will not repeat that affront. As for God's peace…" She bit her lip.

What has troubled you so, Eleanor wondered, noting that the woman's eyes were red with weeping and her face pale as if she had just received some shocking news.

"I regret that I am unable to speak with you at the moment. This is the time of day I have vowed to remain silent in contemplation of my sins." Luce turned away as if eager to be alone, then looked back with an expression drastically changed. "Might you come again tomorrow?" she whispered, her voice trembling. "Your comfort would be most welcome then."

"Of course," Eleanor replied. She wished to say more, but caution held her back. She had read two conflicting messages in the wife's manner: dismissive annoyance and a deep need for the solace offered. Since she had just chastised herself for giving too much credence to flawed impressions, she decided she must obey the wife's reasonable request to return tomorrow even though her heart suggested otherwise.

The steward's wife bowed her head and quickly slipped back into her room.

Eleanor stared at the closed door. Again she heard speech from within but no distinct words. Did one of the voices belong to a man, or was it the servant, whose quality of voice had sounded deeper than most women? Realizing that she had stood there too long, she walked away, gesturing for Thomas to approach.

"We should go to the chapel, Brother," she said. "I fear we have often missed the Offices with all the turmoil since our arrival." She switched to Latin. "I have news for you as well, but let us truly turn our souls to God for a while. All of a sudden, I have grown very weary of the world."

And the deceitful nature of mortals, she thought as a curious detail suddenly came to mind. If Mistress Luce had dedicated this time to solitary silence, why had the servant just arrived with two cups?

◇◇◇

The time spent on her knees did nothing to ease Eleanor's spirit. That night she slept fitfully, her overwrought mind racing in frantic circles like some kitten chasing his tail—and with just as much effect. If only she were back at Tyndal in her chambers where her own cat, a creature far too wise to chase anything without purpose, might settle into her arms and soothe her path to sweet dreams with his rumbling purrs.

Instead, a dog barked outside. Half in jest, she blamed the beast for chasing away what remained of slumber, as it most likely had some wandering nocturnal thing.

She sat up, arms about her knees, and listened to the rasping breath of Mariota sleeping nearby. Not wishing to awaken the recuperating young woman, Eleanor did not rise and pace, a method she often used to increase fatigue and thus fall back asleep with ease.

So she prayed, then prayed some more. There were enough sins of which she was guilty to spend many dark hours telling God how much she abhorred her mortal weaknesses. Yet her remorse was forced this night, and she knew God would not be fooled. Her thoughts were less on her sinful nature than on the guilt of whoever had attacked two people and had most certainly killed one of them.

In any case, Mariota is safe enough, Eleanor concluded, as long as I am with her. The killer has only attacked solitary souls, at least so far.

Panic grabbed at her heart. All around her, wavering shadows taunted her. Satan owned the bleak hours and peopled them with his imps who took joy in infecting men with terror. Shaking her head to dispel fear, she repeated what her aunt had taught, that shadows were but illusions, crafted by demons, and would melt away with the sun's rising. She willed her thoughts away from fallen angels and back to mortal murder.

What was she missing? She felt as if she had been given a skein of spun threads, knotted and hopelessly tangled, to unwind. There were too many answers to the question of who killed Tobye, although perhaps too few to the identity of Hilda's attacker.

The most obvious choice for the groom's murderer remained the steward, but his demonstrated concern for the cook argued against his involvement in the violence against her. Perhaps he was unaware of the adultery, although Eleanor found it odd that he would be. Yet some husbands did refuse to give credence to slanderous tales for reasons known only to themselves, and others in this place certainly had equal cause to kill.

Tobye might have tried to gain something from either Mistress Luce or Mistress Maud in exchange for his silence. As for the steward's wife, she could have killed him if he had grown bored with her body and had found a fresh bed partner. If either woman was guilty of cutting his throat, however, the only reason for attacking Hilda was if she were witness to the crime. That was not improbable. Sadly, the possibility that the cook might soon regain consciousness and reveal the name of the person she saw was growing ever more unlikely.

Yet Maud had surrendered her own bed to Hilda, swearing to stay by her side until Death came or God granted a healing hand. That act still spoke more of kindness than murderous guilt, especially since Hilda had not yet been conveniently smothered. Eleanor did not discount the use of clever deception, but her heart refused to cease its strong argument for innocence behind caring acts.

On the other hand, had the steward's wife shown any interest in Hilda one way or the other? Eleanor had not raised the matter with Mistress Luce, but wasn't it odd that the steward's wife had not even mentioned that she would add Hilda's name to her solitary prayers today? Whatever their own sins, most wives cared enough about those who served them to at least list their names for God's attention whenever something dire occurred. This omission by the steward's wife therefore troubled the prioress.

As for Huet, she dare not dismiss the possibility that he was a killer. He had lied, knowing Brother Thomas would catch him out, a likelihood he seemed not to mind. On brief acquaintance, he appeared a clever, talented, and pleasing young man, but the Devil was charming too, Eleanor thought ruefully, and the reasons for Huet's abandonment of his priestly education as well as the details of his wanderings outside England remained unknown. Perhaps he lied simply to see what her monk would do. This younger son might yet prove to possess a heart grown cancerous with disinterest toward anything not of direct value to himself.

Now, of course, there was reason to suspect he was the widow's lover—or perhaps his stepmother's—or even both. Eleanor cringed at the latter. Like his father, however, he had also defended Hilda, albeit with a lie, and she truly could see no reason to do so if he had then tried to kill her.

The prioress could no longer bear to remain so still. She rose and quietly slipped to the window. Easing open the wooden shutters, she looked down on the silent courtyard. Storm clouds must have shrouded the moon, she thought. Even that dim light had been banished.

A rude wind from the north nipped at her cheeks, and she drew back. Shuttering the window to keep the cold from her sleeping charge, Eleanor sat back on her heels and rubbed grit from the corners of her eyes.

And what should she conclude about the quarrel she had witnessed earlier between the steward's wife and Mistress Maud? Why had Luce summarily ordered the older woman from the manor grounds? Was it a petty thing or had she learned something malign such as an affair between the widow and Huet? Was the cause of the dispute something else entirely with nothing to do with murder? Perhaps she would learn more from Luce in a few hours.

In any case, Maud had not left that night. The prioress had seen her enter the room, where Hilda lay, with a small tray containing the ingredients needed for potions and poultices. Perhaps this quarrel was nothing new between the two women and Eleanor should dismiss it as irrelevant.

As for Mariota's care, the usual servant had arrived with instructions from the widow on the herbal doses needed for her recovery. Both herbs and portions seemed safe enough, she thought, grateful to Sister Anne for teaching her something more of healing than a woman's usual knowledge.

And then there was the question of the second cup on the servant's tray when Eleanor was refused entrance to Mistress Luce's chambers. Was there someone in that room, a person the steward's wife did not want the prioress to see? Or was she expecting another visitor soon whom she did not want Eleanor to meet on the way? She shrugged and hoped she did not really need to resolve this particular question.

At least Brother Thomas had found a witness who saw a person enter the storage hut. With a start, however, Eleanor realized that she did not know what shape the presumed imp had assumed. Was it a man's or a woman's? The boy had not said. Would he have mentioned it if he thought it was a woman's?

"How could I have been so foolish?" she groaned softly. They could have eliminated suspects if only she had thought of this one simple question. Brother Thomas might have gone back to ask the boy yesterday, but now that detail must wait for resolution until morning. Could he find the boy alone again? In fact, despite his argument that the lad might safely tell tales of seeing the Devil to a priest, the boy's parents might not want their son to speak anymore on this matter.

If only she could count on Sir Reimund to seek the truth of what had happened here, a man far more knowledgeable about the details of life and relationships in this manor than any stranger. Even if she and Brother Thomas discovered the killer's identity, would the sheriff listen unless the perpetrator was someone guaranteed not to offend the owner of this manor or his steward? How could she force him to render honest justice? She must find a way.

All logic still demanded that she let this matter go, but her heart clenched in outrage at the very thought. Hilda had been chosen to hang, yet her guilt might rest only in the witnessing of something that could reveal the true killer—that and a woman's weakness for a handsome man.

But the latter was God's business alone. Tobye had had no wife and thus Hilda's only sin was a passing but secret lust. Sin enough, for cert, but a minor one and easily purged with confession and penance. Neither king nor bishop would have demanded death for that.

Eleanor stilled her rushing thoughts, but silently staring into the graying darkness did not enlighten her. Everything she had considered was far too complicated and must be hiding the simpler answer, but her mind baulked from further pursuit. She would give up the attempt until dawn broke.

Eleanor slipped back to her bed, lay down, and shut her aching eyes against the growing light. Perhaps sleep would come now, although it was surely time for the Morning Office.

And thus it might have been, had God wanted his prioress to rest.

Instead, loud shouting from the courtyard sent Eleanor out of her bed and back to her feet.

Chapter Thirty-Three

The naked body of Mistress Luce twisted with each gust of wind that surged through the stable. Her face was a dusky red, her legs stained brown with foul-smelling excrement.

The steward turned away. "Cut her down," he ordered.

Sir Reimund gestured at one of his men to climb into the loft to the beam where the hanging rope was tied.

Near the open door, Thomas stood next to his prioress and looked up at the body. He was often drawn to a corpse's unblinking eyes. Sometimes he could read fear in a dead man's stare, while others left the world with wonder frozen in their gaze, but Mistress Luce seemed to have greeted Death with incredulity. Was there meaning in this difference, he asked himself, or did no one quite comprehend the nature of eternity until the soul first looked into it? He shook the thought away and concentrated on details more pertinent to the dangling corpse. And indeed he found an interesting one.

"My lady, I do not think she..." he began.

She put a finger to her closed lips. "I concur."

Mistress Constance, who stood near the ladder to the loft, began to sob, the sound akin to a wailing hiccup. The physician's widow walked to her side and put an arm around the woman's shoulders, but Constance shook off her attempt at comfort and moaned yet louder.

The steward glared at his daughter-in-law and muttered something incomprehensible, but whatever he said failed to moderate the woman's cries.

Again, Eleanor cursed herself for ignorance of common practice in this place. She had learned that it was Constance who had discovered the body, rather than a groom. What reason had she to come to the stable at such an early hour? Surely her duties did not extend to the care of horses.

The man sent up to the loft had reached the beam where the rope was knotted. He pointed to it and shouted a question down to Sir Reimund.

"Just cut through it," the sheriff replied, then put his hand sympathetically on Master Stevyn's shoulder. "Might she have killed herself?" the sheriff asked in a hopeful voice.

"She had no cause," the steward replied, facing the man with an angry look.

"Nor was she likely to have done so," Thomas added, then looked down at his prioress with silent apology for speaking against her command.

"Continue," she murmured. "As Eve's daughter, I am bereft of logic. While you and the sheriff engage in disputation, I shall seek to give Mistress Constance a woman's comfort." With a conspiratorial smile, she walked off toward the two women by the ladder.

"Shouldn't you be on your knees in the chapel, praying for Mistress Luce's soul?" Reimund snarled at the monk. "Leave this matter to me. You have a most unfortunate tendency to interfere in secular matters, Brother."

"If she committed self-murder, she cannot be buried in sanctified ground," Thomas replied, his voice tense with defiance. "Surely Master Stevyn would find some comfort in knowing that his wife was both innocent of this particular sin and might find rest in a proper grave. Would you deny him that?"

"On what do you base your belief, Brother?" The steward gestured for the sheriff to remain silent.

"If we look at the position of the body in relation to the loft, we can see that she could not have jumped from there and killed herself."

"Stop!" Master Stevyn shouted up to the man who had begun sawing at the rope from which the dead wife was suspended.

The man hesitated.

Sir Reimund quickly nodded concurrence although his expression suggested reluctance.

"Go on, Brother," Master Stevyn said.

"If she was determined to kill herself, she would have made sure the rope stretched down far enough to break her neck as she jumped from the loft. Instead, the noose was only a few inches below the planks of the loft. Had she wanted, she could have pulled herself back to safety when she began to choke. In any case, she would have dropped only far enough to bruise her neck and perhaps frighten herself but not to die."

"Women are deficient in logic, Brother. As distressed as it makes me to conclude this about Master Stevyn's wife, I fear she may not have understood what she was doing and thus bungled the entire matter." Reimund did manage to look suitably grieved.

The steward snorted in disgust. "Have you all noted what Brother Thomas has observed and heard his skillful argument?" Stevyn pointed to each man standing nearby. All nodded concurrence. Now satisfied that there would be no finding of self-murder in his wife's death, he turned in triumph to Sir Reimund. "You may now cut her down."

The sheriff allowed his man to finish cutting the rope. Mistress Luce's body dropped to the stable floor with a dull thud, her legs spread and her sex exposed.

Her husband covered his eyes.

Several gaped.

"Have none of you a charitable heart?" Mistress Maud hurried out of the shadows and threw her cloak over the corpse. Then she spun around and glared at the sheriff. "As mortals, women may be both foolish and sinful creatures, Sir Reimund, but that does not mean the body of Master Stevyn's wife should be left exposed and gazed upon as if she were no more than some common whore."

"I want her prepared for honorable burial," the steward said, his voice catching in a swallowed sob.

Maud gave instructions to those who came forward to take the body away.

The crowd began to disperse, their curiosity sated.

"This was no accident?" Maud suddenly cried out to Thomas. "You believe it to be murder?"

Heads quickly turned, and faces lit up at the prospect of more fodder for gossip.

"That is the most likely conclusion," the monk replied. "Lacking in reason or not, most mortals of any gender are more likely to grab at the chance for life when they find themselves unable to breath. She would have saved herself."

The sheriff still looked eager to argue the point.

"Let the monk finish," Stevyn growled, his fist raised as if longing to find something to strike.

Sir Reimund wisely stepped away.

"Even assuming she wanted to die, she would not have chosen to choke slowly to death. She would have pulled herself up and reset the rope so she would drop farther and commit the act quickly. If we examine the body, I think we will find that she was dead before she was hanged and the killer bungled the deception."

Reimund bent to pull the temporary shroud back.

"In the name of God's mercy, let a woman do that!" Maud snapped. "She is the steward's wife!"

Eleanor left Constance and walked toward the physician's widow. "Mistress Maud could examine the body for any signs of foul play," she said. "With her experience as apothecary under the guidance of her physician husband, she has learned good skills, and I will be happy to assist. Thus propriety will be maintained."

Maud nodded. In the weak light, her face was a faded gray.

"We will share our observations with Brother Thomas, and he can resolve questions or doubts as well as correct our faults. His work at Tyndal's hospital is well known," the prioress carefully added.

"Then do so," the steward said, looking at both women with pitiful gratitude. "After you finish, your monk should bring the findings to me. I must attend other matters until he has need of me, and Sir Reimund is free to return to his many other pressing duties until summoned."

Looking into Stevyn's narrowed eyes, the sheriff must have known he had little choice but to agree.

Chapter Thirty-Four

Eleanor rushed back to the manor, her faithful guard hurrying in silence behind her. The swiftness of her pace was born of impatience to view the body as well as her anger over this latest, and quite needless, cruel death. While the sheriff fussed over his tender ambitions, a killer stalked. Would this violence never end?

Nor could she ignore her own failings that contributed to Luce's death. Had she but insisted on counseling the woman yesterday! But that was past, and penance would be done. In the meantime, she hoped that she was finally getting closer to a solution.

While her monk presented his arguments to the sheriff and steward in the stable, Eleanor had gone to soothe Stevyn's daughter-in-law who had been left alone to cower in the shadows. For once, the woman's rigid certitude had cracked, and she trembled like a doe sensing danger.

Eleanor's conversation with Mistress Constance had been too short, and rather troubling, but the woman had begged leave to go to the chapel for prayer. Eager though the prioress was to question her and clarify details, this plea was not something she would refuse.

"Patience is a virtue," the prioress now whispered aloud, knowing how often she needed the reminder. At least the woman had seemed willing to talk later.

Eleanor shuddered. Wasn't that the same request made by Mistress Luce?

She stopped so quickly that her guard almost ran into her.

And now the steward's wife was dead. But surely Mistress Constance would be safe enough in the brighter light of day, the prioress decided, then continued on her way as she pondered what she had heard in the stable.

The cause of Constance's distress most certainly was not the sight of her mother-in-law's corpse. On that discovery, the woman firmly declared she was glad Mistress Luce must face God with all her sins intact. Eleanor was not surprised there had been no affection between the women, but the statement was indicative of a spiteful heart and most unworthy of one who claimed to be pious.

Other than that one statement, Constance had said little that made sense, but Eleanor did pluck one potentially helpful detail out of the woman's babbling: she had apparently followed Luce to the stable. If she had pursued her mother-in-law, Eleanor suspected the woman hoped to catch the steward's wife with a new lover. From what she knew of Ranulf's wife, she could well imagine the woman's expression of sanctimonious pleasure when she confronted Master Stevyn with irrefutable proof of his wife's latest sins. But perhaps she was just being uncharitable toward Constance, and the woman had meant only to stop Mistress Luce before she once again committed adultery.

When the prioress tried to find out why Ranulf's wife had followed Luce, and how she even found out what her mother-in-law was doing, Constance retreated into wide-eyed silence. Eleanor could not shatter it. Had Constance seen something that would help identify the killer? Prayer would surely calm the woman enough to let her speak of it.

Yet the possibility of a new lover might be important as well. If Luce had found a replacement for Tobye, was he another man of low rank? Or might he have been Huet, someone else Constance disdained? If so, the revelation of such great sin between two people she hated would certainly give her great satisfaction.

As much as Eleanor hoped such a relationship did not exist, she was forced to consider the possibility. Huet had not demonstrated any interest in Luce, while her attentions to him were of questionable nature. Was it all quite innocent or was he simply better at dissemblance than she? He had proven his talent at that when he entertained them by skillfully imitating the ways of several different people. She could not discount the relationship as completely as she wished, and, although many had gathered to see the excitement surrounding Luce's hanging, Huet was notably missing. Was that absence meaningful? Unable to come to any conclusion in that matter, she went on to consider another problem.

How had Constance learned that her mother-in-law was going to the stable at that hour? Although it seemed unlikely, Eleanor did wonder if Ranulf's wife had actually been told by Mistress Luce. Might she even have been the visitor for whom the second cup had been brought by that rude servant?

Eleanor doubted the two women were ever in each other's company, unless some event or custom demanded it, and was thus inclined to dismiss the idea of such a meeting. There was little enough privacy in any dwelling, and much was overheard that ought not to have been. It was possible that Constance had listened in on some conversation meant to be private or had accidentally overheard it.

When the prioress tried to discover why she had gone to the stable, however, the woman had retreated into terrified moans. Even though Eleanor rephrased her questions to gently include promises of God's forgiveness, Constance had cried out in tremulous voice that she must go to the chapel for prayer before she spoke any more to mortals. Without pausing for more than the conventional courtesy, she had then pushed past the prioress, mumbling that she might seek her later, and rushed away,

The entire encounter had been bewildering to say the least—and yet so promising.

◇◇◇

As the prioress climbed the stone stairs to the chambers above the main hall, she set aside all thoughts of Mistress Constance and concentrated on her next problem. How might she handle the examination of Luce's corpse with the physician's widow, a situation fraught with its own difficulties?

Eleanor bade her guard remain without, then entered the room where the body had been taken. The steward's dead wife lay on the top of a large storage chest, her body both naked and still filthy. Someone had put lit candles around the corpse, both for light and to mask the stench of body waste. Nearby, on a small table, there was a basin of water that sat in front of a crude wooden cross, resting against the wall.

Mistress Maud knelt beside the corpse.

Apprehensive in the presence of a woman she liked but could not disregard as a murderer, the prioress left the chamber door open and walked to the widow's side.

"What is your opinion on the manner of her death?"

"Murder is a cruel act. We all should have the chance to cleanse our souls before dying, and her sins were no worse than those of many others. She did not deserve such lack of mercy."

"Then you conclude she was murdered?"

"Your monk was most observant. Indeed, he is as clever as he is handsome." Maud smiled.

The smile was infectious, and the prioress returned it despite the grim discussion and her chaste vocation. "Why do you agree with him?"

"As Brother Thomas noted, someone attempting self-murder usually repents as soon as he begins to choke and tries to save himself by loosening the noose or trying to climb the rope to safety. There are no scratches around her neck from fingernails, nor are there rope burns on her palms. I think she was dead when hanged." Maud brushed her hand over the corpse's eyelids to shut them. "And the one who killed her was a poor dissembler."

"How do you know such things?"

"A fair question. Have you seen men hanged for their crimes?"

"A common enough event," Eleanor replied. "On my travels outside the priory, I have passed by gibbets where the condemned still danced in the air as well as those left as fodder for birds."

What she did not say was that the sight troubled her and she had never stopped to stare.

The widow fell silent and tears began to flow down her cheeks. "They claw at their necks…"

The prioress touched her arm in comfort.

"Forgive me, my lady," Maud said, rubbing her cheeks dry. "I also accompanied my husband when he was summoned to examine those who died by their own hand as well as at the hand of others. Being a weak woman, I did not have his strength to look on their faces without emotion. Yet…" She straightened her shoulders and went on, pointing to Luce's neck. "Now look here."

Eleanor could not help thinking that the widow was showing courage enough now. Was it because she disliked the dead woman, or perhaps had even killed her? Or had she simply mustered the strength of will because a knowledgeable eye was required? The prioress bent to look at the two marks Mistress Maud was indicating.

"See this bruise? And the one here?" She shifted the body so Eleanor could see the back of Luce's neck. "See how my hands might almost fit the marks? And the rope burn is minimal. It does not cut as deeply as it would if she had leapt from the loft and let the noose take the full weight of her falling body. I would say that Mistress Luce was strangled, then hanged to hide the finger marks."

Eleanor knew she must consider whether or not this woman was the killer. As argument in favor of that conclusion, the prioress noted that Maud's appearance in the stable had been swift, yet her entrance unseen. The widow might be Huet's lover, however she had never exhibited any greater affection for Mistress Luce than had Constance. The steward's wife had also ordered Maud from the land, a command that had been blatantly ignored.

Against such a supposition, the prioress knew that few murderers would be so willing to argue that a body, which might yet be deemed a suicide, was the victim of foul play. And were she to take heed of her own observations, Eleanor would conclude that the bruises were too far apart to fit the span of Maud's fingers no matter how she stretched them.

Taking a deep breath, Eleanor decided to trust her instinct and believe this woman to be innocent. The elimination of even one suspect was progress. As for the value of Maud's testimony in law, it might not be taken with the seriousness granted a man of like background, but Brother Thomas would listen to her and give weight to her conclusions by taking them on as his own.

"You know everyone at this manor, Mistress. Who do you think had cause to kill the groom, attack the cook, and now murder the steward's wife? Proof is still required for any finding of guilt, but your considered opinion might help bring a swifter end to these horrors."

Maud stepped back from the body and turned her face to the window as if seeking some guidance from the light outside.

Eleanor continued to press for an answer. "I know Sir Reimund would prefer to find the slayer amongst the servants, but I fear the culprit may be of higher birth than that."

She studied Maud, longing to read some hint of an answer in her expression. But the widow would not meet her eyes and remained as motionless as Lot's wife when she was turned into the pillar of salt.

"Forgive me if I impugn an innocent, but I must ask if Master Stevyn might have committed all or one of the killings."

Maud spun around, her face pale as she stared at the prioress with obvious shock. "Never, my lady! Flaws he most certainly has, but he would not have killed his wife or the groom. As for Hilda, she has long been in his service and high in his esteem. He would never have harmed her."

"Surely he knew that Mistress Luce had put the cuckold's horns on his head. Many would say such a betrayal gives any man just cause for killing the lover, even the wife. Less reason, perhaps, for what was done to Hilda."

"I swear to you that he could never have killed either her or Tobye. Aye, he knew of the adultery, but he is innocent of murder!"

"I do not doubt your word but must understand the basis for your belief. Once more facts are made clear, perhaps they will point to another suspect. How can you be certain that he did not commit either crime?'

Maud began to twist her hands together as if trying to scrub an offensive stain away.

Eleanor tilted her head and remained silent, patiently waiting for the widow's evident distress to birth an explanation, one she believed would surely be of import.

Bursting into broken sobs, Maud fell to her knees and lifted her hands, her expression piteous and pleading. "My lady, my soul is most wicked. I beg for your prayers and pity for I have a confession to make!"

Chapter Thirty-Five

The killer must be a man, Thomas decided. Stepping aside so a shepherd with his dog and many bouncing sheep could pass, the monk leaned against a white plaster wall, rough with cow hair, and considered the options.

In fact, Tobye might have been killed by either man or woman. Although the actual site of the murder had been befouled by the sheriff's incurious men, the body itself bore no marks of any struggle. Thus Thomas felt it reasonable to assume the groom had been asleep when his throat was cut. As long as the killer approached without any sound, only stealth would have been needed to overpower him. A woman could have done it.

But Tobye must have made many enemies amongst the men here. The groom's transgressions were more likely to enflame another man to revenge, if the groom had bedded someone's wife, sister, or daughter. A jealous woman might have slit his throat, but the use of a knife was more a man's way. That said, the manner in which it was done was cowardly, dishonorable.

Thomas was a priest, but his view on how insult should be dealt with was born in his youth, surrounded by men who reacted to perceived dishonor with swords and lances. Even amongst those of lesser rank, an honest man would demand the issue be settled by a fair and open fight. One less than honest might lie in wait with cudgel in hand after the sun had set. Yet, by either method, Tobye would have had a chance to defend himself. Slitting a man's throat when he slept was a despicable act.

In any case, the potential number of suspects was significant and included every man in the vicinity who might have a beddable woman under his protection. Did the assault on Hilda diminish that number at all?

Pushing himself away from the wall, he sighed with frustration. If only he knew more about the people here, their kinships and ways, he might be able to answer that question with ease. He walked on, his head bent in thought, carefully avoiding the steaming dung left by several of the sheep.

As for eliminating any who were ignorant of her arrest, he could not. Hilda had been taken to the shed in full view of everyone working here. Few would have been ignorant of where she was held, and thus knowledge of her temporary prison was widespread.

There had been a local man set as guard by the barred door, but that turned out to be a weak defense. He had gotten drunk and fallen asleep for part of the night, which the sheriff discovered after the wounded Hilda was carried to the manor house. Thomas later heard the man's cries as he was beaten for his negligence. Perhaps the fellow was lucky he had not been hanged, although the beating might have been severe enough to kill him anyway if sweet mercy was lacking in the heat of Sir Reimund's fury.

Certainly the killer would not have taken long to notice that the guard was deep in a drunken sleep. Perhaps he even made sure the ale was waiting for him, knowing the weakness of this local man for strong drink. Getting into the shed had been far too easy.

The lack of evidence of any struggle suggested that Hilda knew her assailant well and, unlike Tobye, had been awake when she was stabbed. Indeed, she had felt safe enough to turn her back to the man. Might she have even expected him to free her? She did lie very close to the door and facing it. Had the door been left open to raise false hope that she might escape?

Briefly, the monk wondered if the culprit had been the sheriff. The man might have arrested her solely as a scapegoat, but there could be more to it. Had she seen him kill the groom?

The possibility pleased Thomas, but he chastised himself for malice. There was no indication that Sir Reimund was nearby until he came with his men later in the morning. His fury at finding his best suspect dying was far stronger proof that he had a better motive for keeping her alive—at least long enough to hang for the crime. Forcing himself to let logic win over his dislike of the man, Thomas reluctantly decided the sheriff had not tried to kill the cook.

So who did? If Hilda witnessed Tobye's killing, or saw the man leave the stable, she would fear him. When she saw that familiar face enter her rough cell, she would assume he had come to kill her and would not have turned her back on him. She might even have fought him off. The cook was not a slight woman, and her arms were well-muscled after years of hacking animal carcasses with heavy cleavers.

Thomas stopped and stared up at the heavy clouds. Might the man have eased her fears by offering to bribe her? Did he promise enough money to allow her to escape and find safe haven far from here? If he convinced her that no one would believe what she had seen and that she would hang in any case, she might have accepted, deceiving herself into believing he would let her escape unharmed. If this is what happened, the man must have enough influence and coin to make such an offer believable.

"How clever of me to think of that," Thomas muttered bitterly. "Such a conclusion eliminates most of those living here, but leaves no one I think likely to have assaulted Hilda as well." Glancing at a nearby flock of pecking chickens, he was overcome by a feeling of kinship with the weak-minded fowl. With somber courtesy, and only half-amused, he nodded at them in familial greeting.

The murder of Mistress Luce, in conjunction with that of Tobye, pointed very specifically to Master Stevyn as the most likely suspect. Men, who discovered that their wives had cuckolded them, sometimes did kill both parties to the adultery, and judgements just as frequently found the husbands innocent of homicide, other men being sympathetic to such humiliation.

The steward would surely know all this. Since he must also realize that his humiliation was public enough already, he was clever enough to see the wisdom in admitting the deed and pleading for mercy due to the circumstances. This, he had not done. Did that mean he was innocent of the crime?

Perhaps. If the steward was the killer, he had behaved oddly for a man who had murdered two and perhaps a third. He had defended Hilda from the beginning. His shock and grief over the discovery of his wife's body did not point to a man who had wantonly taken her life. With some men, Thomas might have concluded that Satan had so possessed their souls that they could feel no guilt, and thus sport the face of innocence, but he did not think that was the case here. Those men remained dry-eyed, as if hellfire had burned away all tears. Master Stevyn had wept.

As he considered the next logical step in his analysis, Thomas rounded the corner of the stable—and found himself face to face with the steward himself.

◇◇◇

"Master Stevyn." Thomas bowed his head in greeting.

The steward's eyes were sunken deep into their sockets with weariness, and his hair had dulled to a grayer shade. He seemed a man of little joy, one who walked the earth solely out of habit.

"Ah, Brother," he sighed, "tell me the limits on God's forgiveness."

Thomas hoped his surprise at such a remark was well hidden. "If a man is contrite and understands the horror of his sin," he carefully replied, "God forgives much. Hard penance may be required, but such a man will welcome it to lift the unbearable guilt from his soul and keep it from the flames of Hell."

Frowning, Stevyn folded his arms. "Then answer me another question, if you would be so kind. Does age make a man more reflective because the stink of death grows stronger in his nostrils? It seems we care little about what we do until our strength falters, our bellies sag, and our hair drops out." He smiled, but the expression was a melancholy thing. "For most of my life, I never thought of myself as an especially evil creature. Like most men, I spent my youth in lusty pleasures. When a man dared to jab at my pride, I fought him. Yet I have worked faithfully for my lord and honored my marriage vows more than many other men do." He fell silent and studied the monk as if expecting something.

This speech was a far longer one than Thomas had ever heard before from this man. Hopeful that the steward would say more, he emulated Stevyn's firm silence.

"I fear you are waiting for a confession, Brother."

"If that is your wish, I suggest we go to the quiet of the chapel where others will not overhear what is rightly said in private by a man to a priest and thus on to God's ears."

The steward laughed, the sound akin to that of an angry hound's barking. "Why should I seek privacy? To admit that I am one of God's more flawed creatures?" He jabbed his thumb at the stable. "If the servants and craftsmen of this manor dare not say to my face that I am imperfect, the horses will be honest enough."

"God demands it, Master Stevyn. When we sin, we forget His might, but silence chases away all worldly concerns and distractions. In silence, His power may be rediscovered to the benefit of our souls."

"You speak well, Brother, and I beg forgiveness for my mocking tone. Nothing ill was intended, but I am a simple man, one who spends his days considering whether seeds should be planted now or a week hence, whether the harvest will provide enough for the beasts to eat over winter, and, as leisure, where the conies are that my lord allows me to hunt on his land. I do not have a scholar's skill in disputation. To men like me, a matter is either this." He gestured with one hand. "Or that." He raised the other. "I have little understanding of much in between."

Thomas was not fooled by this demonstrably false claim of simplicity, but he did hear acute sorrow in the man's voice and to that he responded. "I heard only the cry of a tired spirit, longing to find lost peace."

Master Stevyn's lids closed with fatigue so heavy that he struggled to reopen his eyes. "Would you go to the manor hall and wait for me, Brother? I have one matter requiring my immediate attention but shall join you soon. Then we will share some wine, and I will beg your patience in hearing my tale." He stretched out his arms with evident discomfort. "Aye, this air is very chill with rain. My old joints ache today more than usual."

Sympathetic to the man's complaints, Thomas smiled, nodded his concurrence, and walked back toward the hall. As he reached the steps of the manor, he turned around to see where Stevyn had gone.

The steward had disappeared.

The monk cursed himself. Had the man's light jesting about the aches of old age lulled him into complacence? Thomas had reason enough to suspect the steward of murder. Should he seek him out to make sure he did not escape? At the very least, he ought to have noted where Stevyn went.

The monk shook his head and turned again in the direction of the manor hall. After all, where could a man of his reputation go to hide and what more ill would he cause, assuming he was guilty of murder, now that his faithless wife and her lover were dead? As he had thought before, Stevyn might even be innocent.

Walking into the house, Thomas decided that the steward would keep his word and meet him soon. His conscience did seem troubled enough and eager to confess something. And Thomas would not fail to ask where the steward had been last night, about the time of his wife's murder.

Chapter Thirty-Six

Constance lay on the chapel floor and clawed at the rough stone. Her nails might be ripped and bleeding, but she felt only the writhing agony of her soul. What should she do? Dare she speak out? Where did her duty to God lie?

"Lust," she groaned. "All this has been caused by it. Punishment I may deserve, but surely my sins have been fewer than most. Do I not spend more time than other women on my knees in prayer? Did I not urge my husband to brighten the parish church with chalices and drape the priest in fine robes? Haven't I valiantly fought for virtue, railing against festering sin, and did I not argue for abstinence in my marriage? And do I not loudly condemn the wickedness of creatures like Master Stevyn's wife and the physician's widow?" She turned her gaze to the base of the altar and cried out: "My mortal body may be sinful, but my soul is virtuous. I deserve better than this from You!"

From the soft shadows came a brittle laugh.

Constance fell silent, unsure she had heard that sound. "Who dares to ridicule my righteous longings?" she whispered. "If it is the Prince of Darkness, you shall not claim victory over my soul because of one little weakness, vile though it was!"

"One? You lie, Mistress," the voice mocked, "and that is a black enough sin."

Dragging herself to her knees, she turned and squinted into the darkness.

Nothing moved.

Had that been the voice of Satan, she wondered, her body trembling. Or did it belong to a mortal? The rasping sound was familiar, but she could not identify it, coarsened as the whispering was with cruel scorn. Surely it was the Devil, she decided. He was attempting to trick her, and she raised her chin in defiance.

"I do not understand what fiendish ploy lies in your accusation, Wicked One, but you know I tell the truth. Aye, I may have followed the adulterous wife more than once and watched as Tobye swyved her. But evil should have a witness, for it must not remain secret, and did they not couple like dogs or perversely with Eve above Adam?" Her voice hoarse, she licked her dry lips. "It sickened me!"

"Why then did you go to him and beg to be taken yourself in stable straw as filthy as your lust?"

Clutching her breast, Constance roared in protest. "Never did I grow so weak in flesh that I went to Tobye and asked…"

"Ask? Nay, Mistress, you did not *ask*. You beseeched him! Then, like any wanton, you dragged him down on you, spread your legs wide, and bucked…"

"A lie!" She threw back her head and wailed. "You mock me!"

"Do not deny what you did. Adam's sons may be weak in flesh, but the progeny of Eve light Hell's fire in men's groins and drive them wild. Oh, didn't you make the Devil dance that night with your writhing!"

"You and your imps had but little cause to frolic for that," she whimpered.

Silence fell. Then the voice continued with a tremor. "You did not couple with the groom?"

"Surely you jest, Evil One! The night before Tobye died, I confess I hid in the stable, as I oft did, to watch him sin. But he caught me and, with harsh ridicule, accused me of watching him couple with women because I longed to join in the sport. Shamed by his discovery, I fled." Taking a deep breath, she howled with profound misery. "Had you not entered his mouth and used his tongue to speak those vile insults, that low-born creature would never have dared utter such obscenities to a woman of my rank. How dare you continue humiliating me!"

"Why did you not return to your husband, chastened, and embrace him in the marital bed, as God allows, thus bringing the joy of male children?"

Her sole response was the shrill laughter of contempt.

The sound echoed in the darkness.

"Oh you adulterous whore! Perhaps you did not lie with the groom, but your body longed for his. Rather than welcome your lawful husband, you found wicked pleasure by watching others in unnatural acts. Was that not why you followed Mistress Luce to the stable last night, hoping to see her seduce another man into corruption?"

Constance rubbed her cheeks with her bloody fingers and moaned. Her guilt so overwhelmed her that it crushed a gnawing suspicion, tiny as a nibbling worm, that this voice belonged to a mortal.

"How did you learn she was going to meet another?"

"I overheard Mistress Luce…"

"And thus you ran after her, although you told all that you would spend the night in the chapel for solitary prayer. Jezebel!"

She swallowed with pain, all moisture vanishing from her throat.

"Your sins shall drag you down to Hell. Had you not lied and gone to the stable, you would not have seen the one she met and what happened—nor would you have been observed. Now is the day of reckoning!"

Constance tried to speak but managed only a croak.

The figure moved swiftly from the shadows.

Her eyes widened and terror froze her in place. Unable to scream, her mouth opened and shut like a gasping fish lying on a fisherman's boat.

Clutching her shoulder, the man smiled—then plunged his dagger into the exact middle of her faithless heart.

Chapter Thirty-Seven

The crackling branches spat out a merry warmth from the nearby hearth. Although he was a young man, Thomas was grateful for the heat that chased the dampness from his bones. He rose and walked closer to the fire, stretching his arms wide to embrace more of the comfort. A cup of watered wine would be welcome as well, he decided, especially if he must hear an admission of murder.

"Wine!" a voice shouted.

Thomas turned to see the steward limp into the hall.

From the shadows behind a pillar, a servant rushed off to obey.

Stevyn approached the hearth, rubbing his hand against his side.

"You have cut yourself," Thomas said, seeing smears of blood on the robe when the man drew closer. "I should make a poultice for that wound before it festers."

"Nay, Brother. You are kind, but it is a minor thing." He scowled at his hand, as if it had offended him, and picked out what seemed to be splinters. "I tripped and scraped it against the rough wood of a wall, trying to keep balance. In my youth, I would have righted myself easily, but my legs buckled. Like my youngest son returning from his studies, my body often rebels against my wishes."

Thomas smiled in response.

The servant arrived with a pitcher and two cups. Stevyn grunted and waved him away with the injured hand.

Thomas concluded the wound must be insignificant enough.

The pewter cup Stevyn handed him was of plain design but fine crafting and filled with a dark wine that turned out to be excellent. Thomas nodded with surprised pleasure.

"From Gascony," the steward replied to the unspoken question. "Now, Brother, sit back and let me tell you a tale. Women like them to be filled with handsome knights and courtly love, but I fear this one is about a simpler fellow."

Raising his cup, Thomas grinned. "As a monk from a priory near a seacoast village, I know more of that ilk than I do of knights, Master Stevyn."

The steward raised one bushy eyebrow to express affable doubt, then settled into his chair, drank his wine, and began the story.

"Long ago, but near to this place, there dwelt a lad and a lass, both sinners by birth but as close to Eden's innocence as youth can be. They fell in love, but he was a younger son of a landed knight, and his father had higher ambition for him than a merchant's daughter. A worthy spouse with a little property was soon found for him, and the lovers were forced to part, innocent of lewdness but wounded in heart."

He drained his own wine, glanced over at the monk's cup, and replenished both before continuing. "The lad was now a man in possession of some earthly wealth. His new wife also owned a good soul. She prayed much, gave alms to the poor, tended to the sick, and dutifully bedded her husband for the sake of heirs. She bore one in great agony, then failed to quicken again. Indeed, bedding her husband grew so painful after that hard birthing that he took pity and ceased demanding payment of the marriage debt."

Stevyn stopped and looked into his cup with a disappointed expression as if surprised not to find therein an answer to some question.

"He bore no fault for the pain his wife suffered," Thomas said. "Sometimes God brings suffering to the good for reasons only He knows." His heart always ached whenever he said this, and thus he used the argument as little as possible, but he suspected the steward would only take the words as rhetorical things.

In fact, the steward waved them aside. "There is more, Brother, much more."

Thomas gestured for him to go on.

"Although the man did not love his wife, he honored her and sought remedies to heal her pain. When pilgrimages and trips to noted healers failed, he desperately turned to his former love. By this time, she had also married a good man at her parents' behest and then gained some reputation as a woman skilled with herbs."

He rose and paced without speaking, drained his cup, and refilled it. His hand visibly shaking, he spilled wine and muttered a mild curse. "Aye, a physician would have been the better choice, but the man's wife had begged for a woman to attend her, confessing that her modesty had been offended enough by the questioning of one of the male healers."

Thomas drank in silence.

"This desperate measure failed as well, and the man's wife did not regain her health. As it turned out, it was a dangerous mistake. While the man's wife prayed for relief, Satan found a fertile field in the hearts of the husband and his old love. At first they felt only comfort in each other's company, then hellfire manifested as lust enflamed them beyond endurance. It was not long before they committed adultery, not just once but again and again."

Although guilt colored the steward's cheeks, Thomas briefly glimpsed something else in the man's face. For just an instant, the wrinkles etched in his face smoothed and the brightness of youth flashed in his eyes. Did sin ever bring peace, the monk wondered before fear banished the blasphemous thought with just speed.

Stevyn sat back down and shook his head. "Unlike Huet, I tell tales badly, Brother. Let it be said, simply enough, that the wife learned of her husband's sin and, like a true Christian, forgave him. God cursed him, however, and the good wife grew increasingly weak and finally died, leaving the husband so befouled with wickedness that he lost all reason. Blinded by the Devil, he turned selfish and took a young wife, whom he neither loved nor ever learned to respect, but whom he could swink at will like a boar in rut." He closed his eyes, the illusion of story-telling grown as sheer as worn cloth.

"And when he learned that she was swyving another?"

Stevyn's face turned a wine-red hue as he slammed his cup on the wooden table.

"Might he not have killed her because of the horns she put on his forehead? Many men have done just so and few have condemned them for it."

"Someone else has done this, Brother. As I now think on it, the crime ought to have been done by me. For the sake of my honor, I confess I might even wish that it had been, but I have learned something from my sins toward my first wife. I..."

"...chose to forgive?" The question was dutifully asked, as his vocation demanded, but Thomas knew well enough what the reply would be.

Stevyn snorted. "Nay, I am not a man inclined to turn the other cheek, no matter how often our priest reminds us of that duty. I contemplated sending her to a convent for her sins, with a dowry large enough to guarantee acceptance and everlasting enclosure behind thick walls, but never did I want to kill her. And if you doubt me, Brother, as you most certainly have reason to do, I ask that you consider this. Why would I have publicly strung her up naked for all to see her shame, which is mine as well? That is an act of someone who must have had cause to wound both my wife and me."

Thomas nodded. For a husband to stab an adulterous wife in bed with her lover, or to suffocate her without leaving plain evidence of killing, were more common methods. Yet he was puzzled about one thing. "When did you learn of the adultery? I have heard it continued for some time."

"You are a young man, devoted to God. This may be difficult for you to understand." The steward shifted uncomfortably, then reached for the pitcher and poured himself another full cup.

Thomas refused the offer of more. This was not the time for a wine-dulled mind.

"It became obvious to me that she bore my swyving as a despised duty." He smiled, but his eyes closed from the shame of the admission. "She was a lusty young woman, but her body was as dry as a desert after I tried to please her. Even the Church says a husband must give his wife joy in bed, but I failed and, in truth, she soon began to bore me." He tilted his head to one side, some pride returning to his look. "Isn't it odd, Brother, that I should find more joy with a woman who is beyond child-bearing and can never give me sons? Yet I have, although no man ever has sons enough. My wife's adultery came after I had left her bed for that of another. If I learned late of my wife's betrayal, it was because I was lying in the arms of the woman I have loved for far too many years."

"Is your beloved now free to marry?" Thomas asked, a chill shuddering through him despite the warmth in the hall. Was he wrong in thinking the murderer must be a man? Might it be a mistress who longed to take this man as lawful husband at the church door? Although the Church frowned on marriages between a man and his mistress, it was a prohibition ignored often enough amongst those of lesser rank.

"Aye, she is, but, before you ask the question, Brother, I swear to you that she did not kill my wife either. A gentle woman, she has told me that she is willing enough to remain my leman. I have found great peace, lying in her arms, and her company soothes my angers and renders me a kinder man. I do not understand how this is possible, considering our great sin. Perhaps you can explain it to me?"

The monk chose to ignore the question for the moment. "You believe this woman did not kill your wife, but did she have the opportunity to murder either Tobye or Mistress Luce?"

"I cannot address the night of Tobye's death, because I had fallen into chaste enough sleep by my wife's side. But the night of my wife's murder, I was in my lady's arms." Scowling, he leaned forward, his arms resting on his thighs. "Surely the one who killed my groom also attacked Hilda and murdered my wife. Why would there be two—or three—such evil men at large?"

Thomas turned his head away. The question was valid, but could he believe the steward's protestations of innocence? Inclined though he was to do so, he also knew how fortunate it was that the man and his leman should be together on the night of Mistress Luce's murder. Neither would admit that the other was ever out of sight. Either or both together might have killed.

And how convenient that Luce, the one able to provide the steward with a reason to be far from the stable the night of Tobye's death should now be murdered also. As for the testimony of servants, they would never speak against the master either.

A movement caught the monk's attention, and he looked up to see a man at the entrance to the hall.

"How much have you heard?" Stevyn called out to the figure, and then gestured for him to come forward.

"If you choose to recount any of this story, Father," Huet said, "you had best tell all of it."

Chapter Thirty-Eight

Maud wept.

Kneeling beside the physician's widow, Eleanor embraced her, murmuring words she hoped would soothe, and regretted that she had so quickly sent her guard to bring Brother Thomas out of fear that what she was about to hear was a tale of murder. Maud had her own confessor for the comfort she truly required, but the monk was a gentle priest, a man known in Tyndal for his compassion when told of mortal failings. Perhaps it was wise that she had sent for him. He might well bring this woman immediate peace.

"Does Huet know he is your son?" she whispered.

Maud sat back on her heels, her sobs quieting, and rubbed her cheeks dry. "Not until his recent return home, my lady."

"I am amazed that no one knew of this and must ask why the secret was necessary. Even if you needed to conceal the birth for your own reasons, your son could have been passed off as another woman's child by the steward. Bastard sons are often brought into the father's family."

"Master Stevyn knew his wife could not bear another, and he loved the boy from the moment he heard of my quickening. He wanted him to have a legitimate son's status, a deception that would harm but little. Huet was a younger son, thus taking a trivial inheritance from his wife's beloved Ranulf and nothing the elder would resent."

"Other wives may have taken on the care of a husband's by-blow, but few have been so willing to pretend the child is of their own body. Why?"

"She was a saint in her forbearance and willingness to forgive. Her husband was very grateful for her unique charity in this matter, as was I."

Eleanor understood charity but acting the mother to Huet so well that no one suspected his bastardy was an act most generous by any measure. Had the woman believed this unusual deed would bring her soul special merit? Indeed it should.

Noting the prioress' reflective frown, Maud explained further. "She was a devout woman, my lady, although her reputation as a mother was based more on the piety she required of her offspring than celebrated for the affection she bestowed. Methinks she hoped to wrench Huet's soul away from the Prince of Darkness and into God's hand. Considering his birth, she must have believed that he would be more likely to follow evil ways if she did not intervene."

As she considered both the steward's sons, Eleanor hoped his first wife never witnessed how imperfectly they interpreted her instruction. The eldest might be pious enough in outward ways, but she found him brittle of heart. Huet, on the other hand, was quite unsuited to the vocation chosen for him. That said, Brother Thomas had probably taken his own vows with a less than ardent calling, but he honored his oaths more faithfully than many who claimed greater purpose. Might Huet eventually become a similar cleric?

"Does something trouble you, my lady?"

The prioress realized she had been lost in her thoughts too long. "The sons are so very different…"

"She favored Ranulf, of course. He took after her in his piety, and she showered him with praise, especially when he wailed over his sins. As for my Huet, he was not so inclined to prayer, being a boisterous lad much like his father, and thus he seldom found the comfort of a mother's arms."

How hard this must have been for Mistress Maud, Eleanor thought, hearing the woman's pain as she described what maternal warmth each boy had received. "Then you saw your son on occasion?" she chose to ask.

"Before Huet's birth, my husband and I were invited to join in feasts to celebrate God's grace, or when sickness attacked the manor tenants. That practice continued afterward. If my husband had no immediate need of my services with herbs, Master Stevyn's wife let me play with my son and did not take it ill when Huet ran to me when I opened my arms."

And thus the steward's wife did demonstrate an even more unusual kindness, Eleanor acknowledged. The lady knew she did not have room enough in her own arms for the little boy, but she did not prevent Mistress Maud from giving him what she could not. Many women would not have dealt with this situation so. "The deception seems to have been skillfully performed to remain secret, but how was the matter of Huet's birth handled?"

"When I could no longer conceal my quickening, I moved away on the excuse that a far-away cousin required my care. Master Stevyn's wife pretended a pregnancy at the same time and, when I sent news that my time had come, she took a short journey so that she might feign birthing some distance away. My babe was smuggled in by a loyal servant, her sole attendant, and thus became hers."

"This servant…?"

"She was well rewarded but died of a fever many years ago. The pretense was successful."

"Did no one question that a woman who was so frail might give birth to such a healthy child and suffer no further ill-effects herself?"

Maud's lips turned into a sad smile. "She was most devout, and all assumed that God had performed a miracle, much as he did for the aged wife of Abraham, and blessed her with one last son."

Eleanor nodded, unsure whether she should condemn such deceit or conclude that God had been kind to the babe by allowing him to stay with a father who loved him and a woman who was willing enough to show kindness if not love. "You had no further issue yourself?"

"God punished me for my sins, and I never bore another child during the years when I was able."

"Were you not married at the time of Huet's birth?"

Maud rose and walked over to the bed where Hilda lay. Gently she stroked the cook's ashen cheek and sighed, a sound troubled enough to match the wounded woman's rasping breath. "Aye. My husband was much older than I and a better man than I deserved, my lady, one for whom I felt much affection and gratitude even if my heart resided with another and my body sinned."

"How could your husband not know of this? He was a physician and thus not easily fooled about such matters."

"Did he know?' She faced the prioress, her smile twisted with self-contempt. "As you suggested, he must have, but he never spoke of my long absence, nor did he question me about a cousin whom he had never before heard mentioned. When I returned home at long last, he greeted me at the entrance to our house, his bearing formal and proud, but his eyes filled with tears. My wretched heart broke, and I cried out to him. Before I could beg his forgiveness, he touched a finger to his lips, took my hand in his, and led me into the house. Once inside, I fell to my knees and wept, swearing I would never leave his side again, one promise I did faithfully keep. He never once spoke of that absence, nor did he condemn me for any sin."

"And you were still married when Master Stevyn's first wife died." Eleanor's remark was less a question than an observation.

"My husband did not die until after Master Stevyn had married Mistress Luce."

"A young woman who could give him more sons," Eleanor said. "Did you think he might confess Huet's bastardy if he had other, legitimate issue?"

Maud's cheeks flushed. "Our adulterous union might suggest we are faithless in honoring all oaths, but I did not doubt that Master Stevyn loved our son. When my husband and I visited the manor, I saw much evidence of Huet's place in his father's heart. He would never have cast our lad out."

Eleanor joined the widow at Hilda's side. Looking down, she observed a tinge of pink now coloring the cook's cheeks and feared a fever had set in. She quickly offered a silent prayer for God's mercy. "There are many tales about Mistress Luce's infidelity. Some say she longed too much for a child, a babe her husband did not seed in her quickly enough, and thus played the whore," she said, her thoughts returning to the current discussion. "What do you know of those rumors?"

"I have no right to give credence to any stories nor to criticize."

The prioress shook her head. "I am not indulging in idle gossip; rather I seek reasons for why murder was committed. As for the pointing of self-righteous fingers, no mortal is so blameless that any have the right to cast stones. That said, observations lacking in malice are not sinful. Please tell me yours."

"It was well-known that Mistress Luce and Tobye were lovers, yet he was unmarried and she…In truth, I can think of no one who has a greater motive for killing Mistress Luce than I."

Eleanor raised her eyebrows.

Maud took a deep breath. "I was angry, bitter, and jealous when I learned that Master Stevyn had taken such a young woman to his bed, but after my worthy husband gave up his soul to God so suddenly that I could not send his spirit off with a final kiss, I knew He was punishing me for my sins. All my evil thoughts melted into grief while I mourned the loss of that honorable spouse." She briefly covered her eyes. "Had I wished to kill Mistress Luce, my lady, I surely would have done so after the marriage, not waited until now. Master Stevyn has since regretted the choice of wife, and I have armored my soul against Satan's pricking."

"Why were you here when I arrived?" As much as Eleanor wished to believe this woman, there remained too many details, still inadequately explained, that troubled her.

"You have reason to ask that question, my lady. Not long ago, Mistress Luce's behavior changed and she grew quite erratic. As I learned, she would be melancholic and refuse to share a bed with her husband one night, but the next might swell with wild lust and beg to couple with him most wantonly. Master Stevyn feared illness, perhaps even possession or madness. When he questioned her during one of her calmer moments, she claimed to have quickened. He begged me to attend her for the sake of her health as well as that of any child."

The prioress gave her a look so incredulous that it needed no other statement.

Maud nodded. "Of course, I knew I should not come, but my husband had been the only physician nearby and he had died. Under his guidance, I have gained some small reputation as a healer and had often acted as midwife. For all his faults, Master Stevyn is not a cruel man and wished each of his wives to receive the best care possible. Thus I did agree to attend Mistress Luce, but only after I told him that my own door would be firmly barred at night."

"An oath you kept?" Eleanor's look was skeptical.

Her cheeks reddened. "Despite the firm resolve with which I locked that door, I silenced my conscience one evening and welcomed him to share wine and then my bed. Master Stevyn and I may no longer have youthful bodies, but we should have realized that aging flesh may still spark with lust. Leading us into temptation was easy enough labor for the Devil."

Eleanor shook her head but refused to be distracted from the direction of her inquiry. "When you examined Mistress Luce, what did you find?"

"She refused to submit to an examination. Had a physician met with her, he would have asked her questions only and thus she might have kept her secret longer. Like any competent midwife, I would have discovered the truth the moment my hand felt her womb. That, she knew. Of course, I quickly suspected she was not pregnant, and I had heard whisperings of her affair with the groom. Just before she was killed, I told her that I believed she was not with child and must cease all deception with her husband. My phrasing was ill-spoken for she thought I was speaking of her adultery."

"Was that when she abused you in the courtyard and ordered you to leave this place?"

"I fear you were not the only one who overheard that conversation."

"Including Master Stevyn? If he did not hear the argument, he was surely told of it."

The woman stiffened. "My lady, I know you must suspect him of murder as well, but he did not kill his wife. We may be guilty of adultery, deception, and foolishness, all evil enough, but they are the worst of our sins. Aye, he was unwise to bring me here, and I was imprudent to agree. After that first night, we often slept quite chastely in each other's arms, as we did the night his wife was killed. Lust we do feel, but the burning in our loins is more temperate than when I could bear children, and satisfaction of our longings gives us a different contentment. It is not a passion that spawns murder."

Eleanor turned away, not out of contempt for the woman's admission, but from need to think without distraction. Was Maud lying to her, assuming that an older woman could easily fool a younger one, especially a prioress who had forsworn carnal love? Her own passion for Brother Thomas was achingly hot and most certainly did not resemble such tranquil longings described by the widow. Eleanor could find nothing in her own lust that might instruct her in the truth of theirs.

Yet as she thought more on that, she remembered Sister Beatrice's premise that mortal love may have many manifestations. Hadn't the time spent with her monk during this unfortunate journey been both chaste and sweet? Had she not found as much joy in that as she did agony in her lust? The realization gave her pause.

Making a swift decision, she faced the widow once again. "Sir Reimund will not want to point an accusing finger in your direction even if you each did have cause to kill Mistress Luce and colluded in her death," the prioress said.

"My lady! Master Stevyn would never commit such a vile…"

She gestured that she had not finished her thought. "My observation about the sheriff is little different from a remark you recently made to me. Nonetheless, I believe you both to be innocent." Silently she prayed that such a conclusion was not badly mistaken, but the woman's unselfish attempt to defend the steward's innocence before that of her own suggested a heart that held goodness in it.

Maud looked as if she had just been given a reprieve from the hangman.

"If not the two of you, tell me who else might have had cause to murder? Surely the deaths of Tobye and Master Stevyn's wife, as well as the attack on poor Hilda, are connected. You know the people here well. I must have your opinion."

"Not my Huet!" Maud whispered, her voice mixed with both fresh relief and reborn fear.

"Although I choose not to condemn the deception of his birth, others might decide otherwise. For that reason I must ask if anyone, including Mistress Luce, Hilda, or the groom, knew Huet's secret." If any did, Eleanor thought, he might well have had cause enough to kill.

"None of them. I swear to it!"

"You said your son did not learn that you were his true mother until just recently. Why tell him at all?"

"Although Huet was happy enough as a boy, sorrow darkened his soul when he became a man. He fathered a child on a woman who was unsuitable as a wife in his father's eyes. She died birthing a dead babe, and Huet believed it was all God's curse for his own sinful lust. He went quite wild with grief, but the noble de Lacy had noted his talents and offered to send Huet to Cambridge where he might become a priest or, barring that, a clerk in his service. My son thought of it as penance. His father was delighted, seeing it as a fine opportunity for a younger son with little inheritance to advance in the world."

"An education and a calling your son soon rejected, apparently choosing instead to wander abroad as a common minstrel until his recent return."

"The boy was confused! When he arrived home, filled with doubt over the path on which he had been placed, he found a father too distracted to offer kind advice and a stepmother who cared only for herself. Even I had little time for him, struggling as I was with my own sins. Master Stevyn most certainly greeted Huet with harsh words when the lad returned, but the steward was deeply grieved, fearing that our son would lose his lordship's favor and thus any hope for a decent living. It was then he said to me that I must tell Huet the truth of his parentage. The shock of learning he was a bastard, with no right of any inheritance from his father, might shock him into a wiser path than he had been following of late."

"When did you tell him?"

"The night Tobye was killed, I slipped away from Mariota's side to meet with Huet in my chambers. His longing for a sweet word and gentle direction was piteous, and it was not easy for me to tell him the story. Although I had not intended to leave my vigil over your charge for so long, I fear even the owls had ceased their calling before we finished our discussion."

"God must have smiled on your efforts. Indeed, Mariota suffered no harm." Eleanor reached over and gently touched the woman. "But do tell me how he took the news."

"I expected outrage or grief. Instead, his countenance softened, and he said he was much comforted by the news."

"Although this meant he had no right to his father's estate should Ranulf die without issue, as his wife has yet to bring forth heirs?"

Maud clutched her hands together. "He said he was grateful that the woman who reared him was not his mother," she whispered. "Sinful though this may be, my lady, I found joy in his happiness. As for his bastardy, he grew merry about it, jesting that the truth was just considering his wayward nature."

What a strange reaction, Eleanor thought as she looked down at Hilda and touched her cheek. Although the skin had regained a suspicious coloring, she was relieved to note there was no feverous heat. "Might he have told this news to anyone else?"

"To whom, my lady? He and Ranulf are not close, and he has not sought out any boyhood friends due to the reasons for his sudden return. He is wise enough to stay silent in any case." Preparing to defend her lad's good sense, Maud tensed.

Not having any cause to debate this, Eleanor nodded, and then grew thoughtful. Perhaps Huet's response had not been so odd. Jests were an honored means of speaking truth through laughter. Even wise kings encouraged their fools to do it, thus allowing bitter honesty to counter the honeyed words of flatterers. The manner in which Huet had defended Hilda had been similar. Maybe he knew how difficult this confession had been for his mother and he had simply tried to make her laugh. That would point to a kind nature and not one prone to murder.

"Indeed, I soon saw hope that Huet might return to Cambridge. As we spoke more in private about the matter, he listened with the grave earnestness befitting a man. When I reminded him that a position with the Earl would bring him a comfortable lot in life, whatever the truth of his birth, he said he would refuse to take even one mazer of a true son's inheritance from Ranulf."

"You tell me that you and Huet were together the night Tobye was murdered. Brother Thomas has argued persuasively that Mistress Luce's death could not have been by her own hand, but you and Master Stevyn were together the night she was killed. Finally, I see no reason why any of you would attack Hilda." Eleanor threw up her hands in frustration. "Who, then, is the murderer?"

Chapter Thirty-Nine

"I had cause enough to kill my step-mother," Huet said, leaning back against the stone wall. He sampled the wine and then pointed to his cup. "Congratulations on finding an honest wine merchant. In university, they gave us vinegar, although some claimed drinking it was intended to be a foretaste of Hell."

"Why are you trying to put the hangman's noose around your neck? You have no reason to kill anyone," Stevyn snapped.

"If you were to ask Ranulf, or his pious wife, they would say that a mortal as stained with sin as I am must be capable of any foul crime. When the shepherd culls his flock, they declare the black sheep are slaughtered with more joy than the white ones, and that the Devil thinks the former taste better roasted on the spit. Never mind that white sheep are not so pure in hue, nor black ones as dark." He shrugged.

"This is nothing to jest about!" The steward spun around to Thomas. "Don't listen to him!"

"But he must," Huet countered, winking at the monk. "Does our dear brother not have ears?"

"As do asses," Thomas replied, "but I am a priest, not a sheriff, and thus prefer saving souls to hanging mortals."

"And a priest who reads what truth there may be in any man's smile, I think." Huet produced a patently false grin.

Thomas gave Huet a look advising caution.

The steward uttered such a deep growl that one passing dog yelped, then skittered off with tail between its legs. "Do not be fooled by a tonsure, my son. I have never known any monk who would try to stop a condemned man from hanging." Stevyn shook his finger at the young man. "Brother Thomas has been asking enough questions to suggest he wants a murderer hanged for the killings here, whatever his claimed interest in the cleansing of souls."

"Will you forgive my sins, and then lead me by the hand to Sir Reimund, Brother?" Huet gazed at the monk over the edge of his mazer, a look that could be interpreted as playful—or carefully feigned innocence.

Thomas suddenly lost his own patience with Huet's glib responses, although he suspected the son's motive was less frivolous than a very sober attempt to turn suspicion away from his father. How long would it take before the son gave up the noble effort? He decided to test Huet and see what truths that method might reveal. "Explain your purpose in killing Mistress Luce."

"How dare you!" The steward took a step toward the monk.

"Please, Father. Let me speak freely."

"I have no wish to falsely entrap your son. If he is innocent, his words will prove it."

"No matter what he says, he had no part in this violence," Stevyn replied, then reluctantly nodded his permission for Huet to continue.

"My brother has always longed to buy a space in Heaven, and his wife will not even countenance lust long enough to produce heirs. In addition, most would conclude he is less capable of managing an estate than your prioress' donkey is of winning a race against my father's horse. As a second son, I might have hopes of inheriting my father's position as steward, and the lands he holds in his own right, if the saintly Ranulf turns his back on the world and takes vows."

"You should know better than to assume your brother would do so. He may have calluses on his knees, but he is no saint," Stevyn muttered. "I never told his mother of the times I caught him pleasuring himself in full view of the laundry maids."

Huet gave his cup to his father for more wine. "Even if Ranulf never forswears lust, he may die without issue unless his wife relents on her refusal to pay the marriage debt. As the second son, I would inherit." He turned to Thomas. "As you have now learned, Brother, I may be my father's son but Mistress Maud birthed me instead of a wedded wife. That fact, once I learned it, was reason enough to kill Mistress Luce to prevent any new and legitimate heir from displacing me."

Thomas gestured at the fuming steward to remain silent. "Should Master Ranulf take vows as penance or die without issue, you would inherit over any son of Mistress Luce as long as the truth of your birth remains secret."

"And if my bastardy is revealed now, or the truth is subsequently discovered, I would be stripped of the inheritance and Mistress Luce's child would gain all. That is reason enough to kill her before she breeds."

"You would never…you could not…you are not…" Stevyn's eyes grew wider with each dismayed protestation.

"There is more to this," Thomas replied. "All you have said is true, Huet, but you are not a foolish man. Being perceptive enough to think beyond the moment, you would not have waited until now to kill her. If you wanted to avoid losing any part of your inheritance, you would have murdered her shortly after the marriage and before there was any chance that she might grow big with child. Why wait until you returned home? By then, she had much opportunity to quicken in your absence."

"But I did not learn of my true parentage until recently, Brother. Were this a simple matter of losing some minor inheritance because my father's new wife bore sons, I would agree with your logic."

Thomas smiled his concession of the point. "Yet men are often greedy beyond reason and will kill for a clipped penny as quickly as for a jeweled ring. Even if I agree with you on this, however, you must still explain why you stabbed Hilda. Did you not profess love for her and even defend her innocence before the entire manor? Why do so if she witnessed your foul deed and might be hanged for it instead of you?"

Huet began to argue further, but his shoulders hunched and he fell silent. The expression on his face declared that he had lost all taste for this dispute when asked to confess the stabbing of a woman he cared about.

Yet Thomas had seen how well this man took on the nature of others for the sake of entertainment. Dare he believe this particular show of emotion to be honest?

"Will you now end your foolishness, my son? If you are trying to save me by building a case for your own hanging, there is no reason to do so." Stevyn stretched his hands toward the monk. They trembled with his pleading. "Tell him that you do not suspect me of killing my wife!"

For a moment, Thomas hesitated. Was he convinced of the steward's innocence? Did he believe his story? Finally, he nodded agreement. "Your father was elsewhere the night Mistress Luce was killed, a story easily confirmed. As for Tobye, however, you might have had good reason to kill him. Surely you heard that he was swyving your stepmother?"

Some enigmatic emotion flickered in Huet's eyes. "I might have beaten Tobye for taking that which did not belong to him, but kill him? Nay," he whispered. "It was my stepmother who dishonored my father's bed. The groom only took what was thrust at him. I might have killed her for the pain she gave my sire, had my attention not been redirected to the matter of my bastardy." Sighing, he stood up, walked over to his father, and gently placed a hand on Stevyn's shoulder. "Father, I do not condemn you, my mother, or your first wife in this matter of my birth. My true mother gave much love to me as a boy, and you gave me your favor. As for the woman who called herself my mother, she taught me the meaning of charity, even if I had to learn how she practiced it after her death."

"Where were you while Mistress Luce was being murdered?" Thomas asked softly.

Master Stevyn looked up at his son. A rising of tears now glistened in his eyes.

Here was a man accustomed to facing many trials without flinching, Thomas thought. Now he quakes with fear for the safety of his beloved Huet. He hoped the ordeal would soon be over.

Huet squeezed his father's shoulder in reassurance. "I was at Hilda's side. Mistress Maud asked me to watch over her when a servant came to her door, calling her away. I did suspect you had summoned her and thus I promised to watch over our cook in case Death came for her and a priest should be called. That is where I was when I heard the hue and cry from the courtyard." Turning to Thomas, he met his gaze without blinking. "I even prayed that she regain consciousness and name her attacker. Sadly, she did not."

"Very well," Thomas said after a moment. "If you both are innocent of sending unshriven souls to Hell, who might have done the deed?" He looked first to the steward, then to the son. "Surely you have suspicions."

Stevyn sank into the bench and rubbed at his eyes.

Huet fell into a contemplative stance.

"Brother Thomas, I have finally found you!"

Startled, the monk turned to look behind him.

His prioress' guard stood at the door.

"Prioress Eleanor begs you come immediately!" the man cried. "To the room where the cook lies. There has been a confession."

Thomas set off at a run.

Huet snatched a dagger from the table, the blade flashing in the hearth firelight, and followed close behind.

The steward stared after them, his hands trembling as if a severe palsy had just struck. Then he threw his head back and cried out like a wounded animal alone in the forest.

Chapter Forty

Eleanor gasped in shock.

"Forgive me, my lady. I have no wish to point an accusing finger at an innocent," Maud said. "Although I do find the creature obnoxious, I mention the name only to suggest there were others who might have had cause enough to do violence."

"What reason would Constance have to kill anyone? I thought her eyes looked only to Heaven, however benighted her vision of it might be."

"Mistress Constance hated her husband. I was not the only one who heard her loudly refuse to lie with him and plead that they take vows of celibacy for the salvation of their souls. Yet she was not without carnal longings and had a hot eye for a well-formed man. When my son first returned home, now more a man than the boy who left here, she even gazed upon him like a hungry traveler might look upon an innkeeper's savory stew. Then he bluntly told her that he would be no woman's supper." Her lips briefly twitched with a smile.

Eleanor mind began to race with this new possibility. Ranulf was quite certain he had seen a woman visiting the groom the night he was murdered. Might it have been the elder son's wife? Yet surely he would have recognized her. There must have been too little moonlight to identify the person. Perhaps he had just assumed it was Hilda?

But Constance was a slight woman, unlike the cook, and thus more like the steward's wife at a glance. How could he have confused such different women? As for Luce, now that she had been murdered, she was unlikely to have been Tobye's killer. Indeed, this mysterious woman visiting Tobye might be innocent as well. The killer could have arrived later.

Eleanor wiped her face as if removing an annoying cobweb. "Tobye had quite the following of women. Was Mistress Constance one?"

The widow might be mistaken for Hilda in poor light, the prioress thought. As much as she believed Maud was innocent, dare she finally eliminate her from the list of suspects? Aye, she could. What Mariota had seen was not a lover's embrace but that of mother and son. In light of what she had just heard about the longtime relationship between steward and widow, she doubted Maud would invite Tobye to her bed. What she knew of the widow just did not suggest the woman was a killer.

Then whom had Ranulf seen?

"There is much common gossip," Maud said with evident hesitation. "I do not want to spread malicious untruths."

"I am a stranger here and thus seek to learn what others know. If you believe the tales are born only of spite, I have no wish to hear them. That said, I beg your opinion on how much truth lies in others."

The widow sighed. "There was a rumor that Mistress Constance was obsessed with the groom. Even Tobye laughed about her with his fellows, and I did overhear him once jest that her eye was often on his groin while she bent her knee to God. Whether this was true, I cannot confirm." She looked at the prioress as if hoping this was sufficient.

"Did he ever claim to have lain with her?"

"I can avow no direct knowledge of that, my lady, although I never heard such a story. Perhaps there was pleasure enough in telling the tale that this stern and pious wife might chase after a lusty groom. What I did notice, however, is that his jests about her, which I overheard from others, grew quite cruel. One might think he had grown weary of her longings?"

"Public mockery is hard enough to bear for any mortal, but more so to one who purports to be righteous," Eleanor replied. "The humiliation has most certainly driven some to murder. And a woman could slip up on a sleeping man and slit his throat. Perhaps she is also the one who drove a knife into Hilda's back. But I wonder if Mistress Constance was strong enough to strangle a younger woman and hoist her body to simulate a hanging? Ranulf's wife was too slight, was she not?"

"Aye, but might not jealousy add strength to a hand already driven by shame? Surely she had heard that Tobye was bedding Mistress Luce."

"Although envy is a very malignant sin, especially when joined to lust and public shame, I am not convinced that Mistress Constance is our murderer. Out of fear, a woman might strike a man with a dagger, or even in a moment of rage, but she does not usually choose that means to kill and Tobye's death was most certainly planned."

"Yet Jael, the wife of Heber, drove a nail into Sisera's head…"

"…with the strength of God's hand to save Israel. Nonetheless, you may be right. Yet is it truly reasonable to conclude that a woman could strangle another, one who would fight back with equal vigor, and then pull her dead body…?" Eleanor gasped.

"My lady?" Maud stretched out a supporting hand as if she feared the prioress had just been stricken with illness.

"I am well enough, good mistress, but have reason to curse my slow wit! There is another I have never considered, one whose motives for the violent acts are becoming clearer now."

The door to the chamber crashed open.

Both women whirled around.

Master Ranulf was bolting the door shut behind him.

Chapter Forty-One

"Whores. The women were but whores," he snarled. "I successfully sent all their souls to hell, with God's blessing, saving only that cook who still breathes there and whom you have wickedly tried to save. I shall now finish my task."

"Does He not grant everyone the right to repent their sins?" Eleanor asked quietly, noting the knife he held in his right hand. "By what right did you assume God wanted any quivering soul condemned without the chance for mercy?"

"God is wrathful and sends His fire down on all who defy Him like the foul creatures in Sodom and Gomorrah." Ranulf's eyes glittered. "What lusts do you hide?"

The prioress winced at this accurate blow, then modestly lowered her eyes, hoping to cool his rage with meek humility while she concentrated on the more immediate problem of staying alive. "Being mortal, we all sin, but surely God wants us to recognize the evil we have done and strive never to repeat those errors." Glancing to her left, she saw a jug and basin on a nearby table.

"Women are Devil-spawned, bitches in heat!" Spittle flew from his white-flecked lips. "Adam would still be in Eden were it not for his fickle wife."

Theological debate with this man was clearly not the path to travel, and Eleanor prayed for the calmness needed to discover how best to protect Hilda, Maud, and herself from his frenzy.

"Our cook was guilty as well?" Maud asked in a timorous voice. "Teach me, Master Ranulf, for I do not understand her sin."

"The Devil bought her soul and thus she lusted after the groom! The breath she exhaled befouled the air like some stinking mist and rotted the souls of other daughters of Eve when they came near her. Even the food she cooked for those at the manor was contaminated by her touch." He gulped air. "The proof of that lies in the number of women who coupled with Tobye. She has to die."

"And when God sent an avenger to slay the groom, did her profane eyes witness the deed?" Maud clutched her hands together as if in prayer. "Did she also have to suffer because no one so foul should look upon the splendor of righteous vengeance?"

The steward's son frowned as he considered those words, and then nodded as if pleased to agree.

Keeping a diffident silence, Eleanor backed toward the table.

Suddenly, Ranulf spun to face the prioress and gestured at her with his knife. "You! You whited sepulcher that leads men into all manner of mortal error, daring to question the cook's guilt when I spoke out on the side of virtue! What Order founded in God's rule would allow a woman to rule over the sons of Adam? Satan hides in your robes." He stepped forward. "I smell him."

Eleanor retreated another couple of steps, put her hands behind her, and felt the edge of the table.

"Then it was you who wielded God's sword against Tobye!" Maud's cried out, extending her hands toward Ranulf in supplication. "But wasn't he Adam's heir, like you? Surely he deserved mercy. Why punish him when it was women who tempted him beyond endurance?"

Ranulf turned away from the prioress, lowered the knife, and blinked as if he had not thought about that aspect.

Eleanor took advantage of the moment and stretched a hand back in the direction of at least one of the items that lay behind her.

"But you killed Tobye on God's behalf, did you not?" Maud's tone quivered with submissiveness, as if longing only to be taught and belying any accusatory intent.

"Aye! He was low-born, yet all the women lusted after him while I..." The man began to swallow convulsively.

Eleanor was grateful that Ranulf had hesitated, showing more reluctance to attack the widow than he had her. Perhaps Maud had given him comfort when his mother's pious demands were too much for the young lad to bear. Would that past mothering now save them both until Brother Thomas and the guard could arrive?

Then fear chilled her heart as she stared at the wooden bar lying firmly across the door. Two men could not break through such reinforced thickness. Either she or Maud must somehow open that door from the inside.

"And Mistress Luce? Why kill her later?" Maud's question was ever so softly spoken.

"Because she made me burn with lust for her," he screamed. "While she wallowed like a sow in the stinking mud with that man, she had Satan send a succubus in her shape to torture me. Once Tobye was dead, I believed she would repent her sins and turn to me for comfort."

And what difference in transgression was there between a groom's lust and that of a step-son, the prioress wondered as her fingers groped for basin or jug. Couldn't the man see that adultery compounded with the sin of uncovering the nakedness of a near kin was even fouler in God's eyes? No wonder Mistress Luce had not wanted to be widowed and left alone with Ranulf as her only protector.

"And this she failed to do?" Maud glanced at the prioress.

"I begged for her embrace, but she turned from me with pale disgust. It was then that my heart hardened with virtuous fury. If the whore could not see the difference between me, a man who honors God, and Tobye, I knew it was my duty to send her soul to Hell, along with that succubus."

"How did you draw her to the stable?" the widow continued.

"I suspected that she lusted after my shameless brother, since wantonness is attracted by depravity, and thus used her wickedness against her. I told her that Huet wanted to meet her there that night. When she expressed doubt, I explained that he had good news for her but feared the steward's anger if he saw them together. After all, he was not in our father's favor after his sudden return home." Ranulf smirked.

"She believed your tale, kept the tryst, and discovered you instead."

He gnawed at his lips.

Eleanor grasped the handle of the jug, hesitated, then recalled that God had never condemned David for battling against Goliath.

"And once again rejected my offer. She was no different from all other women, preferring to lie with a baseborn man than me!" Ranulf shouted and spun around, pointing his finger at the prioress and raising his knife to strike. "Like you, she was the Whore of Babylon!"

Eleanor flung the jug at him, striking him squarely on the side of his head.

Maud swung her foot into Ranulf's groin.

As the man fell to the ground with a high-pitched howl, Eleanor leapt to the door and unbolted it.

Thomas and Huet were but a few feet away when she swung the door wide.

The monk ran to the squirming man, whipped the belt from the man's waist, and quickly bound Ranulf's wrists behind him.

Stepping inside, Huet put his hands to his hips, in unconscious imitation of Mistress Maud, and grinned.

"Well done, Mother!"

Chapter Forty-Two

Although Sir Reimund was surely accustomed to horses, he shifted uncomfortably in the saddle.

Standing beside him, in the company of Brother Thomas, Eleanor wondered if the sheriff had just bitten into something bitter when he winced, his eyes focused on the scene at the manor house door.

Two of his men pulled Ranulf, hobbled and arms bound, through the entryway.

Close behind strode the steward, his head bowed.

Mistress Maud followed Stevyn, as he approached the sheriff's horse, and gently touched his arm, the gesture so swiftly done that most in the courtyard would have missed it.

The steward glanced down, his grim expression softening as he felt her comfort. "Hang him, Sir Reimund," he said, looking back at the uneasy sheriff. "He may be the son of my loins, but I have cast him from my heart. Yet, when the day comes, I'll be there. The only favor I ask is that my men be allowed to pull his legs so his neck will break and some family dignity retained. No one who bears my name should dance and buck for common amusement."

Eleanor looked at the pitiful creature to whom the steward referred. Surrounded by the sheriff's men, Ranulf was ragged, bent, and reeking of his own filth. According to Thomas, Ranulf had been rolling naked in his excrement and howling like courtyard scavenger dogs when the monk visited him at dawn for prayer and confession.

"I wish the outcome of these crimes had been otherwise," Reimund said, carefully looking at a spot over the steward's head.

"No less than I," Stevyn retorted. "But he killed three people, three whose sins were God's to punish, not his."

"Three?" Reimund blinked.

"His wife," Maud said, her voice catching. "We found her corpse in the chapel, stabbed through the heart."

"A deed that Ranulf admitted with some glee as we locked him safely away," Thomas added, his eyes narrowing as he nodded at the trussed man. "All the ones he slaughtered cry out for justice, but one murder is crime enough in God's eyes."

"Perhaps the total will be four. Hilda's fate is still in God's hands," Eleanor said. Indeed, she offered many prayers for the cook last night, and Hilda's eyes had opened this morning. Nonetheless, there was no recognition in the woman's gaze, nor had she spoken. The prioress lowered her eyes to hide the tears they held. If God took Hilda's soul, He would most surely treat it with infinite mercy and pull it gently enough from this world. Yet mortals will grieve, and her laughter would be sorely missed.

The sheriff nervously cleared his throat.

Startled out of her thoughts, she looked up at this man, who weighed the cost of justice in the scales of ambition, and found she was not yet capable of forgiving him.

"My lady, if the guard I set to protect you offended in any way, please let me know. I shall punish him accordingly."

Eleanor swallowed her anger. That he was so willing to cast blame on another, one who had no choice but to obey orders, meant this wretched sheriff had learned nothing. "He was most courteous, Sir Reimund, and, most worthy of reward for his care. I am sure that a larger bit of land from you, so he might marry again and support a growing family, would not go amiss. When I tell my father of the events here, I will mention his name." Thus you dare not treat him ill for the kindness and good service he did render me, despite your spiteful intent. With a pleasure she knew was wicked enough to require confession, she fell into a pointed silence.

"Then I hope you bear me no malice, my lady, for my wish to keep you safe with a killer about."

She tilted her head and smiled but said nothing more.

A flush rose from Sir Reimund's neck and bathed his face with a scarlet hue. He waited for a very long minute, then bowed his head. "You are most kind, my lady," he muttered, willing her indifferent smile into a sign of favoring grace to him.

Quickly, he gave the order for his contingent of men to leave. When the sad party moved toward the manor courtyard gate, a man poked at Ranulf to indicate he must walk on as well. Staggering forward, the elder son of Master Stevyn neither cried out, nor did he turn to give any farewell to his father.

As she watched the small procession, Eleanor realized she was saddened by the thought of hanging this man. Without doubt he had murdered several people, but Satan had so blinded him with obscene obsessions that he could not see it was Evil who had directed his hand against those victims, not God. According to Brother Thomas, the man's wits had fled, leaving him utterly possessed by madness, and thus rendered incapable of repentance or confession.

Would Ranulf ever be able to feel the horror of his crimes and beg forgiveness, even when the hangman draped the rope around his neck? Shouldn't all men have the chance to cleanse their souls? Perhaps she should not grieve for him, murderer that he was, but her heart was not easily silenced on the matter. To distract herself from the murmurings of that womanish organ, she turned to consider whether there had been a lesson in the events of the last few days for her.

She thought back on all the times she had involved herself in mortal crime and wondered if she had committed the same error as Ranulf when she decided she knew better than others what God's justice meant. Had the Prince of Darkness blinded her to the dangers of her own arrogance?

In this case, her motive for interfering with a matter of justice, which belonged under the jurisdiction of an earthly king, was not pure. The sheriff had treated her with disrespect, and her pride in rank had been offended. Had she been less concerned with thwarting the sheriff, might she have saved Mistress Luce's life, perhaps even that of Ranulf's wife? Had her failure to discover the truth in time been due, at least in part, to her own sinful motivations?

Just a few months ago, after Martin the Cooper was poisoned, she had been blinded by her jealousy and failed to see events with needed clarity. If she finally succeeded in conquering her own lusts and pride, would she not serve God's justice better?

Yet the mortal heart had much to teach, especially about the power of love. From old Tibia last summer, she had learned the force of a mother's love. Even Ivetta the Whore had demonstrated loyalty, albeit to a man who little deserved it. This time, Stevyn and Maud had lessons for her. But finding the jewel of love amidst the dross of sin required a craftsman's skill, and Eleanor felt so pitifully ignorant.

She folded her hands, closed her eyes for a moment, and begged God for forgiveness. When she returned to Tyndal, she promised to ask a hard penance from her confessor for her failings. In the meantime, she would pray for Ranulf, as difficult as that would surely be. When the steward's son died and his quaking soul discovered that his true master had been Satan, might God still grant him at least some mercy for having lost all reason? Or was that a blasphemous hope?

She looked up. The gates to the manor were closed. The sheriff's party was well along on the road with their prisoner.

Eleanor turned away, pressed a hand against her heart that ached with unhappiness, and walked back to the chamber she shared with Mariota. During those days and years of prayer she owed God, there would be many questions for which she would seek answers. The truth of this particular situation was one, relegated to that shadowy corner of her mind where it would await His enlightenment.

Chapter Forty-Three

The cold air nipped their cheeks, but there was enough promising blue in the sky to suggest that this journey home to Tyndal would have a good beginning.

Eleanor and Maud stood next to each other, the shared regret at the parting tinged with additional sadness that the bond of their emergent friendship had been forged in such tragic circumstances.

"Would you give me your blessing, my lady?" Maud bowed her head and eased herself down on her knees.

"With a heart most willing," the prioress replied.

As the widow rose, they both began to weep and drew each other into a warm embrace of farewell.

"I shall never forget what you have done for my charge," Eleanor said, standing back and wiping her tears away. "Nor will I cease to be grateful to you for saving my life."

Maud folded her arms, her expression amused as if she had just won a friendly argument. "My lady, had you not struck the man with such force and accuracy, I would never have had the chance to fell him so. Methinks it was your vigorous attack that saved us both."

"This weak creature?" the prioress replied, looking at her hands with mock amazement. "I believe we must thank God who gave my arm an unwomanly strength. Did He not do so for Jael, the wife of Heber, when she drove the nail into Sisera's head?"

"This manor is but a sparrow compared to the eagle that is the land of Israel…" Maud's words began as a jest but her abrupt silence suggested she had been overcome with uneasiness.

"I pray that He brings comfort to you and Master Stevyn." The prioress grasped the woman's hand. "Violence has claimed too many here, and the pain must be intensified by the identity of the killer."

The widow turned her head away. "I fear this scourge has been the result of our sin."

"Some would concur, and I should not presume to counter those deemed far wiser than I," Eleanor replied, "yet my woman's imperfect heart stubbornly rebels against the conclusion. That you sinned is indisputable, but you saw the error of your ways with clarity and repented with sorrow. Ranulf did not and howled so loudly over the wickedness of others that the noise drowned out the cries of his own soul. Then he bathed in their blood as if violence would somehow make him a less tainted mortal. I cannot see that you and Master Stevyn were to blame for all that."

"Then I must ask this question, my lady. Is it sinful for us to marry? We hoped to do so after a proper mourning for Mistress Luce."

Perhaps she should confirm Maud's fears that some in the Church might argue against that comfort, Eleanor thought, falling silent as she watched servants help Mariota into a cart and arrange blankets to keep the girl warm. Yet de Lacy was a powerful man, and Stevyn had found favor with his faithful, competent stewardship. Were there a problem with the union, a priest to marry them would be easy enough to locate. After all, he might conclude they had vowed themselves to each other in a marital bond many years ago and thus any subsequent marriage by each was defective. The prioress was well aware that the donation of a valuable chalice would help cast such logic in a strong light.

"I would think it wrong if you did not," she said at last. "Indeed," she continued with a gentle smile, "I will pray that you live your remaining years together in God's grace."

With that, the women embraced one last time.

◇◇◇

"Brother!"

Thomas spun around and saw Huet hastening toward him. His eyes stung, and he quickly rubbed at them. Why was he not stronger about hiding his failings? A traitorous moisture remained on his cheeks.

As the younger son stopped in front of the monk, the two men looked at each other in awkward silence.

"I shall miss you," Huet said at last, his voice hoarse.

"You only regret the departure of my admiration when you sing and tell fine tales, but others, who have a finer ear for your talents, will replace me soon enough." Thomas smiled but he knew his jest had fallen flat.

"Now that my brother is off for hanging, I must trade my lute for accounting rolls and a horse for a minstrel's ill-shod feet." Huet covered his eyes and groaned. "That remark was foul with cruelty, and I shall do penance for it. Ranulf is my brother, and, despite our differences and his crimes, I grieve over his fate."

"I did not doubt it." Thomas hesitated, then asked: "No one will learn the truth of your birth?"

"There is little reason to fear the revelation. My father speaks of giving his own lands to some monastery in exchange for prayers after he and my mother die. As for my future, the Earl of Lincoln had promised me a place and now that shall most likely be here as his steward. He has that right, whatever my birth."

Thomas nodded. "Will you return to Cambridge?"

"More likely to study outside the university walls where I shall better learn how to manage lands." His look suggested he was less than pleased.

"Will that be so hard?" Thomas asked gently.

"Ah, Brother, how I wish you could remain and give me counsel, for I am a man who dwells in some middle land, suited neither to a priory nor to the world."

"Your priest…"

"…sees men as warriors, religious, or servants to great lords. It was he who advised I give my body to God when my woman and our babe died. It was a choice I discovered fit me ill."

"Yet I have heard you followed his guidance gladly enough."

Huet shook his head, began to answer, but then hesitated as if having second thoughts. "I cannot blame our priest for my decision. It was I who chose the path—for the wrong reasons."

"Grief over the death of beloved ones leads many men to seek comfort in His service. Yet, whether you take final vows or remain in the world, God will provide balm for your wounded heart if you let Him."

Huet looked away.

Thomas grasped the man's shoulder. "As you see, I provide sorry advice, but I have faith that you shall find another who can give far better."

Huet tried to hide his tears but failed. "I shall miss you, Brother. That is all I can say."

With trembling hands, the monk drew him into a rough embrace, then pushed him back and walked away.

◇◇◇

With prayers for a safe journey from those gathered to say farewell, the party of horsemen started down the road, the prioress on her donkey riding next to the cart that carried the young Mariota.

Eleanor looked down at her charge, now warmly bundled against the brisk wind. In the past, she would have urged this reluctant postulant to pray for the strength and faith to continue in the vocation, even though her heart longed to stay in the world. Many times this was the wisest advice, for acceptance of the inevitable made a woman's life easier. Yet the experience of Maud and Stevyn had taught her something about the tenacity of mortal love, a persistence that was not always without merit.

Although the pair had most certainly sinned, they had shown a stubborn fidelity to each other. Despite their transgressions, Eleanor believed their marriage would be a strong one. Each would provide the other with the fortitude to continue through whatever life demanded of them, until Death arrived to steal their souls.

In many ways, they reminded her of David and Bathsheba, although Master Stevyn had not sent Maud's husband off to die. For cert, God had demanded repentance from that famous couple, but afterwards He had blessed their union with a son named Solomon. On the other hand, Ranulf and Constance might have bent their knees at the altar with notable fervor, but their faith had grown putrid with brittle sanctimony. Matters were often not as simple as some would wish, and perhaps that was one more lesson God wished her to learn.

Mariota's swallowed sob brought the prioress back to the moment. "What troubles you, my child?" she asked, noting the girl's eyes were full of tears.

"I have caused much grief to the innocent, my lady."

"Although I concur that you would have been better advised to speak earlier of your illness, I cannot say that God did not have a hand in directing us to the manor. He knows men's hearts and may well have sent us there to render His justice where men would fail."

"It was I who suggested that the embrace of Mistress Maud and Master Huet was sinful. I feel deep regret for my error."

"You told me what you saw, and I interpreted the information with my own blindness. The fault lies with me." She tilted her head in surprise. "How did you learn it was otherwise?"

"Master Huet suspected I had seen them and did not want me to be troubled, fearing for my health. Before we left, he explained that Mistress Maud had taken on the role of a mother to him, after his own had died. She had been comforting him as she would any son when he confessed his soul's torments."

"He was thoughtful to care about your weakened state," Eleanor replied. "She taught him well, as his own mother would wish, and I know she will continue to guide him on the right path."

The two traveled on in silence for some moments before the prioress turned back to Mariota. "May I say, however, that I suspect your thoughts continue to drift to your own situation?"

"My selfishness has been revealed. I fear you are correct."

Eleanor reached out to stroke her donkey's neck and was answered with a contented bray, not a pleasing sound to most but a delight to the ears of his particular rider. "We shall pass through the town where your family lives, and I had hoped to rest there briefly. They would be most happy to see you, and your diminished strength does require a less strenuous journey. We would be well-advised to take an extra day on the return to Tyndal Priory."

"As much as I would love to see my mother and brother, I fear they will be deeply disappointed over my ongoing doubts…"

"…doubts you might be wise not to express during this visit. I had hoped to talk with your brother, Mariota. Although I cannot promise anything, I want to suggest to him that honoring your father's wishes might be fulfilled by other means. Many believe that enforced prayer brings steel to the soul and merit to those who demand it, but the Devil finds fertile fields for his wickedness in unwilling hearts. On the other hand, God rejoices when mortals feed and clothe the needy. If you and the man you would marry prove diligent and honorable, you may find that prosperity follows and generosity to the poor and other noble causes may serve God's commandments far better."

And thus the two women continued in easy conversation, hope entering the heart of the younger and compassion the soul of the elder.

◇◇◇

When the travellers rounded the turn in the road that led eastward, Thomas pulled back on his horse's reins and turned around for one last look at a place he might never see again.

A small figure now, Huet stood alone at the manor gate and raised his hand in farewell.

The monk returned the gesture and watched the steward's son retreat into the courtyard and his new responsibilities.

I shall miss the man, Thomas thought. Should he allow himself to dwell on it, he knew he would grieve over this parting as much as Huet had seemed to do. Not since Giles had he felt so at ease with another man, one with whom he might have founded a pleasurable friendship had they been clerks together at another time and before he had suffered so cruelly.

But he willed himself not dwell on an occurrence that would not happen and, perhaps, one that should not. Instead, he urged his horse to travel on and mulled over all that had happened during the last many weeks, including the murders at the manor.

How strange, he thought, that his wayward spirit had been so peaceful during this ill-fated journey, and he tried to examine what had caused such a change.

One reason was surely the service he had been able to render his prioress. Although she had relied on his knowledge of charters and other legal issues before, never had they worked as closely as they had in these weeks, determining the proper action to take on those matters involving priory lands. Once their task had been completed, she had expressed much appreciation and even unusually warm regard for his efforts.

Then they had arrived at the manor and, once again, she had turned to him for consultation and assistance. In the past, Sister Anne or Crowner Ralf had been by her side to help bring a murderer to justice. This time, she had only him, and, again, she had seemed well pleased.

Had he been a man filled with the usual ambitions, he might have used this regard to advance in his vocation. He was not. In fact, he knew he was fortunate to have survived his time in prison, and his greatest aspiration was to ease the melancholy he so often suffered. Were he to make use of Prioress Eleanor's pleasure in his service, perhaps he should ask again for permission to spend a year as a hermit?

But did he still want to escape the world, even the world in a priory? If he were honest with himself, he would confess that he had enjoyed these many days outside Tyndal, befouled as some of them were with murder. He rather enjoyed investigations into crime of greater and lesser evil. Were it not for his malignant grief over Giles and the troubling nature of his feelings for the man in Amesbury, might he not have found his work as a spy both satisfying and challenging?

If that were the case, he realized with a pang of fear, perhaps he was not suited to the religious life at all. Might he find more contentment in the world, working instead for the king?

Although he longed for a simple answer, there was none.

Briefly, he looked back in the direction of the now invisible manor. Huet had been right in a way. Perhaps he did understand the man's confusion, having neither a strong religious vocation nor a comfort with the demands of a worldly life. Yet he had found neither peace nor satisfactory answer to the difficulty himself and thus had no advice for another.

How would Huet resolve his quandary over the Church? As his father's presumed heir in the stewardship, his path lay in the world, and the Earl of Lincoln would surely find a way to let him ease out of any vows taken. Huet dare not let his doubts rule him. He must make choices and wise ones at that. Indeed, Huet's travails might well enlighten Thomas. If anyone was bereft of counsel, the monk thought, it was he. And for that reason alone, he would miss the steward's son. All other reasons, he would lock away in the dungeon of his melancholy.

He sighed. Nothing had ever been uncomplicated for him, and he had no cause to think that would change. All men owed God allegiance, whether king or villein. For those sent to a religious house, even the ones who doubted or felt undeserving, they must bend the knee and find ways to pray. And he was most certainly one of the most unworthy to enter any priory.

Yet Anchoress Juliana had given him both direction and hope with her advice. Patience was a virtue he was trying to learn, and he could only wait for something to happen to guide him into the right choices. Friends he most certainly had in this life and now, it seemed, the favor of his prioress. With grim humor he considered how often she was placed in the middle of unnatural deaths. If he wanted adventure, he might be well-advised to stay at her side.

With that thought, Thomas took a deep breath, urged his horse forward, and followed his prioress and their company on the road leading back to Tyndal Priory.

Author's Notes

No matter how bleak the events in this story, the months following were the beginning of a far more disconcerting historical time.

By August 1284, Edward I had finally arrived home and was crowned. While his father, Henry III, has never been considered one of England's more talented monarchs, Edward ranks with the most noteworthy. A fascinating and complex man, his reign would be marked by both greatness and brutality. On one hand, he was the "Hammer of the Scots" and known for castles, like Harlech and Beaumaris, which he built in an attempt to beat the Welsh people into submission. In 1290, he cruelly expelled the Jews from England after he bled them dry from taxation. On the reverse side, he was the "lawyer king", renowned for his efforts to codify and strengthen the rule of law after the lax administration of his father.

For those who became adults under Henry III's comparatively quiet reign and the waning influence of the vibrant intellectual atmosphere of the twelfth century, the 1300s would prove an era less inclined to tolerance or acceptance of even reasoned dissent. There were many causes for this, all common ingredients in the creation of fear and uncertainty which often lead to the blunting of reason and inventiveness. Some of these were the frequent wars, a little ice age that wreaked havoc with agriculture, and the Black Death. That said, no shift in attitudes or behavior is ever born without intimations of its coming, yet those living during the evolution are often amazed when the change becomes obvious. Eleanor and Thomas have some interesting times ahead, and their storyteller does feel much sympathy for what she plans to put them through.

But, to return to the current tale, there are some less dramatic, but nonetheless interesting details worthy of more explanation.

A steward, or seneschal, acted as a deputy in estate management to men of high rank, both secular and ecclesiastical, whose lands were scattered all over the country and sometimes the continent. A secular steward was often a knight, but sometimes a younger son, and was chosen for his prudence, loyalty, and skill in farming, law, accounting, and the direction of subordinates like craftsmen, bailiffs and reeves. In charge of several properties, he visited each several times a year to preside over manor courts, review the farm work needed with the local bailiff and reeve, arrange for property repairs, and gather information needed for the annual account due his lord on Michaelmas (September 29) which was the end of the agricultural year. A good steward was highly prized and well paid, often earning enough to buy small properties of his own or gifted with same by his lord for profitable service rendered. If Tyndal Priory acquires any more property, Prioress Eleanor will also have to find a cleric to act as steward so she will not repeat the unfortunate trip she took in this book.

Since the era was primarily agrarian, we often assume that people learned farming and property management, virtually from the cradle. Imagine my delight, therefore, when I discovered that there were actually courses for the "man of business" and treatises on good farming practices. Although universities were geared to the religious career, there were sometimes teachers in the surrounding town who offered courses in the drafting of contracts, the holding of a court, accounting, writing, business Latin, and other skills useful to the small middle class entrepreneur and those who would run estates. According to Margaret Wade Labarge in *A Baronial Household of the Thirteenth Century*, there were such instructors near Oxford in the reign of Henry III. The course lasted six months to a year.

As for treatises on farming, Walter of Henley was one of the most famous writers with his *Husbandry*. Bishop Robert Grosseteste wrote his thoughts on the subject, compiled as *Rules of St. Robert*, and an anonymous author included particular details to help stewards in *Seneschaucie*. These are just a few of the known "how to" manuals of the era.

In modern times, under laws founded in English jurisprudence, children may be legitimated by the subsequent marriage of their biological parents unless the mother was married to another at the time of conception. This was not true in the thirteenth century, nor for some time after. The most famous example involved the Beauforts, children of John of Gaunt and his longtime companion, Katherine Swynford. In 1397, Richard II signed Letters Patent legitimizing them, although the parents had married in 1396 and received papal legitimation from Pope Boniface IX. Despite this official recognition, they still remained barred from succession, and many never did accept them as legal offspring. Thus it is unlikely that Stevyn and Maud, Huet's true parents, could ever prove Stevyn's paternity since the boy was conceived and born during his mother's prior marriage. The truth of his birth will probably remain secret.

Regarding the issue of adultery, we assume medieval law was pretty brutal to women who committed it and more tolerant of the men. From the available documentation, this is largely true. As household head, the husband was responsible for disciplining a wife or servant who showed disobedience or disloyalty. This meant he could beat either for "good cause" and, if he killed the individual in the course of his chastisement, he might be found guilty of no greater crime than manslaughter—if he was found negligent at all. A woman who killed her husband in the process of defending herself against the blows, however, was guilty of petty treason and might be burned at the stake.

That said, we must recognize that legal records show only the cases where there was an accusation of murder. They do not include the larger number of wife-beatings that did not result in death, the deaths of husbands deemed "accidental", nor those situations where husband and wife came to some other resolution. In this book, I wanted to show a man who did not resort to violence, to balance out popular assumptions about the era. Had Luce not been murdered, Stevyn might well have arranged "a religious vocation" for her. As a solution, it had the merit of being non-violent, and, from the medieval perspective, "saved her soul".

Many of us know something about jongleurs and minstrels but less about theater before the famous York Cycle of a later century. Although the Church frowned on plays as pagan things, they also recognized that enactment of an event is a powerful teaching tool. Thus we have a tenth century nun, Hrotsvitha of Gandersheim, writing didactic dramas in the manner of Seneca, and liturgical dramas in the thirteenth century that remind one of early opera. As a university student, Huet would have known scholars who put on amateur performances of popular tales. When he visited Arras, in the area called the Artois and on the River Scarpe, he would have discovered the secular dramas of such masters as Adam de la Halle and Jehan Bodel. The tale he tells of the prodigal son is probably based on a popular play, *Courtois d'Arras*.

Garderobes may have been privies or latrines, but, in some cases, they were also storage places for clothing and furs. According to a pamphlet from Old Soar Manor in Kent, the stench was believed to keep moths away, an early and equally unpleasant form of moth balls. Some might even wonder which method was more toxic—to humans as well as to insects.

And in conclusion (a phrase beloved by any who suffer through interminable speeches, common to business and politics), I must add a *mea culpa*.

Not long ago, a reader in England pointed out, with graceful kindness, that I had, in my *Author's Notes* to *Wine of Violence*, retired Eleanor of Aquitaine and Eleanor of Provence to Amesbury Priory at the end of their lives. Since both queens were notably strong-willed in life, thus likely to be possessed of equally formidable and incompatible spirits in death, they had the good sense not to die in the same place where I so foolishly put them. Instead, they wisely put the English Channel between them. Although Eleanor of Provence did spend her last years, from1286 to 1291, at Amesbury Priory in Wiltshire, Eleanor of Aquitaine retired and was buried at Fontevraud Abbey in Anjou some eighty-seven years before.

Bibliography

Once again, I would like to list a few books that might be of interest to readers and ones that most certainly gave me many hours of pleasurable reading. Any erroneous use of information is my fault alone and sincerely regretted.

Life on the English Manor by H. S. Bennett, Cambridge University Press, 1937.

A Medieval Book of Seasons by Marie Collins and Virginia Davis, Harper Collins, 1992.

A Common Stage: Theater and Public Life in Medieval Arras by Carol Symes, Cornell University Press, 2007.

The English Medieval House by Margaret Wood, Studio Editions of Random House UK Ltd, 1965.

To receive a free catalog of Poisoned Pen Press titles, please contact us in one of the following ways:

Phone: 1-800-421-3976
Facsimile: 1-480-949-1707
Email: info@poisonedpenpress.com
Website: www.poisonedpenpress.com

Poisoned Pen Press
6962 E. First Ave. Ste. 103
Scottsdale, AZ 85251